THE ANIMAL... NOVELS BY
THE "INCREDIBLY
TALENTED JILL SHALVIS"*

"I'm a big animal lover, and this series is centered on animals. Animals and hot heroes. How can you not love a romance like that?"
—*Jaci Burton, *New York Times* bestselling author

## PRAISE FOR
## ANIMAL ATTRACTION

"Definitely a good way to spend a few hours with some sexy characters." —*USA Today*

"A delightful read full of cuddly animals, hot men, and confident women . . . This book is definitely a must-read for fans of contemporary romance." —*Fresh Fiction*

"Funny and hot as hell . . . Moving, empowering, and engaging." —*All About Romance*

"Fast-paced, filled with great dialogue, a strong story line, and most of all some really sexy scenes . . . I can't wait for the next book in this series." —*Fiction Vixen Book Reviews*

"It was beautifully written and had me tearing up . . . [It] totally met my expectations. Jill Shalvis has become one of my 'go-to' authors for contemporary romance. Her stories are fun, sexy, moving, and always put a smile on my face." —*The Romance Dish*

*continued . . .*

## ANIMAL MAGNETISM

"A captivating story that will have you laughing out loud, rooting for a happy ending . . . and hoping that this won't be your last visit to Sunshine."  —*Romance Reviews Today*

"Jill Shalvis's signature light tone and terrific sense of humor are alive and well."  —*All About Romance*

"That rare find—an excellent, straight-up contemporary romance. From the small-town setting to the fun (and intriguing) supporting cast to a fabulous hero and heroine— everything works. This book is an entertaining and romantic story you won't want to put down!"
—*The Good, The Bad and The Unread*

"Anyone remember those funny, fluttering-butterfly feelings you get when you're in love for the first time? That is what I felt while I was reading *Animal Magnetism*. If you love a true romance with amazing characters that leaves you wanting more, go out and grab a copy of *Animal Magnetism*. It is so worth it!"  —*Joyfully Reviewed*

"*Animal Magnetism* ramps up the pet-friendly book trend . . . [A] steamy, romantic barn burner."
—*Library Journal*

"There's plenty of sizzle . . . An entertaining read and a good choice for readers who like cooing over cute animals as well as a cute romance."  —*Publishers Weekly*

## SLOW HEAT

"*Slow Heat* may be about baseball, but you certainly don't have to be a sports fan to enjoy it. If you like reading fun, sexy contemporaries, then this one fits the bill quite nicely. Pick it up and enjoy the game!"  —*The Romance Dish*

"Exactly what a romance story should be."  —*Dear Author*

"Light, funny, sexy, and just plain enjoyable to read."
—*All About Romance*

*Berkley titles by Jill Shalvis*

**THE TROUBLE WITH PARADISE**
**DOUBLE PLAY**
**SLOW HEAT**

*The Animal Magnetism Novels*

**ANIMAL MAGNETISM**
**ANIMAL ATTRACTION**
**RESCUE MY HEART**

# Rescue
## MY HEART

Jill Shalvis

BERKLEY SENSATION, NEW YORK

**THE BERKLEY PUBLISHING GROUP**
**Published by the Penguin Group**
**Penguin Group (USA) Inc.**
**375 Hudson Street, New York, New York 10014, USA**

Penguin Group (Canada), 90 Eglinton Avenue East, Suite 700, Toronto, Ontario M4P 2Y3, Canada
(a division of Pearson Penguin Canada Inc.) • Penguin Books Ltd., 80 Strand, London WC2R 0RL,
England • Penguin Ireland, 25 St. Stephen's Green, Dublin 2, Ireland (a division of Penguin
Books Ltd.) • Penguin Group (Australia), 707 Collins Street, Melbourne, Victoria 3008, Australia
(a division of Pearson Australia Group Pty. Ltd.) • Penguin Books India Pvt. Ltd., 11 Community
Centre, Panchsheel Park, New Delhi—110 017, India • Penguin Group (NZ), 67 Apollo Drive,
Rosedale, Auckland 0632, New Zealand (a division of Pearson New Zealand Ltd.) • Penguin Books,
Rosebank Office Park, 181 Jan Smuts Avenue, Parktown North 2193, South Africa • Penguin China,
B7 Jaiming Center, 27 East Third Ring Road North, Chaoyang District, Beijing 100020, China

Penguin Books Ltd., Registered Offices: 80 Strand, London WC2R 0RL, England

This is a work of fiction. Names, characters, places, and incidents either are the product of the author's
imagination or are used fictitiously, and any resemblance to actual persons, living or dead, business
establishments, events, or locales is entirely coincidental. The publisher does not have any control over
and does not assume any responsibility for author or third-party websites or their content.

RESCUE MY HEART

A Berkley Sensation Book / published by arrangement with the author

PUBLISHING HISTORY
Berkley Sensation mass-market edition / November 2012

ISBN: 978-0-425-25581-0

BERKLEY SENSATION®
Berkley Sensation Books are published by The Berkley Publishing Group,
a division of Penguin Group (USA) Inc.,
375 Hudson Street, New York, New York 10014.
BERKLEY SENSATION® is a registered trademark of Penguin Group (USA) Inc.
The "B" design is a trademark of Penguin Group (USA) Inc.

PRINTED IN THE UNITED STATES OF AMERICA

10  9  8  7  6  5  4  3  2  1

**ALWAYS LEARNING**                                                    **PEARSON**

# One

There was a fine line between being exhausted and being comatose, and Adam Connelly had just about found it. He'd been two nights without sleep, half that without food, and his shoulder hurt like hell where his shirt was sticking to his open wound.

It was hard to feel much past the heart-pounding adrenaline surge still making his limbs quiver, but the pain managed to creep through. The freezing burn of the sleet slapping him in the face didn't help either as he opened his pack and shoved in his gear. Later, he'd have to take it all back out again and carefully repair, clean, and repack everything after the unexpected rescue, but for now he wasn't particularly inclined toward much besides getting the hell out of there.

Milo stood at his side, still in his search and rescue vest, attentive to their surroundings even though he had to be as done in as Adam. Knowing it, Adam forced a few deep breaths to try and slow his heart rate. "What do you think?" he asked, pretending he wasn't fighting his still knocking knees to hold him up. "Food, sleep . . . or a woman?"

Milo nudged the pocket of the daypack where his food was kept.

Adam shook his head, finding some humor in the day, after all. "You always vote for food."

The ten-month-old yellow Lab seemed to smile at that. He was a search-and-rescue dog now, but not too long ago, he'd been nothing more than a scrappy, unwanted pup. In Milo's world, food still trumped everything else.

Adam got that. After all, like tended to recognize like. Besides, sleep was overrated, and it wasn't as if a woman had been on his calendar, anyway. Hell, a woman hadn't been even a glimmer of a possibility in too long to contemplate.

His own fault. "Food it is, then," he said, and realized in spite of still shaking and sweating, he was starving, too. That was a good sign, he decided. It meant that the PTSD had been kicked down to a lowly 3 on the scale, when two years ago it would've been at a 10.5, not to mention wholly consuming him.

Progress.

Besides, he'd never been able to resist a good adrenaline rush. After all, some of his fondest memories were born of adrenaline rushes—being five years old and running like hell from a pack of Rottweilers that he and his brother Dell had accidentally roused while climbing fences. Or at fourteen, getting caught underage drinking and "borrowing" a '69 classic GTO—a joyride that had landed him in juvie. Hell, for most of his teenage years, fathers everywhere had feared Adam's influence on their impressionable sons and mothers had locked up their daughters on Saturday nights. And then it had all caught up with him in one horrifying, tragic evening that had changed the direction of his entire life.

Good times.

Footsteps came up behind him: Kel, the local sheriff and good friend. Hooking his radio back on his hip, he squinted through the wind and freezing rain whipping at them, rippling the surface of Bear Lake into a frenzy in front of them. "Nice job."

"It wasn't a job," Adam reminded him. They'd just happened to be scouting out this area for new rugged terrain to be used in search and rescue training. They'd been doing a complete two-day run-through when they stumbled into a real rescue situation. "It was just sheer dumb luck."

"*Good* luck," Kel corrected. "All those years you spent overseas with the National Guard saving the good guys' asses left you like a machine. Man, the way you shimmied down that sheer rock to get to the kid before he slipped . . ." Kel shook his head in marvel. "And how the hell did you hold on to him like that until I got the ropes to you without popping your shoulder out of the socket? You do that Superman shit in the military, too?"

*Among other things*, Adam thought, but he merely shrugged, a movement that caused the laceration on his shoulder to split further. *Some machine.*

"Well, however you did it," Kel said, "it's damn good to have you back."

Yeah, well, there was back, and then there was *back*. Adam couldn't have gripped a rope right then to save his life. He could no longer hear the thump-thump-thump of the vanishing helicopter airlifting the ten-year-old and his father out of this remote area, which was good. His foster brother, Brady, was behind the chopper's controls, which alleviated any concern about the increasingly bad weather. Brady, an ex–army ranger who'd retained all of his skills, could fly in and out of the eye of a needle if he had to. From here to Coeur d'Alene would be a picnic, oncoming storm or not.

Kel shouldered his pack. Adam did the same but much more gingerly. Normally, there'd be hours of post-rescue takedown, but everything had happened too fast. As the region's coordinator and S&R team leader, Adam hadn't even had time to set up an incident command post or mobilize a search. There weren't the usual myriad trucks or equipment or people it generally took to run an S&R, and for once, that was a good thing.

They could go home right now, and Adam could stop expending all his energy on appearing to be fine, when what he really wanted to do was pass out and pretend today hadn't happened. Because although he made a living teaching and training search and rescue, and he had more accredited initials after his name than the alphabet was long, he hadn't actually been *active* in a rescue in two years. Not since Afghanistan, when he and his unit had been called in to rescue a group of British soldiers stuck on the side of a godforsaken mountain. That day they'd dropped in from helicopters and rappelled down cliffs and into the caves.

And straight into enemy fire.

Most of the time, that memory was buried deep. But today, thirty minutes ago, Adam had faced his nightmares in broad daylight. He'd had to rappel down a cliff to save that kid, and being forced into an active role like that, hanging off those rocks at the mouth of the caves, *barely* grabbing the boy in time—it had all brought him back to a very dark place.

Milo pushed his wet nose into Adam's palm and leaned against him, something the dog wasn't supposed to do on the job. Adam didn't correct him for it, didn't have the heart. There hadn't been much softness in Adam's life, and even less affection, and though he didn't yearn for either, something about the damn dog got to him every time. He looked down at Milo, who was panting happily up at him, his brown eyes clearly saying, *Dude, concentrate! Food!*

And Adam had to laugh. "Right. Food." Always food. And proof that even a dog had better sense than to hang on to the negative shit.

They all headed back to Adam's Polaris Ranger, a four-wheel all-terrain vehicle that could get them in and out of just about anywhere—at least until the heavy snows came. "Up," Adam said to Milo, but the dog leaned on him again. Worried. And Adam realized the dog wasn't fooled by Adam's cool exterior but was picking up on his lingering anxiety. With a sigh, he crouched and hugged the dog. "I'm fine. You're fine. We're all fine. Now up."

Milo leapt into the small backseat of the ATV and Adam angled in behind the wheel. With Kel riding rifle, they four-wheeled out of there. By the time Adam dropped Kel off at his station in their small hometown of Sunshine, the adrenaline was definitely wearing off. Pain was a dull ache in his shoulder, right behind his eyes, and in his heart, but he told himself to suck it up because at least this rescue had a happy ending.

A gust of wind brought in more icy rain, and the first few flakes of snow. Yesterday it had been sixty-five degrees. Today, snow. Welcome to early December at the base of the Bitterroot Mountains in Idaho. By the time he off-roaded to the property he owned with his brothers, the snow kicked up a little bit in intensity, the landscape going soft and white and quiet.

He loved quiet.

He pulled into Belle Haven, which spanned thirty acres and was big enough to house their large vet clinic and stable their horses. Having been gone two days, Adam needed to poke his head in the office to pick up his messages and check on things.

And then sleep.

With any luck Dell would've treated all his patients for the day and locked up by now so that Adam wouldn't have to see anyone and talk about what had happened. Unfortunately, he'd run out of luck a long time ago. When he pulled into the lot, Dell's truck was still there, next to Adam's in fact, which was freshly washed and shiny clean as always.

Not Dell's. Dell's was covered in a fine layer of dust and

filled with crap. Work equipment, sporting gear, yesterday's fast-food lunch wrappings . . . It boggled Adam's organized mind. But then again, Dell hadn't gone into the military and had the discipline drilled into him. Dell, two years younger than Adam, had gone to vet school, and had gotten used to practically living out of his truck while trying to make it through. Old habits died hard.

Adam strode into the animal center, with Milo on his heels. Their reception area was large and airy, with wide planked wood floors lined with comfortable benches for waiting. At one end was a long counter, behind which was the hub of the entire place. Jade's arena. Jade was their drill sergeant slash office manager and also Dell's very significant other slash better half.

At the sight of him, she stood up, a strawberry blond pinup girl in eye-popping pink, phone in hand. Adam considered himself tough as hell and street-smart. Jade was both tougher and smarter than he, and most competent at running his world when he needed her to.

"He's back," she said into the receiver, no doubt reporting to Dell. Dropping the phone, she came around the counter, eyes on Milo, whom she crouched low to hug. "Hi there, handsome."

"Right back atcha, beautiful," Adam said.

This earned him a smile as Jade slipped Milo a dog cookie.

Milo snarfed it down and licked his chops, eyeing her hopefully for a second, even though he knew the rules. One cookie at a time.

A young cat sat on the counter next to the cookie jar. Beans ruled the place with the same fierceness Jade did.

Milo whined up at her. The pup wanted to be friends so bad he could taste it. But Beans eyed the dog with the same general disdain she held for the rest of the world before lifting a leg to wash her Lady Town with quiet dignity.

With a sigh for the lost cause, Milo plopped to the floor, head on his front paws, eyes soulful.

"So," Jade said to Adam. "You look like hell. You need a cookie, too?"

"Need something."

Her expression softened. "I have leftover chicken in the kitchen. I'll make you a plate." She grabbed his messages. "The IDRA called. They want to publish your latest article on S&R dog training."

Adam was a certified instructor and evaluator for the Idaho Dog Rescue Association, both for handlers and dogs, and had provided much of the site's public education content. "Tell them that's fine."

"Oh, and that reporter from the *Coeur d'Alene Chronicle* called—Cynthia Withers. She wants to know if you'll pose in their annual Hot Outdoorsmen calendar this year. She said she asked you last year and you said—"

"Fuck no."

Jade grinned. "Yeah, that. Shame, though. You could totally make the cover, especially with that two-day scruffy, smoldering glower you've got going on right now."

Adam didn't react to this. Reacting only gave Jade ammunition. But he did feel an eye twitch coming on to go with his headache.

"Damn, you're no fun today." Jade tossed that message to the trash and read the next one. "Oh, yeah. Liza Molan enjoyed your puppy training class so much that she wants *private* lessons this time. For herself, not her puppy," Jade clarified, looking like she was thoroughly enjoying herself. "She said, and I quote, 'You're a most excellent master, and she's most eager to be . . . *mastered*.'"

Yeah. A definite eye twitch. He gave Jade a long look, which didn't bother her in the slightest.

"Hey, don't shoot the messenger," she said. "You know damn well that you look like a fallen dark angel. The price for that, you poor, *poor* baby, is women wanting you. You ought to try dating some of them—that would scare them off in no time."

Yeah, yeah, message received. But he wasn't big on socializing and hadn't been in a while. Watching half his unit be blown away in a war zone tended to do that to a person, he'd been assured. He'd get back on the bike soon. Things would get better. Time would heal all his wounds. Blah, blah, blah, he'd heard it all. Some of those old adages might actually be true, but most of the time it all felt like a load of bullshit to him.

Dell stepped out from the back, tailed by Gertie, his one-year-old, happy-go-lucky St. Bernard. "You tell him about the calendar offer?" Dell asked Jade.

"Uh-huh," she said. "He says he can't *wait* to pose."

Adam shook his head at his brother. "Your woman thinks she's funny."

"Hey, I'm my *own* woman," Jade said.

Gertie made a beeline for Adam, his welcome-home committee in a one-hundred-pound package of joy, exuberance, and slobber.

Adam held up a hand. Gertie, eager to obey him, skidded in her efforts to stop. She failed, and ran into Adam's legs, nearly taking him out. Panting, Gertie regrouped and sat obediently, looking up at him in adoration.

Milo hadn't left his position at Adam's other side, his training too strong to break posture, but he stared at Gertie with the same love that Gertie lavished on Adam.

With a soft laugh, Adam crouched low and gave Gert a full body rub that had her falling bonelessly to the floor in ecstasy. "Come on, then," he said to Milo, who happily joined the lovefest.

Beans looked unimpressed.

Dell extracted Adam's messages from Jade, leaning in to nuzzle and then kiss her jaw as he did. She cupped his face and kissed him softly before heading to the back, her heels clicking as she left Dell and Adam alone.

Or as alone as one could get surrounded by all the animals. Dell eyed his dog flat on her back, trying to entice Adam to rub her down again. "She missed you guys."

"I see that." Looking at Dell was a whole lot like looking in the mirror. Same dark hair, dark eyes, and dark skin they'd gotten from their Native American mother, who'd given them up as young boys to go back to her reservation. Same big, broad build they'd gotten from their Texan, all-American football player father, who was long dead. Same matching commitment and authority issues they'd gotten from their unstable youth.

"You had a long few days," Dell said casually.

The equivalent of a welcome-back hug. Adam shrugged and then sucked in a pained breath as the movement jarred his shoulder. He concentrated on the fresh warm blood that trickled down his back instead of his brother's intense gaze.

Kel might have been a little clueless on exactly how long it had been since Adam had been on the active side of an S&R mission instead of running it, but Dell was not.

"So you saved the kid," Dell said.

"Milo found him."

"Clinging to the cliff that you then had to climb because no one else was close enough."

Adam blew out a sigh. "Brady called you."

"Brady called," Dell confirmed. "Said you were favoring your shoulder and that you looked like you hadn't eaten or slept in two days." Dell paused, his gaze scanning the length of Adam, the doctor eyes carefully assessing. "He also said you were in a mood."

Adam ignored this and snatched his messages from Dell's fingers.

"So . . . how are you really?" Dell asked.

"I'd be better if everyone would leave me the hell alone."

He flipped through the notes. Several state S&R agencies wanted him to run some training for their staff. He did a lot of that, traveling across the country to set up systems and training. He also had some new sign-ups for the dog obedience class starting next week. Two more wanted to attend his tracking and agility class. A breeder was looking for advice. And three calls from . . . "Holly?" He stared at the name on the paper. "Holly Reid?"

Dell nodded. "She's been here twice today looking for you."

Adam kept his face carefully blank. As far as Dell knew, Holly was the daughter of one of Adam's clients. And she was. But she was something else as well—a blast from Adam's past, one that never failed to evoke an entire slew of emotions in him, not a single one of which he was equipped to deal with on the best of days.

Which today definitely wasn't.

Most of Adam's errant, misguided youth had been a blur of resentment, anger, and wildness. Growing up in a series of foster homes had turned him into a ruffian thug in the making. He'd thrived on trouble, all kinds, and he'd been exceptionally good at it.

In comparison, Holly had come from another planet. She was the daughter of Donald Reid, an extremely wealthy businessman who'd bought up a bunch of failing ranches in the state and turned them around. Holly handled the business side of her father's ranching conglomerate. Which in no way explained the blast of fury she unloaded on Adam every time their paths crossed. It had been twelve years since they'd been young and stupid—emphasis on stupid—a virtual lifetime. She was settled and successful.

And married.

So he had no idea why she hated him.

Well, maybe he had *some* idea. But it would take some thinking about, an inner reflection that he wasn't up for at the moment.

Or ever.

In the meantime, he had no idea what the hell she'd want with him. Her dad, Donald, was a big, old softie who often fostered young S&R puppies for Adam until they were old enough to be trained and adopted. The problem was Donald had been spending a lot of time up north helping upgrade his sister's ranch, leaving Holly to handle the entire Reid empire, puppies included. Maybe that was it—she needed help. But he knew he was the last man on earth she'd come to if she needed something. Shrugging it off, he turned to the stairs.

Milo immediately leapt to his feet, ready to roll. The stairs led up to the loft above the animal center. At one time or another, each of them had lived there, but it was Adam's at the moment. It was large, running the length of the center, and quiet. It suited him.

"So what does Holly want?" Dell asked.

"No idea."

"Whatever it is, she's not going to give up."

No shit. When Holly sank her teeth into something, she was like a pit bull—the prettiest pit bull Adam had ever seen. Once upon a time she'd sunk her teeth into him, and he'd loved it.

And then he'd been an idiot and pried her loose. He'd done it for her own good, not that he'd gained any credit for that. So, no, he really couldn't imagine what she wanted. Hell, she was married. *Married*, living the life as one half of a couple, sharing a place, sharing a bed.

Which he really didn't want to think about. "Whatever she needs," he said, "*you* handle it."

Dell laughed softly, his tone suggesting that Adam was *still* an idiot.

Probably true.

Bessie came through, pushing a broom. Bessie was their cleaning lady, and somewhere between fifty and one hundred years old. They'd inherited her from Sol Anders, who'd been Adam and Dell's favorite foster parent. Bessie came up to Adam's elbow and was about as wide as she was tall, but she could clean like no one's business, and she never took shit from anyone. A bonus in the Connelly Casa. She gave Adam a long look up and down, then shook her head. "You done it again, huh?"

"I didn't do anything," Adam said, automatically reacting like the guilty teenager she'd gone after with her broom a time or two.

She cackled. They both knew he was guilty as hell of *something* on any given day.

Adam started to climb the stairs. Aware that both Bessie and Dell were watching, he forced himself not to groan, but every single step jarred his shoulder, and he gritted his teeth against the pain.

"That's not good," Bessie said conversationally to Dell. "You see that?"

"I see it," Dell said, sounding grim.

"It's nothing," Adam said to them both.

"You need food?" Dell asked.

"Jade's already on it, Mom."

Bessie snorted. They all knew Dell was about as unmom-like as they came.

"I'm coming up," Dell said. "So don't bother locking me out. I've got a key."

"I'm fine."

"Don't look like it," Bessie said. "You're bleeding through your sweatshirt."

Adam entered the loft and shut the door harder than necessary. He strode directly to the small kitchenette at the far end, where he poured Milo a big bowl of water and food. Then he headed to the bathroom, stripping as he went. He cranked on the water, and while waiting for it to heat up, checked out the back of his shoulder in the quickly fogging mirror. He had a two-inch-long gash that wasn't going to kill him but definitely needed stitches.

Shit.

Rifling through the medicine cabinet didn't yield much. He'd long ago tossed all the various meds the doctors had foisted on him after Afghanistan: the anxiety pills, the anti-depression pills, the sleeping pills. He'd never wanted any of them, and seeing them in the cabinet day in and day out had only made things worse.

All he had in there now was a bottle of aspirin and a razor. Since he'd never been one for slitting his own throat, he shook two aspirin into his palm and then added two more. This was definitely a four-aspirin type of situation. Swallowing them dry, he stepped into the shower and hissed out a breath as the water hit his abused body.

While scrubbing up, he found an assortment of other cuts and bruises. Deciding he'd suffered much, much worse, he let the hot spray soothe him until the water cooled. He turned it off and heard the impatient knocking on the door.

Meddling Dell.

Adam grabbed a towel and his first-aid kit and left the bathroom. Milo had eaten and was curled up in the middle of Adam's bed. "Five minutes," he warned the dog. "And then I'm taking over that whole thing."

Milo cracked open a single eye but didn't appear concerned. On duty, the dog was attentive and polite. Off duty, he was lazy as hell.

Another knock. Milo just lay there, not a growl or even a heads-up. "No, don't get up," Adam said dryly. "I'll get it."

The yellow Lab rolled to his back, his head landing onto Adam's pillow. All four legs in the air, he immediately began to snore.

The knock came a third time, much harder and firmer now. "What the—" He reached for the door. "Since when do you knock—"

Not Dell.

The leggy blonde in front of him wore a pale blue down parka, painted-on jeans tucked into knee-high leather boots, and a tight frown.

Holly Reid, looking city hot and as untouchable as ever. It was her shield, that sophisticated New York air, and she was exceptionally good at using it. Adam knew this. He expected this. Which in no way explained why his heart did a slow roll in his chest at the sight of her. He thought of all the long nights he'd spent somewhere out in the middle of hell, not knowing if he'd make it back alive, and how he'd often imagined a moment just like this to make it through.

Whenever he played that particular mental game with himself, it had always been Holly. He didn't know the implications of fantasizing about her and wasn't sure he was up for knowing, anyway. "Let me guess," he said, propping his good shoulder against the doorjamb, casually crossing his arms. "Your daddy's out of town and the two golden retriever puppies he's fostering for me are on your last nerve."

She flushed at the reminder of the last time she'd shown up at Belle Haven, a wriggling puppy beneath each arm, her blue eyes spitting fire. "Thing One and Thing Two are fine," she said, and nudged him inside with a hand that, hello, had no wedding ring on it, not that he was noticing, and entered his loft.

In those high-heel boots, she clicked her way across the wood floors to the wide wall of windows that overlooked the property, which at the moment was nothing but dark looming shadows only hinting at the remote beauty beyond.

Pretty much like the woman in front of him.

She wasn't particularly fond of him, and he couldn't much argue with that. Adam wasn't particularly fond of himself, either, but whatever her reason for being here, it was pissing her off.

She turned and faced him then, and he realized she wasn't angry at all.

She was scared.

## Two

Holly's heart was pounding against her ribs, hard and way too fast. Her stomach hurt a little bit, too, but this might have been the fast food she'd grabbed for lunch on the run. Or the fact that because of said fast food, her jeans were a little too tight.

Normally, she prided herself on being in control, but that control deserted her completely now that she stood toe-to-toe with the tall, dark, and attitude-ridden Adam Connelly.

She'd faced him before, of course. Just last month she'd seen him here at Belle Haven, a memory burned in her brain. He'd been outside in the yard surrounded by a pack of dogs all suited up in their S&R vests.

Adam had been training them off leash, putting them through their paces on an obstacle course. The animal center behind him had been packed with dogs and cats and various other four-legged and not-so-four-legged creatures coming and going right past the training session, and yet the S&R dogs' attention never wavered from the calm, confident Adam.

He'd obviously built a relationship with each of them based on trust and respect, and Holly remembered exactly how he'd looked working them in a pair of battered Levi's, sweatshirt with the hood up against the cold, and five-o'clock shadow on his jaw. He'd looked good. Too good.

Now he stood in front of her in nothing but a towel and a few water drops. Sweet baby Jesus, he was built. As a teenager, he'd been lanky lean, almost too lean, though even back then the breadth of his shoulders had indicated he had more growing to do.

He'd come into that promise. He'd filled out in all the right places, leaving his body as good as a body could get, born from a life of outdoor, physical labor. Dark eyes, dark life.

Adam had been her first crush. Her first dance. Her first date. Her first kiss. Her first everything. And once upon a time she'd loved the wild, adventure-seeking troublemaker with all her eighteen-year-old heart. She'd have done anything for him and he'd known it.

He'd chosen to rip out her heart and stomp on it.

But that was in their past. She'd since grown up the hard way, and so had he. By all accounts, the military had beaten back the wild, reckless part of him, molding him, leaving him guarded. Stoic. He wasn't the same, and neither was Holly. She reminded herself of that, even as her gaze drank in the sight of him.

*Focus*, she ordered herself. She wasn't here for a walk down memory lane. She needed help. Needed it badly enough to come to him.

Unlike her, Adam didn't appear unsettled by her presence, although he was the master of hiding his feelings so it was hard to tell. He stood there quiet, calm, expression impassive, tracking her with that always-aware-of-his-surroundings air he had.

A battle-ready soldier.

And the best tracker she knew. Actually, the only tracker

she knew, other than her brother Griffin. But Grif was on the other side of the world, still in Afghanistan.

"I need your help," she heard herself say, her voice not nearly as strong as she'd have liked.

Adam arched a brow. He didn't like to waste words. She imagined that was what made him so good at what he did. He was pragmatic, confident, and utterly irritating. "My dad's missing," she said. "He went hunting three days ago and didn't return."

He relaxed very slightly, making her wonder what he'd expected. "And . . . ?" he asked.

She knew what he was really asking. Her dad vanished all the time on hunting trips. In fact, he used the term *hunting* as an excuse to be alone—his favorite state—and everyone she'd approached in her worry had assured her that he was fine. He'd always been fine. "I can't explain it," she said. "I just have a really bad feeling. And you're the only one I know who can track. Please," she added, hating that it was Adam she was having to beg. "Something's wrong, I know it."

"Has something happened, did something change that would make this trip different from his others?"

Fair question. "Two days before he left, Deanna broke up with him," she said. "I don't know the details, but he was upset."

"He's got other women."

Holly squelched a grimace. Her dad was a known womanizer. But this thing with Deanna had hit him hard. Her dad was a cowboy at heart, a good old boy who'd never shown much in the way of emotion unless it was about his horse or dogs. He loved women, too, and his family, of course, but he'd never been one for needing them around, not like his animals. "Yes, he has other women," she said, "but apparently Deanna was his favorite. We had dinner together and he wasn't himself. He left the next morning, taking his usual gear and the two dogs he's fostering for you. They got into his ATV, so I know he was planning on off-roading to wherever he was going. And then he didn't come back." She caught Adam's slight head shake and hastened to go on before he refused her like everyone else had. "I know, nothing unusual. But he's rarely gone this long without at least checking in, and we've heard nothing. Not a single radio or cell call, nothing." The words rushed out of her in a worried river, and embarrassed her. She'd managed to be cool and calm while talking to Red, her dad's ranching manager, to Kel, to her dad's friends . . . everyone.

But now, with Adam, she was falling apart. She drew in a deep breath, willing herself to keep it together.

Adam studied her for a long beat. "Donald goes out all the time," he finally said. "He's been doing so for years. Is there anything besides the Deanna thing that makes you think he's in trouble?"

"This morning there was a board meeting, and he missed it. Didn't even call in to check on how it went."

Adam nodded. They both knew Donald loved business, all of it. He had great employees and wasn't required for any day-to-day action, but he kept up on everything. He'd turned sixty-five this year and still insisted on attending all the important meetings. Just as he also insisted on riding the wildest of his horses, herding cattle, wining and dining too many women, four-wheeling into the wilderness to go hunting . . .

Until last year, Holly had run the business side of things from New York. She'd grown up in New York under the watchful eyes of her mother, who'd passed away five years ago, one of the many women Donald had gone through in his heyday. Holly had remained on the East Coast, an arrangement that had worked well for everyone. She got her beloved freedom, and her dad got the same.

But then he'd pressured her to move to Sunshine, reminding her that he wasn't getting any younger, and with Grif still overseas, he wanted her—his only other family—nearby.

It had been a blatant manipulation of Holly's emotions, but she'd come, anyway. Maybe because her personal life had been in the toilet. Maybe because the memory of the one summer she'd spent here as a teen made her nostalgic for the last time she'd felt truly happy.

"And there's something else," she told Adam. "Deanna called me looking for him as well. If she's been calling him like she says, he'd have answered."

*If he could . . .*

Adam's dark eyes never wavered from hers and she felt a most annoying pull of the same sexual magnetism that had always been between them. His state of undress didn't help, he was sex on a stick—not that she intended to go there. She didn't. Not ever again. She'd been burned by him, badly. And even a silly eighteen-year-old could learn not to play with fire—no matter how attracted to it she still was.

"I feel like something's happened to him," she said, "and I need to find him before tomorrow night's storm hits."

"What did Kel say?" he asked. "Did you fill out a missing-persons report?"

"I tried, but everyone knows he takes these damn trips all year long, in worse conditions than we have right now. So no one's particularly concerned. This is just for me—I need to go out there and make sure."

Adam turned his head and made a point of looking out the window.

Pitch-black, of course.

Again he met her gaze, his own ironic.

"I don't care what time it is," she said. She'd go by herself, except that it had been a long time since she'd roamed these mountains during the day, much less at night. The Bitterroots were among the most gorgeous in the world, and also among the most remote, isolated, and dangerous. There were miles and miles of land accessible only by foot. Not that she wasn't capable, but she was rusty. It would take her a lot longer than Adam to get to her dad's favorite hunting haunts.

But asking for help was hard. She'd been taught to handle her own problems, thanks in large part to her mom, who'd spent her life pretending everything was okay even when it wasn't. Her brother had also had a hand in teaching her how to be tough. So had her dad himself, Mr. Never Ask for Help.

And then there was the man who'd been the hardest on her of them all. The one in front of her who was now wearing nothing but that low-riding towel and a few water drops sliding down the chiseled body that made her mouth dry up even as other parts of her dampened.

"No one's going out there tonight," he said.

It was true that the wind had kicked up since she'd gathered her courage to come here, battering at the windows. It was also true that only the craziest of the crazies would want to be out in this. "But—"

"No one, Holly." His eyes never left hers as he stood there in that very still way he had. "Where do you think he went?"

She hated knowing that it wasn't safe to go out now. That she'd have to wait until daylight to take action, but she did take heart in this question because he wouldn't ask if he wasn't going to help, right? "He didn't say." And of course he hadn't left a note or a message. "But his favorite places are Diamond Ridge and Mount Eagle."

"Diamond Ridge and Mount Eagle are twenty-five miles apart."

"Yes," she said, turning to stare out the window into the black night. "I'm going to start with Diamond Ridge—it's slightly closer. Mount Eagle has that deserted ranger station he likes to camp in, so that's my second guess."

"You remember how to get there?" Adam asked.

She craned her neck so her gaze met his. And held.

On that fateful long-ago summer, her dad had been busy. A lot. She'd been bored until she'd met the sexiest ranch hand she'd ever known—Adam, working part-time on one of the Reid ranches. There'd been instant chemistry between them, made all the hotter since her dad had forbidden her from dating any of his men.

So they'd kept it a secret. She, because she didn't want her dad to kill him. And Adam, because . . . hell, who knew. Adam tended to keep his own counsel. In any case, he'd taken her out on the mountain, to the deserted ranger station at Mount Eagle. She'd been seated behind him on his dirt bike, hands clutched at his waist, legs straddling his lean hips, the power of the engine rumbling up from beneath her. It had been a sensual, erotic, heady thrill of a ride, and once they'd gotten there, he'd given her another sort of ride altogether.

To her eternal annoyance, the memory still rated as her top sexual experience. "I remember," she said softly.

His gaze dipped down to her mouth, and she chewed on her lower lip to keep from saying more. She didn't want to beg. Wouldn't beg.

Surely he knew that.

She'd only ever asked him for one thing. When his circumstances had changed and he'd gone into the military, she'd asked him not to break up with her. Go if he must, but keep her in his heart.

He hadn't.

He'd left without looking back: no letters, no contact, nothing.

He'd moved on, with shocking ease.

So she'd moved on as well, with the opposite of ease, foolishly getting sucked into a bad marriage with a bad-for-her man. Just like her parents' marriage, it had been a sham, a façade, and one hell of a hard-learned lesson. These days Holly no longer ran with scissors or led with her heart.

Or let a man have power over her.

But as her father always said, *Reids don't quit.* "So will you help me?" she asked.

"Where's your husband?"

Not the question she'd expected, not from him. But not all that surprising. She'd kept her private life to herself— or more accurately her *lack* of a private life—out of self-preservation. And in any case, thinking about Derek never failed to make her feel vulnerable and stupid, and like a complete failure. "I'm no longer married," she said. The rest was on a need-to-know basis, and as far as she was concerned, no one needed to know. *Especially* not Adam.

He studied her thoughtfully. "So why does everyone here, including your father and brother, think you are?"

Adam was still tight with her dad, and Grif as well. "I don't know," she said. A lie, because she did know. It was pride, of course. Hers. She'd come from a fractured family, had been asked to choose between her parents, but never really getting either of them.

Then Grif had left as well.

And then Adam.

The lesson learned had been clear—any sense of happiness, family, and security was an illusion. Heartbroken, she'd gone back to New York for college, where she'd kept to herself for a year. Then she'd met a man. Her professor. Derek had been romantic and nice and kind. He'd been gentle and . . . beta—a complete change from all the alphas who had always been in her life. He'd sucked her in with that slow charm and sensitivity. God, how she hated remembering how easy of a mark she'd been. A lonely, scared, vulnerable college girl, looking for love. Derek had dazzled her, completely, and even more so when both her dad and Grif had tried to tell her that she was being played. The three Reids had one thing in common—they were stubborn to the end. So of course they'd battled, and her dad and Grif had pushed Holly hard.

Holly had pushed back, being young and stupid enough to marry Derek at nineteen, giving him all she had, including her already trampled on heart. She'd settled in for her happily-ever-after, but that hadn't been the ending she'd gotten. Derek had indeed played her with his quiet, passive-aggressive ways, so completely it had taken her taken several years to realize her dad and Grif had been right about him.

She hadn't been the only student in her professor's life.

Crushed, embarrassed, and completely ashamed—especially at how long she'd been fooled—she'd never told her dad or Grif that they'd separated. Pride before the fall and all that. For a long time she hadn't even filed for divorce because she'd never intended to get married again. It had suited her, being free but not available.

She could only assume Derek enjoyed the pretense of being married as well, because he hadn't made a move to divorce her, either.

But then a year ago she'd come back to Sunshine for her dad. And in doing so, she had decided to learn to live in the moment and not just pretend everything was okay like her mom had always done. She wanted to take full control of her own life, and be happy. Her way. So she'd filed for that long-overdue divorce, certain that after all this time Derek would agree to it.

He hadn't.

She'd been forced to go to court, which had been a very unpleasant experience. Derek had fought her and then hadn't even bothered to show up for their court date. Twice. Finally, just last week, the judge had agreed to sign off on the case without him, and, as far as she was concerned, the deal was as good as done.

And Holly was over faking her happiness.

Adam was still just watching her. She had no idea what it was about his melting-chocolate eyes, but they had a way of looking at her, as if he could see all the way inside, past her walls, past her guard, past everything, to where her real thoughts and feelings were laid bare.

It was disconcerting.

Terrifying.

Arousing.

"My past isn't up for discussion," she said. "It's . . . complicated."

The very hint of a smile curved his lips. "And what with you isn't?"

She was pretty sure that wasn't a compliment, but she didn't want to go there. To give herself a moment, she walked the length of the loft. He hadn't lit a fire, and the place was chilly. Framed pictures sat on the mantel. Adam with a search dog on either side of him. Another with a handful of guys on a cliff in full combat gear looking into the camera with varying degrees of stoic strength and camaraderie.

But it was the last picture that grabbed her by the throat. It was small, the photo itself a little wrinkled, as if maybe it had spent time in a wallet before making its way to a frame. It was Adam circa his Troubled Years, wearing loose, low-slung jeans and down jacket, hood up. No smile, dark glasses in place, hiding the eyes already old beyond his years. He had his arm slung around a girl.

Her.

She ran a finger over the frame and asked the question she didn't know she'd been holding on to. "So, how is it that you ended up in Sunshine again when you told me you wouldn't ever be back?"

# Three

Holly held her breath for Adam's answer, but he ignored the question and headed toward the far end of the loft, and the tall dresser standing there.

"You're right about the weather going to hell," he said. "It's all over the news."

"Which is why we need to find my dad quickly," she said.

He shook his head. "There's no we."

Disappointment rolled over her like a wave. So he wasn't going to help. "Okay," she said, having no idea why she was surprised. "I'll go alone. It's not like it's the first time someone's walked away when I needed them."

The silence was weighted, and she bit her tongue. She hadn't meant to go there, but apparently she was holding on to some resentment. A lot of resentment. Who knew? Unable to take it back, she strode to the door and, dammit, fumbled with the handle. Before she could get it open, Adam's hand settled on the wood above her head, holding it closed.

He had long fingers, and more than one scar on them. His forearm was corded with sinew and felt too close. Intimate. She closed her eyes and took in the scent of masculine soap and warm, male skin. He wasn't touching her in any way, but she felt him surrounding her just the same. And the bigger problem? Her body remembered his. Remembered . . . and ached. She thunked her head to the door, desperately searching for balance—which wasn't going to happen, not with him so close.

"I didn't say I wouldn't do it," he said.

Processing his words, she turned and flattened herself against the wood, staring up at him, relief filling her hot and bright, so that for a moment she couldn't breathe. "You're going to help me?"

"Yes," he said. "But I go alone." His eyes were shadowed, his mouth tight and grim.

And she realized something else that she'd missed when she'd first soaked up the sight of him, dazzled by his perfection.

He seemed utterly and completely exhausted.

And, she realized in horror when he turned away from her and headed back to his dresser, *injured*. At the sight of his back, she gasped. "Adam."

He didn't respond.

Shock.

She stared at the long, jagged laceration on his shoulder, along with the bunch of other scratches and bruises all over him, as if he'd been dragged over rocks. "You're hurt."

"It's nothing." He pulled a pair of sweats from a drawer.

"It's more than nothing." Her gaze was glued to the blood dripping down his back as she moved close, helplessly drawn in. "It's—"

He dropped his towel to the floor, fully exposing his body in all its bare-ass naked glory.

And there was a lot of glory.

She sputtered, torn between slapping a hand over her

eyes and staring at the finest stretch of broad back and perfect male ass she'd ever seen, while he calmly stepped into his sweats and pulled them up.

Sheer feminine appreciation had won out, of course. She didn't even attempt to cover her eyes—which is how she caught his wince and hiss of breath when he straightened.

"I'll leave at first light," he said, turning to face her.

"Adam, what the hell happened to you?"

Ignoring yet another question, he moved to the door, opening it for her in a direct but silent invite for her to go. "I'll call you when I get to Diamond Ridge," he said.

She shook her head. "I'm coming with you."

"No." He set a hand on her stomach.

She was shocked to immobility at the unexpected touch. Every muscle quivered, and she was completely distracted by it, so that when he gave her a gentle push over the entryway and then shut the door in her face—not quite as gently—she could only blink in surprise.

"Hey." She tried the door, but he'd locked it. She rapped her fist on the wood. "Adam."

No answer. Hands on hips, she stared at the door. "Are you kidding me?"

She could almost hear the proverbial crickets but not a word or a breath from the man inside. "What, are we teenagers and stupid all over again?" she asked through the door.

Nothing. *Unbelievable.* "Adam, you can't be serious."

But apparently he was.

Swearing beneath her breath, she left a strip of her Jeep's tires on the asphalt peeling out of the parking lot. She was halfway home before her wits caught up with her. There were few people on earth who could light her temper. In fact, she could count them with three fingers: her father, Grif, and Adam.

Especially Adam.

Apparently he still had that ability, which really chapped

her hide. It would be one thing if she'd ever, even once, been able to return the favor, but his fuse was notoriously slow and long-burning, and it had never been directed at her. In fact, she wasn't sure she'd ever even heard him raise his voice. Nope, Adam's temper, when it blew, was a quiet explosion.

Internal.

She could remember once being with him when they'd come across someone beating his horse on the trail. Two days later the local paper had printed an article about a horse theft. No one had ever found the horse or caught the perp.

But sure as Holly knew her own name, she knew Adam had stolen that horse.

Fast-forward to the night he'd been late-night drag racing and a cop had died while chasing him and his friends . . . Not twenty-four hours later he'd signed up for the military.

That was the thing about Adam. Despite not ever toeing the line, he had a moral compass that always pointed to Do the Right Thing.

This is how she knew he'd do exactly as he'd said—he'd go out after her dad. Alone. Damn him.

The drive home to the Reid ranch house was on a narrow two-lane road, lined by the Little Eagle River. It was beautiful, and she often stopped at the bridge to watch the river flow by. Not tonight. Tonight she paid no attention to anything but getting home. The place had been built just outside of Sunshine, on the biggest of all the Reid ranches. There were lots of buildings on the land—barns, storage, bunking for the ranch hands, and the Reid offices, which held their staff.

The main house was huge, large enough for each of the three Reids to have their own space when needed, though Grif was rarely here. For that matter, her father was rarely here, either, preferring to travel among all the ranches under his empire.

Holly went straight to her office and began an e-mail to Grif about her plans to leave to search for their dad in the morning, because no matter what Adam thought, she *was* going. But she was surprised to have Grif IM her before she could send it.

> **ShootFirst:** Hey, bossy pants.
> **NYGirl:** Grif! How are you? You okay?
> **ShootFirst:** Fine. You back in NY yet?

Grif would say he was *fine* even if he had limbs falling off, but the New York question made her wince. He kept bugging her about not getting sucked into the ranching business just for their dad's sake, reminding her that she'd gotten out of Sunshine and shouldn't cave to family expectations, that she should follow her own path.

This was because Grif and Donald couldn't spend more than five minutes in the same room without Donald laying on the guilt about Grif not wanting to run the family empire. Their fights were legendary, no doubt having something to do with two alpha males not being able to share space.

For the most part, Holly enjoyed sharing space with her father. The sheer amount of time it took to run his ranching conglomerate grew every year, and she was extremely busy. She had two office staffers to help her, and it took the three of them working full-time to keep things afloat. Gone were the days where she could work from New York or from wherever she wanted to be.

But also gone were the days where she *wanted* to work from somewhere else.

> **NYGirl:** I'm not going back to NY. I'm staying in
>     Sunshine.

**ShootFirst:** Christ, you did it. You let the old man get his hooks in you. What does the husband think of this? Tell me you left that asshole.

Holly would tell him that over her own dead body.

**NYGirl:** Forget about me. Dad went hunting and he's been gone three days. I'm worried. He's not moving as fast as he used to, not that he'd admit it. But Deanna says that his horse threw him last week. He never said a word to me about it. I'm worried he's out there, hurt. What if a wild animal cornered him?
**ShootFirst:** *He's* the wild animal. And he's fine.

*Fine* again. Holly rolled her eyes.

**NYGirl:** He's not answering his phone or returning texts.
**ShootFirst:** Prob no reception.
**NYGirl:** I have a bad feeling.
**ShootFirst:** Like the time you had a feeling about Santa Claus and we had to climb on the roof and wait for him?
**NYGirl:** Hey, you falling off that roof was your own fault.
**ShootFirst:** I nearly broke my neck, not to mention my ass.
**NYGirl:** And yet you live. I'm going to Diamond Ridge to look for him, Grif.
**ShootFirst:** No. There's weather moving in, and the old coot can take care of himself.
**NYGirl:** Why are you keeping track of our weather?
**ShootFirst:** Because Kate's going to the balloon races this weekend. She's got a blind date with one of

the racers, and she's going up in his balloon—
which is pure insanity by the way.

Holly sat back and stared at her computer screen. Kate
Evans was Holly's best friend. Grif had been home exactly
once this year on leave, and he'd stayed for a total of two
weeks. The first week he'd done nothing but sleep. The second week he'd spent in the company of old friends like
Adam and Dell, mostly in the local bars.

Kate was a second-grade teacher. In the presence of a
male older than seven, she tended to get nervous and started
spouting useless science facts. She was funny and smart,
and an amazing friend, but she was swamped with family
obligations and spent exactly zero time in bars. There was
no way she and Grif had managed any time together. Holly
would have known.

*Wouldn't she have known?*

**NYGirl:** How do you know Kate's going to the balloon
races?
**ShootFirst:** Facebook.
**NYGirl:** You're stalking my friend on Facebook?
**ShootFirst:** She poked me. She was being friendly,
sent me a long newsy note. That's what people
think we want over here, news from home.
**NYGirl:** Don't you?
**NYGirl:** Grif?
**ShootFirst:** *Don't* go out to Diamond Ridge or Mount
Eagle alone.

Interesting subject change. Grif wasn't "friends" with
women. He went through women like other men went
through socks. And Kate wasn't the one-night stand type—
though she'd give a perfect stranger the shirt off her back.

If Grif had taken the shirt off Kate's back, Holly would

have to kill him. And that'd be a shame, since she loved her brother's stubborn, nosy, interfering hide. Mostly.

**ShootFirst:** Stay home, Holly. I mean it. I'll get ahold of Adam. He'll check things out.
**NYGirl:** I've already contacted Adam. He said he'd go.

And no matter what he thought, she was going with him.

**ShootFirst:** Let him handle it, then.
**NYGirl:** Grif, you can't micromanage me from 7,000 miles away. Be safe. Love you.

And then, because she'd discovered this was what worked best with both of her two well-meaning but more than slightly overbearing male relatives, she logged off. "Oops," she said out loud. "Bad connection."

She took another moment to send e-mails to her staff and Red, the ranch manager, letting them all know her plans in as much detail as she knew them. She also put in a call to Kel to tell him what she was up to. Because unlike her father, she wanted people to know where she was.

Then she got a backpack together with extra clothes, food, and since she knew exactly how quickly things could change out there, she added stuff for an overnight—not that *that* was going to happen.

Adam had said he'd leave at first light, but she was going back to Belle Haven now because, one, she didn't trust Adam. And, two, she didn't trust Adam. He was likely to take off in the middle of the night just to make sure she didn't tail him. She'd sleep in her Jeep if she had to. Yes, she was being paranoid, but she was also being proactive, tackling the things in her control.

Letting go of the things not in her control.

Or at least *attempting* to let go of the things not in her control. That part was still a work in progress.

The lights were on in the building so she took the stairs again, determined to have a calm and rational *two-way* conversation with Adam about the morning. But when she knocked on the door, it swung open and then she was sucking in a breath, unprepared for the sight in front of her.

Adam was sprawled out facedown on his bed still in only a pair of sweatpants, snug across the best ass she'd ever seen, low-slung enough as to be almost indecent. He was holding stoically still—though swearing viciously into his pillow—as Dell pulled a needle through the skin of his shoulder, stitching him up.

# Four

"Oh my God."

At the soft, distressed female voice coming from the doorway, Adam gritted his teeth. He didn't have to turn and eye the leggy blonde to get his blood pressure rising—her voice was enough. Normally it rose his blood pressure *and* a certain portion of his anatomy at the same time but not tonight. Craning his neck, he glared up at Dell. "You didn't lock the door."

"No," his brother said calmly. "My hands were full."

Milo had been sound asleep, but the yellow Lab lifted his head now, assessing the new visitor. Clearly deciding she wasn't a food source, he yawned and closed his eyes again.

So much for him being a watchdog.

Holly sucked in a shaky breath. "I knew you were hurt," she said. "And now you've got a needle in you."

"Get her out of here," Adam said softly to Dell.

"Little busy right now."

The needle continued to go through Adam's flesh and he gritted his teeth. Something hit the hardwood floor, Holly's keys maybe, but the sound was like a shot. He'd been purposely directing his thoughts elsewhere, so he wasn't sure exactly when his entire body had broken out in a sweat. Or when his heart had begun to race. Or how suddenly the loft faded away and he flashed to a barren, cold cliff in Afghanistan, just outside the caves, frozen into immobility as he watched dead bodies being pulled out—

"Adam."

He blinked at the sound of Dell's voice. "Just one more," Dell said, and the pounding in Adam's chest retreated as he looked up and met his brother's knowing gaze.

"You're good," Dell said. Not worded as a question. Adam nodded. He was good.

Or at least he was working on it. Two years ago, the panic attacks had ruled his life, but they rarely if ever made an appearance these days. He shook it off as Holly walked up to the bed.

"What happened?" she asked, trying to get a look over Dell's shoulder. "Who hurt you?"

If he hadn't been grinding his back teeth into powder at the glide of the needle in and out of his skin, he might have laughed. He was six foot two and built tough enough that few, if any, ever messed with him. He'd made sure of it from a very young age. The way they'd grown up had made it a necessity.

"He saved a kid out at Black Forest River," Dell said to Holly.

"Seriously?" she asked Adam. "You're the guy all over the news who leapt halfway down a cliff to save the boy from falling?"

"Yep," Dell said. "Our very own Batman."

Adam opened his mouth to tell him to shut the fuck up but Dell grinned at him. "He's a bit shy about it though. Has a complex. Doesn't like us to talk about his skills, hasn't since he got back."

Adam slid his brother a keep-talking-and-die look but it didn't stop Dell. Nothing ever did.

"We've got the PTSD under control," Dell continued conversationally to Holly. "But that whole stage-four hero complex thing . . . It stuck. Maybe you should hold his hand. Stroke his hair."

"Swear to God," Adam muttered beneath his breath.

"Why isn't he at the clinic getting this done?" Holly asked.

"He's not big on clinics," Dell said.

If he hadn't been wielding a needle, Adam would've strangled him. Even though it was true. He wasn't big on clinics. He wasn't big on doctors, MDs, or shrinks, even though he owed a bunch of them his life. "Holly," he said wearily. "Go home."

Instead she came even closer, and then the bed compressed as she sat at his hip. "That cut is pretty deep." Her voice sounded funny, and remembering that she was incredibly squeamish about blood, Adam lifted his head to get his first real look at her.

Her eyes were locked on his shoulder and the needle being plunged in and out of it, and a soft sound of distress escaped her. Her skin looked waxen, and her eyes had gone glassy, and if she wasn't careful, she was going to fall off the bed and onto her head. "Holly," he said sharply.

She didn't respond, though she slumped over a little.

"Shit," he said, "there she goes." He pushed up to his knees to grab at her, managing to catch her just as she would have indeed slid to the floor in a boneless puddle.

Dell swore at Adam's sudden movement, but Adam ignored him. Had to, because now there was incidental body contact.

*Full* body contact.

She was soft and warm and flush up against him, and

even though she was sweating, she smelled like heaven. "Holly," he said. "Holly, look at me."

She did, but it wasn't good. Her eyes were dilated and she felt clammy to the touch. Keeping her in his lap, resolutely *not* thinking about how she felt up against him, he pushed her head between her knees. "Breathe," he told her. "In through your nose, out through your mouth."

"Speaking of mouth," Dell said. "Maybe she needs resuscitating."

Adam leveled him with a gaze over Holly's head.

"What, just saying." But Dell moved to her other side. "No worries," he said, reaching for her hand. "Women faint at the sight of us all the time. It's the chiseled good looks. Mostly mine, of course."

She choked out what might have been a soft laugh.

"It's true," Dell said. "They've asked us not to stand too close together, ever. We cause riots."

Holly, color back now, laughed again. Dell was good at that. Making women laugh. Making women feel good.

Once upon a time Adam had been good at those things, too, but he was sorely out of practice, and not too interested in changing that anytime soon.

Holly lifted her head and caught sight of the needle and thread now hanging from his shoulder. Quickly she closed her eyes and dropped her head to the crook of his neck. "Oh, Adam."

He sighed and stroked a hand down her hair, which felt like silk. Not that he was noticing, even if a strand of it had caught on the stubble of his jaw. "It's not as bad as it looks," he said.

"Are you sure? Because it looks bad. And you're pale. You're never pale."

"I've seen him look much worse," Dell said. "Like last year, when I signed him up for this online dating thing. He got all scared. He was pretty pale then."

"Because I was *stalked*," Adam said. "By a crazy person."

"Aw, she wasn't that bad. And she bought you that teddy bear, remember? Because you were her *cuddle umpkins*. How scary can a woman who says 'cuddle umpkins' be?"

Holly laughed.

Adam shook his head. "She broke in and tried to convince me to marry her. With a *Taser*. You always leave that part out."

Holly's damp forehead was still pressed to his throat, and when she snorted, damned if her lips didn't brush against his skin, causing a head-to-toe body shiver to wrack him.

"You sure you don't need to see a doctor?" Holly asked him.

"Dell's a doctor."

"He's a *veterinarian*. No offense," she said to Dell.

"None taken," Dell said. "But no worries, I've stitched up hundreds of animals over the past few years. Including this guy here, more than once."

Because Holly's color was back, Adam forced himself to take his hands off her. She slid off the bed and paced the length of the room away from him. Like errant soldiers, his eyes followed her. She still had a world-class ass . . .

"This changes everything," she said, and turned to face him.

He shook his head. "I can still go."

"Where?" Dell asked.

"Of course you can't still go," Holly said. "You're injured."

"I've got this," Adam said firmly.

"Go where?" Dell repeated.

"Donald's missing." Adam watched Holly gnaw on her lower lip. If she hadn't shown up earlier, he wouldn't have thought twice about her father's disappearance. Donald liked to be alone.

But Holly wasn't much for worrying. Or coddling, for

that matter. She wouldn't have come here, to him of all people, if she weren't absolutely desperate. Clearly her instincts were screaming.

There'd been more than a few times where Adam's own instincts had saved his sorry hide. He wanted to go out into the mountains with Holly like he wanted a root canal, but he couldn't ignore her level of concern.

"Where did he go?" Dell asked.

Holly shrugged. "Hunting three days ago, and he hasn't returned."

"He always goes off hunting for days on end," Dell said.

"This time is different," both Adam and Holly said at the exact same moment.

Holly stared at Adam in shock for a beat, during which he did his best not to stare back. There'd been a time when finishing each other's sentences had been second nature.

That time was long gone.

Dell divided an amused gaze between them. "Okay, so let me get this straight. The two of you are going into the mountains on a search for Donald. Together."

"Yes," Holly said.

"No," Adam said. *Hell no.* "I'm going," he said. "Holly's not."

"Yes, I am," she said, jaw tight, heels digging in.

Adam remembered the last time he'd seen that expression—when he'd told her he was leaving Sunshine, going into the military, and that she wasn't to wait for him. It hadn't been any easier to look at her then than it was now. "I track faster alone," he said.

She crossed her arms but refrained from saying anything. This did not ease his mind in the slightest. She'd grown up with tough men: Donald, Grif, Red, and a bunch of ranch hands. She knew how to handle them, *and* herself. He knew that her narrowed gaze, her tight, sexy, glossed mouth, combined with that stern teacher-to-errant-pupil expression usually worked for her, making even the most stalwart of men cave.

But not him.

Never him.

Dell, still eyeing them both, only laughed softly. He was having fun. He might have no idea that Adam and Holly had once had a thing, but he clearly suspected and could put two and two together. It didn't matter. What did matter was that a joint mission between the two of them would be a disaster of epic proportions. He allowed Dell to push him back to the bed and braced himself as his brother finished doctoring him up.

"*My* stitches," Dell said as he finally set the bandage. "*My* bandage. This means don't touch. If you want to touch, you call me. If you don't think you can manage that, I'm going to put a cone around your neck." He slid a look at Holly. "Soldiers are the worst. They don't rest, they don't listen. They think they're invincible."

She nodded.

Dell turned back to Adam. "So, to recap: touch my stitches or my bandage and I'll kill you. Got it?"

Adam sat up. "So I should remove the bandage and stitches myself, then?"

Dell sighed and began to clean up. "Big storm moving in tomorrow afternoon."

Holly nibbled on her lower lip and looked out the window. "We could go now."

There she went with the royal *we* again.

"No go," Dell said, shaking his head. "Our boy hasn't slept in forty-eight. He needs shut-eye and some fuel. Trust me, if he doesn't get food soon, he's going to get even more bitchy and need Midol to boot."

Adam slid his brother a long look that didn't intimidate him in the slightest. "And for the tenth time," he said to

Holly, "there's no 'we.' I'm going alone. I just need a few hours of sleep and then I'll be good."

Holly hesitated, worry and concern all over her face, and he couldn't stop the thought—had she felt this way when he'd taken off?

*No, you idiot, you'd made sure of that* . . . "I'll find him," he heard himself promise her.

She held his gaze for a long beat and then, without another word, nodded and left.

When the door shut behind her, Adam closed his eyes and let out a breath of relief. Whether she hated him or not, and he was pretty sure she did, she at least was going to let him do this. More relaxed now, he felt himself start to drift off right where he lay.

"Lot of tension between you two," Dell said casually.

Adam ignored this.

"*Sexual* tension."

And that . . .

Dell bustled about, tossing the trash, closing up his medical bag. "You know you're screwed, right?"

"You don't know what you're talking about."

"Okay," Dell said. "But I totally do."

"No, you don't."

"Yeah? Who's the one sleeping with a hot chick every night?"

This was true. Dell had somehow managed to nab the *very* hot Jade Bennett. And mystery of all mysteries, she loved Dell's laid-back, easygoing hide. "You just got lucky," Adam said.

"Yeah, you might want to try it sometime."

Adam would have rolled his eyes, but he was too tired. "Not everyone is meant for a happily-ever-after."

"Yeah, they are," Dell said. "You are. You learned that in your therapy, dumbass."

The only reason Dell even knew this was because he'd

dogged Adam through therapy, going with him, driving him batshit crazy until the doctors swore to Dell that his brother really was better. Adam drew in a deep breath. "What I mean is that not everyone *wants* a happily-ever-after."

Dell stared at him. "Well, that's just stupid."

"It's true."

Dell was quiet for a minute. "Look, Afghanistan was fucked-up," he finally said. "But you're home now. Finding someone, connecting with her, even falling in love—it could just hit you over the head, like it did me. What then? You going to just ignore it?"

Adam let out a low laugh. He had plenty of connections in his life. He had Dell, Brady, Brady's wife, Lilah, and Jade. He didn't need more. "It's not going to be a problem," he said with confidence.

"Man, you totally just jinxed yourself."

"Dell?"

"Yeah?"

"Go away. Far away." And then he gingerly rolled over and fell asleep, ignoring Dell's knowing laugh.

# Five

A half hour later, Holly was slumped in her Jeep, one eye on the old *Friends* episode she had playing on her iPad, the other on Adam's dark loft, when her cell rang.

"Just got your text," Kate said. "You're crazy if you're serious about going after your dad tonight. There's a storm coming."

Holly sighed and adjusted the phone into the crook of her shoulder so she could shift her weight because her butt was numb. "I'm not crazy, just worried." Really worried.

"You're not going to be one of the stupid chicks in those crime shows you love and do this alone, right?"

Kate, definitely the cutest, sweetest person on earth, was also one of the sharpest. She taught at the elementary school in order to take care of her younger siblings, whom she'd had to raise on her own. If life hadn't dealt her that blow, she'd be off chasing big dreams, making the most of the degrees she kept collecting online.

"Not alone," Holly said. She hesitated. "I went to Adam."

There was a beat of stunned silence. "Adam? The guy who broke your heart Adam?"

Holly grimaced. "I can't believe I ever told you that story."

"Yeah, well, we'd just suffered through Suzie Metzer's very froufrou wedding, remember? We were drunk in the bar by eight P.M. Telling each other sob stories was a side effect. Now let me get this straight. You're going into the mountains after your father, into a storm no less, with not only the hottest man in Sunshine but also the only man you ever really loved? Maybe I should come with you. Be your voice of reason."

"I have lots of reason," Holly said. "And you've got work."

"True, but honey, honestly? It's only been three days. Your dad's often gone this long. Are you sure—"

"Yes. Something's wrong, I know it."

"So you and Adam . . . on the mountain. Alone."

"It's not like that." And yet . . .

And yet he had a picture of her on his mantel . . .

"Text me," Kate said. "Often."

"I will."

"And keep your heart zipped up tight. Your pants, too," Kate added. "Oh, and don't wear blue. Mosquitoes are twice as attracted to blue."

Holly laughed. "I don't think it's mosquito season."

"Okay, that's probably true, but you still need to be careful. You've already experienced the dark, bad-boy sexiness that is Adam Connelly."

"A *very* long time ago," Holly reminded her.

"Yeah, but he's improved with age, if that's even possible."

True.

"And we both know you'd have to be dead for it to not be a problem," Kate said.

Also true. And she wasn't dead. Not even close. She

disconnected and went back to watching *Friends*. Half an hour later, she nearly came out of her skin at the soft rap on her window.

Dell looking so much like Adam it stopped her heart. She clutched her chest and powered down the window.

Dell smiled at her, sweet. Affable.

Not like Adam.

"Season five?" he asked, nodding to the iPad. "My favorite."

Hers, too. She turned it off. "Let me guess. You're here to chase me away."

"Adam says you should go home."

"And what do you say?"

"I say the same. Go home, Holly. Get some sleep." He paused and flashed her a bone-melting grin. "Then be back by four A.M. Oh, and don't bother watching his truck. It's the ATV you should be worried about. Park your Jeep down the block, and then be in the ATV so he can't sneak off without you."

Holly jerked awake at the sound of the Ranger's engine rolling over, for a moment completely discombobulated.

Then she remembered.

She'd set her alarm and done just as Dell had suggested: she'd come back to Belle Haven, planting herself and her gear in Adam's ATV so that she wouldn't miss his departure. The vehicle was open on the sides but had a roof. She'd hidden in the back among a tent, sleeping bag, and two carefully folded, heavy wool blankets, all of it covered by a tarp.

According to her watch, it was four thirty. She risked a peek through all the gear to make sure it was Adam in the vehicle and not the boogeyman.

But there was no doubt that the tall, broad silhouette was Adam. He was talking on the phone in his low, steely voice.

"Lilah, are you really calling me at four in the morning to check on me? Seriously? . . . Well, stop worrying. I'm fine . . . Yes, I ate . . . No, I'm not in pain . . . Yes. Yes. Jesus, *yes*, I'll text you. Go take care of Brady instead of me, would ya?"

There was a pause, and when he spoke again, he sounded greatly pained. "I could have lived the rest of my life without knowing how you plan to take care of my brother, but thank you, Lilah. Thank you for that image that is now burned in my brain. I'm hanging up now."

It was the most words Holly had heard him string together since she'd been madly in love with him.

Holly had seen Lilah with Adam a few times at the animal center. The two of them shared an undeniable chemistry, and she'd wondered once or twice if they possibly had something going on. But listening to him on the phone with Lilah now, Holly could tell that the chemistry wasn't sexual. It had the familiar, extremely comfortable feeling of siblings.

Adam tossed his phone aside and Holly went still as a possum.

He didn't look back, but she still didn't breathe. Then the engine revved, and they were off and running. Their first turn was out of the parking lot. The second was onto the main road.

So far, so good.

Then the Ranger abruptly stopped short. Holly slid, bumped her head hard on a cooler, and bit her tongue rather than make any noise. *Please don't let him get out, please don't let him come back here and look—*

Of course he got out. She felt the shift of his weight leaving the ATV, heard his booted footsteps crunching in the predawn ice as he strode to the back.

Crunch, crunch, crunch . . .

Then nothing. Utter silence, and once again she stopped breathing. She huddled into herself beneath the tarp and closed her eyes. *Be the tarp, be the tarp—*

The tarp was abruptly lifted away. A dark shadow loomed over her holding a flashlight. Another shadow leapt into the compartment with her.

A seventy-five-pound shadow that was a dog. Milo put his nose to Holly's ear and snuffled, then licked her from chin to forehead.

"Milo, down," the big, grumpy shadow said.

Milo sighed at the command but followed the request and jumped down.

A sliver of moonlight slashed across Adam's face. Leaner than Dell, he was built more like one of those cage fighters, tough and edgy and hard—except for his face.

An angel's face. Dark disheveled hair, strong features, and a devastating smile when he chose to use it.

He didn't choose to use it now.

There was a long beat during which Holly debated on continuing to play possum or face the music. Playing possum felt like a chickenshit way to go, but then again it was a bit early to face the music.

Or late . . .

And, anyway, facing the music was totally and completely overrated. Maybe a compromise halfway between? So it was with a sigh that she pushed the hair from her face and sat up.

Adam was crouched on his haunches, the bill of his ball cap low enough to completely hide his face except for his square jaw.

Something low in her belly quivered. She told herself it was the fact that she'd forgotten to eat dinner. "How did you know?"

"Your empty Jeep's parked on the street."

Yeah, crap. She should have pulled into the woods.

"I have no idea why I'm surprised," Adam said, calm as you please. Wrapping his hands around her arms, he hauled her out of the Ranger and onto her feet in front of him.

Her heart stuttered at his unexpected touch, and she

grasped at the hard, knotted sinews of his biceps. He'd just taken another shower, she could smell his shampoo, his soap, his clean, warm, male skin.

A few raindrops dotted his head and the shoulders of his heavy winter coat. He wore a black hoodie beneath it, hood up over the ball cap, jeans that were taut over his hard thighs, and ass-kicking boots.

He looked heart-stoppingly amazing.

Twelve years and he still amped her pulse rate. It wasn't fair, not one little bit, and it took more than a little bit of concentration to focus on the task at hand instead of his hard-muscled body. "I was waiting for you," she said. "And fell asleep."

His silence was disconcerting. He was probably trying to figure out how to leave her on the side of the road. She straightened and tried to look unleavable. "I didn't want you to go without me," she added.

"Going without you was the plan, Holly."

"Yes, well, the plan sucked," she said. "Did you get some sleep? Is your shoulder okay?"

He gave her a barely perceptible nod. His posture was annoyingly relaxed for someone who'd just found a stowaway. Relaxed but not amused.

Then their gazes met, and for a minute, being this close to him, she got this grown-up, distant, edgy Adam confused with the younger version.

The version who'd cared about her, however briefly.

It softened something inside her and she found herself leaning in closer without meaning to.

But whatever he caught in her expression—memories, confused emotions, *something*—tipped him off because his eyes went hooded and he pulled back. "Holly," he said quietly.

"You can't make me stay behind."

But they both knew he could do just that if he really wanted. He could make her do anything he set his mind to, thanks to his superior size, not to mention his sheer will. Not that he'd ever force her physically.

He wouldn't.

Mentally . . . well, that was another game entirely. Mentally, he had her.

He always had.

"I need to do this, Adam."

"Holly—"

"No, I mean it. I've got this really bad feeling that won't quit, and . . ." *Dammit*. She let out a shaky breath. "I'm scared, okay? I'm scared and . . ." Her voice broke, which really pissed her off. She didn't want to lose it, not with Adam.

A low, rough sound escaped him, and he reached out, tucking a strand of hair behind her ear, his fingertips brushing feather light across her temple, his thumb at the line of her jaw.

Gentle.

So terrifyingly gentle that it was almost her complete undoing. Not again. She couldn't survive him again.

"You don't have to be scared," he said quietly, and pressed closer, sharing his body heat as he sighed against her temple. "You're not alone."

She pressed her face to his shoulder. Then she remembered his injury and jerked her head up. "I'm sorry—"

"I'm fine."

The *fine* word again. But he *was* fine. And sure. So absolutely sure of himself.

"We're going to find him," he said.

"How do you know?"

"Because you won't let me give up until we do."

There was wry humor in his voice now. She closed her eyes and had to stop herself from pressing her face into his throat and inhaling him in. "Thanks."

"Don't thank me yet." He wrapped his fingers around her ponytail and gently tugged until she lifted her head to his. "We have a long way to go." He paused, and for the first time she sensed a hesitation in him. "Together."

"It doesn't have to be a problem, Adam."

He locked eyes with her, and she got it. He thought it would be a problem for *her*. Oh, hell no. "I moved on a long time ago," she said.

His thumb made a slow pass along the curve of her jaw and she shivered. To make sure he knew that was to be attributed solely to the cold air, she wrapped her arms around herself and took a big step back, both mentally and physically. She was independent now, unwilling to depend on anyone for emotional happiness.

But damned if being with him wasn't making her feel a whole lot of things that she'd forgotten how to feel. She didn't trust those emotions, or him. She'd been fooled, and hurt, by him before, badly.

And then again by her ex.

She refused to do that to herself a third time. At some point, she had to learn. That point was now.

Adam looked at her for another long beat, saying nothing. He rubbed his jaw, and since he hadn't shaved that morning, and possibly not the morning before, either, the stubble beneath his fingers sounded rough.

And sexy.

He nudged her out of the way and rearranged the equipment she'd messed up. "Up, Milo," Adam said.

Milo shot Holly a look of sorrowful reproach, then settled in the back with the equipment.

Holly took the passenger's seat. "Does Milo always behave for you?"

He slid her a look.

Right. Dumb question. Everyone behaved for Adam. It was his voice, low and utterly authoritative. He rarely raised it, he didn't have to. "What if there's a cat?" she asked. "Or better yet, a sexy two-year-old Lab strutting her stuff right in front of him? He can resist a distraction, just for you?"

Her attempt at brevity was met with a barely there smile as Adam hit the gas. "A dog is either trained and obedient, or not," he said. "I don't know how to half train a dog." He glanced at her. "So what's your plan here, Holly? How were you planning on getting to Diamond Ridge?"

"Up Pyramid Hills and then through Shirley Canyon," she said, and wrapped her arms around herself. The ATV was open to the wind and icy air. She was wearing several layers, including her down parka, but she was still cold.

"Shirley Canyon's got rock slides," he said. "And by noon we're going to possibly have snow." He reached behind her seat and then something warm and thick was tossed over her.

A jacket. "Pyramid Hills is suicide at this time of year," he said.

She gratefully wrapped herself in the thick down jacket. "What's a better way, then?"

"Old Crestmont Road."

"I've never gone that way. Isn't it longer?"

"Yeah," he said. "It's also the only doable route in this weather. Mostly."

Gulp. Well, at least she wouldn't be alone. She'd have the best tracker and climber she knew right at her side. "Old Crestmont Road it is, then."

He glanced at her. "Say the word and I'll take you back."

She had to wonder, was he so against her company because it was going to be rough-going and potentially dangerous? After all, even Lewis and Clark had nearly met their end here in these mountains.

Or was it that he didn't want to spend time with her?

*Both*, she decided. "I'm not going back, Adam."

He let out a long, slow breath, and looking resigned, he kept driving.

## Six

They didn't speak, which worked for Holly. She didn't want to talk. She wanted to get this done, find her dad, and go back to pretending she wasn't attracted to Adam in any shape or form.

Since he was quiet, she assumed he felt the same. Except probably he didn't have to pretend anything. Hard to tell with his hat and hoodie up and no expression revealed as he handled the road like a pro. As she had multiple times a day, she tried calling her dad again. Still nothing.

Dawn arrived, a rose stripe where the sky met the purple outline of the majestic peaks. Burgeoning, tumultuous clouds pressed down, muting daylight, warning of the weather still to come. The land was vast and rambling, open but not flat, not by a long shot, and as they gained in altitude with each minute, the wind beat at them.

Holly hunkered into herself. Adam had already cranked up the heater, but after a glance her way, he turned the vents all in her direction. Grateful, she smiled at him, but he was already concentrating on the road again.

She did the same. The rose stripe in the sky widened as day broke over them, and she took in the landscape. This area was the largest expanse of continuous pristine wilderness in the lower forty-eight states. Much of its beauty came in the form of heavily glaciated, rugged, not easily approached peaks. The glaciers had formed steep canyons that opened onto a wilderness valley floor, all of it roamed by small and big game.

Simple beauty. Another world away from New York. Pristine. Pure. She had no idea what it said about her being out here, in the open ATV with Adam, with the wind beating at her and her nose nearly frozen off, with her father missing, with Adam not exactly thrilled to have her along, that she was still enjoying herself more than she had for far too long.

It didn't say anything good, she decided. Especially since Adam didn't appear to be moved one way or the other. *He'd let you come . . .*

The old Holly would have been satisfied with that, with whatever he offered. But the new Holly wanted acknowledgment from him, wanted his undivided attention, things that she wasn't sure he could give any woman.

As if he could read her thoughts, he turned his head toward her. In the morning light, he'd slid on dark, reflective shades so she couldn't see his eyes, but then he fried a few of her brain cells when he pulled off the sunglasses to meet her gaze, his own heated and swirling with emotion.

*Huh*, she thought weakly. So he was somewhat moved. She faced forward again because it turned out that looking right into his eyes was like looking into the eye of the tiger. If you weren't equally strong, you were going down. She'd already been down.

She was now up.

Up, up, up.

She tried to occupy herself with their incredibly beautiful surroundings, but damned if her gaze didn't keep straying back to the man next to her handling the ATV like he'd been born to it. This, of course, was extremely counterproductive to her resolve to stay immune to his charms.

Milo was happy. Behind them, he had his head in the wind, tongue lolling out. Doggy heaven.

Old Crestmont Road was a fifty-year-old, rarely used fire road, narrow, windy, and rutted. And truth be told, "road" was a bit of an exaggeration. The going got rough, but Adam continued to navigate with the single-minded ease of one who'd taken much rougher routes than this.

Which she knew to be true.

He'd had it rough as a kid, too, real rough. She knew that he and Dell had lived with their mom on an Indian reservation for a while but that it hadn't worked out. With their biological father dead, they'd had been bounced around before finally landing in a good, solid foster home. But by then, the wild, restless, badass Adam Connelly hadn't been easy to wrangle in, and he certainly didn't like to play nicely with things like rules and expectations.

To a teenage girl who'd never openly rebelled against anything, this had drawn her in like a moth to the flame.

A few years older than she, Adam had been dark and mysterious in every possible way. He and Grif had been good friends and had hung out together. Holly had been forbidden from doing the same, but once she'd been told that, her fate had been sealed. She'd wanted him.

Needed him.

Loved him.

She'd really believed they were the real deal, that she could tame him, that they'd get married and have babies and a ranch of their own.

Looking back, it was embarrassing to think about how naïve she'd been.

Halfway up Old Crestmont Road, Adam stopped. He gestured to Milo, and the dog leapt out and immediately lifted a leg, anointing the closest tree.

It was late morning now, and with the low lighting, the view was spectacular. So far this winter, the Bitterroot snowpack was trailing badly behind the average depth, but what there was of it was incredibly dangerous. Holly got out and took in the three-hundred-foot drop-off. Far below, the dry valley floor and lower foothills were awash in an arid-lands mix of grasslands, scrublands, and ponderosa pine lining rivers and streams. At the midelevation where she stood, there were stands of Douglas fir, lodgepole pine, and western larch. She took in the faraway glimpses of reservoirs and fast-running streams and drew a deep breath of cool, fresh air. "It's not quite cold enough to snow."

"No," Adam said. "But that will change."

She looked up at the sky. The sun was losing its fight against burgeoning, threatening clouds.

Adam kicked a fallen log closer, gestured her to it, then handed her a bottle of water, an apple, and a string cheese.

"Breakfast of champions?" she asked.

He remained standing, relaxed but definitely taking in their surroundings with the diligence of lifelong habit. She had no idea if it was the soldier in him or just the man, but he was always ready. Prepared. Battle-weary. "That picture on the mantel at the loft," she said softly. "The one of you in your military gear. Was that your unit?"

His expression didn't change. Actually, nothing about his posture changed, but there was a weight behind his single word. "Yes."

She wondered how many of them were gone now and felt a pang deep in her heart for each of them. For Adam, too. Her knowledge of the tragic event had come from the online accounts she could find and also what she could browbeat out of Grif. Adam's unit had been called in to rescue a group of British soldiers stuck in some caves on a mountain in Afghanistan, facing an unexpected, epic storm. Communications between the troops had gone down, but when Adam's unit had gone in for a rescue, they'd been ambushed by enemy fire. Only half of them had made it out alive.

Holly couldn't imagine the strength it took to go through something like that and survive, but she knew one thing. Adam had it. In spades. "I tried to contact you, when you first got back," she said. "You weren't taking calls. I don't remember what I wanted to say exactly. Sorry doesn't seem near enough." She turned and looked at him. "I wanted you to know I was there, if you needed anything."

"I was fine."

They both knew that was a lie. It hung in the air for a long moment before he shrugged. "Okay, so I was pretty fucked-up."

"Was?"

"Yeah." He shrugged again. "Still working on it." He nodded to her food. "Eat up. You're going to need it."

She opened the string cheese, noting Adam did the same for himself but not before giving Milo a doggy treat from his pocket. "I brought food, too," she said. "I didn't mean for you to do all the work. Why don't you let me drive the next leg?"

Milo licked his chops and waited with bated breath for a second treat. A very small smile tilted the corners of Adam's mouth. No clue if it was meant for Milo or her.

"You want to drive, Holly?"

Why did the sound of her name on his lips do funny things low in her belly? He was so freaking sexy just standing there. It wasn't fair. "Yes," she said. "I want to drive." Which they both knew wasn't going to happen because he wouldn't give up that kind of control.

Adam leaned against the Ranger and drank from his water bottle, tilting his head back, downing the thing in a few long gulps that appeared to quench his thirst while making her own mouth dry. "Here it comes," he said.

"What?"

Above them, the sky seemed to swell and darken. A few drops hit her face. And then more than a few drops hit.

"The rain," he said. He tossed the water bottle into the ATV and narrowed his gaze at something behind her.

She craned her neck, but though she had her contacts in, her eyes were dry out here and she still couldn't see much in the distance.

Milo, who'd been playfully bounding around in the terrain about ten yards ahead of the Ranger only seconds ago, began growling low in his throat. The hair at the back of his neck ruffled, and all his muscles bunched as if to charge forward.

"No," Adam said.

The dog stilled, quivering with energy.

"What—" Holly started, but Adam pulled her to her feet in one swift, economical movement, kicking the tipped-over log out of her way.

"Get in the ATV." Then he practically dragged her there himself.

She scrambled into the Ranger and reached for the binoculars she'd seen in the console. That's when she saw them, on the ridge just past where Milo had gone still. Three still forms, watching them all intently.

Wolves.

The middle one tipped back its head and howled, sending a chill racing down Holly's spine as they crept closer. "Adam," she said shakily. The wolves had been a problem this year. Their numbers were higher than in previous years, and, being squeezed out of their usual hunting grounds, they were bolder than ever before. In town, three dogs had been attacked and killed in the past few months. No people that she knew of, but that didn't stop her fear. "Adam. Get in."

Of course he didn't. He was in his protective alpha zone.

He reached into the back and came up with his rifle. "Milo," he said low, calm. Utterly authoritative. "Come."

Milo didn't want to come, not when the wolves were on the move in their direction. The overzealous puppy wanted to show he could protect his pack, too. He ignored the testosterone radiating from Adam and whined, tossing an *Oh please can I?* look over his shoulder at them.

Adam strode to the front of the Ranger, his movements every bit as purposeful and aggressive as the two smaller wolves, still slowly stalking forward toward them.

Adam sighted the rifle, the muscles of his arms and shoulders bunching with the ease of a man who'd performed this action thousands of times.

Holly sat there gripping the dash, blinking through the rain, eaten up with envy. She wanted a big, badass-looking gun, too! Most of her life she'd been protected in some way. By her father. Her brother. Adam. Even Derek had done his fair share of protecting her from the world for a while, and she'd let him.

Then she'd discovered life was so much better when *she* was in charge. Well, she sure wouldn't mind being in charge now, facing down the wolves with the same fearless courage that Adam was.

"*Now*, Milo," Adam said.

Milo jumped into the Ranger in one graceful arch, but he didn't look happy about it. He sat in the back behind Holly, one hundred percent alert, his focus divided between the wolves and Adam.

With Milo inside, Adam lowered the rifle, never taking his eyes off the wolves as he slid behind the wheel. He cranked the engine and the wolves scattered, vanishing into the landscape as if they'd been a dream.

Holly let out a breath. "Would they have gone after Milo with us right there?"

"They were thinking about it." Casually, as if he faced down three crazy wolves every day, he picked up a Camel-

Bak and squirted water into a stream over his shoulder, which Milo caught out of thin air, taking a nice long drink.

Milo licked his chops when he was done and gazed at Adam with love and adoration.

"He's pretty impressive off leash," she said.

"An S&R dog necessity."

So was blind trust, apparently. Milo had trusted Adam to take care of him.

Holly knew the feeling.

Without another word, Adam hit the gas. He drove until the road seemed to come to an end. When he stopped, Holly faced him. He wasn't a bad view, as far as views went. Even beneath his heavy jacket, with water beading off of him, his chest was broad.

Strong.

And she knew from long-ago experience that he would be warm to the touch. And oh how she wanted to touch. She wanted that more than she wanted her next breath of fresh air—and that scared her to death.

But Adam didn't appear to share the yearning, which was good because she didn't think she could resist him.

The wind kicked up and the temperature dropped. Adam pointed to Diamond Ridge ahead, and she nodded. Hopefully, they'd find her dad there and be on their way home by this afternoon.

Another hard, vicious gust hit them and she looked at Adam, wondering why they were stopped, wasting valuable daylight. "The road ends here?"

"Only if you don't know where you're going." He gestured with his chin to what appeared to be a wall of woods. "You can pick it up about a hundred yards north."

She was going to have to take his word on that. He got out of the vehicle and muscled a fallen tree that was in their way. He got back behind the wheel and turned to her. "So, tell me again why you've pretended to be married this whole time."

She blinked. "What does that have to do with anything?"

"Nothing, actually. Answer the question."

She sighed. "I didn't pretend. Everyone just . . . assumed."

"And by everyone," he said, "you mean . . ."

"My dad. Grif." She shrugged, not wanting to talk about this. "Neither of them are exactly big emotional talkers."

"No guy is," Adam pointed out. "But what does emotion have to do with it? You say, 'Hey, Dad, Grif, my husband left me—'"

"I never said Derek left me."

"So he didn't?"

How had they gotten here?

Reaching out, Adam tugged off her reflective sunglasses. She really wanted to do the same to him, but she held back because this felt easier, not having to look into his see-all gaze. She blinked a few times in the harsh day's glare, realizing it was no longer raining. It was too cold to rain.

Adam waited patiently.

So did Milo, head cocked as if he was intently following this conversation. Well, probably *intently* was too strong a word since he appeared to be smiling.

"No. Derek didn't leave me," she finally said, just as a few snowflakes began to drift down. Lazy. Slow. Fluttering through the air like forgotten hopes and dreams. "I left him."

"The marriage was no good?"

"The marriage was no good." She pushed her quickly frizzing hair back from her face. "But the divorce was great." She reached up to try and contain her hair. No luck.

Adam pulled off his hat and slipped it onto her head, tucking a tendril of wayward hair behind her ear. His fingers lingered, stroking gently over her temple, along her jaw. "He hurt you, Holly?"

A rich question, especially coming from him.

And now she had a bigger problem—she was melting at

his touch. *Much* too attracted to him, she leaned back, out of the danger zone.

Actually, she'd have to be on the other side of the planet to leave the danger zone that was Adam Connelly, but she was good at making do. "Not in the way you think."

His eyes never left hers. "What happened?"

Oh no. Not going there. Not with him. "You know, if you're feeling so Chatty Cathy," she said, "let's talk about you. You never answered my question last night—why did you come back to Sunshine?"

"I live here," he said simply. "My brothers are here. My friends and business—"

"Are all here. Yeah, yeah," she finished for him, doing her best to keep the hurt out of her voice. "But you said you weren't going to come back *ever*."

"No, actually. I said I wasn't coming back to us."

A direct hit, and she did her best not to fall out of the Ranger because *that* would have been embarrassing. As if she weren't embarrassed enough. "I see," she managed evenly. "Big difference there, I suppose."

He grimaced. "Holly—"

"Can you just get us there, please?" She turned away from him, arms over her chest. She felt the weight of his stare, but then he finally put the ATV in gear and drove straight into the woods.


Adam drove through the woods with single-minded purpose so he wouldn't think about the woman next to him. She was making a big production out of staring into the quickly thickening forest around them, looking completely engrossed in the gorgeous ambiance. But she was radiating confusion and hurt.

His fault, of course. "Holly."

She pretended not to hear him. She was still wearing his hat, and she looked adorable. Adorably hot . . .

Not *going there, Connelly*.

Shaking his head, he drove on, clearing his thoughts. He'd been taught how to do this in counseling for the times when his brain got caught in a nightmare loop, replaying shit he didn't want to replay but couldn't stop. The technique was to start low, in the toes. He wriggled them. Then moved his thoughts to the arch of his foot. Then his heel. He went on to purposely and carefully categorize his entire body and, in doing so, prevented his brain from hijacking his thoughts.

He was at his own dick when he caught sight of Holly's expression. Pale. Solemn.

Unhappy.

It was worry, he assured himself. Worry for Donald.

And it was also because he was an asshole.

He argued with himself for a minute, then stopped the Ranger. "Holly."

She was still pretending he didn't exist, and doing a fine job of it, too, so he cupped her jaw and turned her to face him.

Her eyes flashed at that. Yeah, she was pissed off, too, and suddenly, the interior of the Ranger felt a little tight. Especially since Milo was leaning forward, blowing doggy breath on them, waiting for Adam's next move.

"Down," Adam said.

Milo's ears sagged, but he lay down.

"Holly, look at me."

She lifted her gaze and he was immediately slammed by her beautiful blue eyes.

"It wasn't you," he said, voice soft. "It was me."

"What?"

"Back when I left. When I said good-bye. It wasn't you, it was me."

Her eyes narrowed. "Are you seriously giving me Classic Breakup Line Number One right now?" She leaned away from him, arms crossed, body language blaring high warnings at him. "Should I feed you your next line, or do you know it?"

He scowled. "It wasn't a line."

"Oh yes, it was. And not a very good one. Line Number Two isn't much better. It's 'I wasn't ready for a long term relationship.'"

Adam couldn't believe he'd been drawn into this conversation, or that he was even here. "I *wasn't* ready for a long-term relationship."

"Oh my God." She turned away.

Milo, always extremely sensitive to tension, leaned forward and licked Adam's ear.

And then Holly's. She sighed and hugged the dog.

Swearing beneath his breath, Adam shoved the Ranger back into gear but didn't hit the gas. He could feel his brain swelling. Probably an oncoming aneurism. "You were eighteen."

"Old enough."

*"No,"* he said, disagreeing. "And I was—"

"A good guy," she said so firmly he knew that she believed it to the depths of her soul.

Something inside him reacted to that, something forgotten so long ago. "A complete fuckup," he corrected. "Did you forget why I had to leave Sunshine?" He knew she hadn't. His wild ways had been legendary. Hell, he'd dragged her into some of them. No one would have believed that Donald Reid's daughter, in Sunshine for the summer, would give a thug like Adam a second look.

But she had.

She'd sucked him into her vortex in the best possible way. And then Adam's wild ways caught up with him one night when he and his idiot friends had gone drag racing out on Highway 89. They'd raced a lot. But on this particular night, the weather had gone to shit. Not that they'd cared. Hell, they'd been invincible.

Thank God, Holly hadn't been with him. He'd been

careful to keep her away from his friends. The accident, when the inevitable had happened, hadn't involved Adam or his car. Nope, that would have been far too easy.

The cop chasing them had slid out on the wet, slick highway, over a three-hundred-foot embankment, dying instantly.

By the skin of his teeth, Adam had been spared legal blame by the court system. The judge had ruled the tragedy an accidental death but had firmly suggested Adam get his act together, and fast.

On a one-track path to hell and already halfway there, Adam had been at a loss on how to do that. Then Donald—clueless as to what Adam and his precious daughter were doing with their free time in Adam's beat-up old truck—had suggested the military.

Adam had agreed, and everyone within a two-hundred-mile radius had breathed a sigh of relief.

Adam could still remember facing Holly after he'd enlisted, looking into her achingly blue eyes, torn by what he felt for her and what he would become if he stayed.

Out of some sense of obligatory self-flagellation, he'd gone about cutting everything good out of his life before he left. He'd told Holly not to wait for him, that he wouldn't be coming back. That she needed to move on.

And damned if, for the first time ever, she'd actually done exactly as he'd told her. When he'd found out about her marriage to Derek, he'd thought, *Good, great, perfect.* She'd really moved on. And while he was happy for her, he hadn't kept in touch, not wanting to hear about it more than he already had.

As for him, he'd gone on to see five continents, learned how to survive in just about any kind of conditions, shoot anything with a bullet, and how to be a detached asshole. He'd also learned the value of discipline and boundaries, the hard way of course, since he didn't know the easy way to do anything. His twenties were a blur of more wild-and-craziness, but this time it had all been sanctioned by good, ol' Uncle Sam. "Did you?" he asked Holly. "Do you remember why I left?"

She looked away, arms crossed as if she had to hold her aching heart inside her chest. "I'm not going to discuss this."

"So you're still stubborn as hell. Stubborn and . . ."

When he broke off, not finishing the sentence, she spun back to him. "Oh, don't stop there," she said, "it was just getting good. Stubborn and . . . what?"

Adam tried really hard not to make stupid mistakes these days. But once in a while, he fell off the wagon. "Clueless," he said, and once again hit the gas.

## Seven

*Stubborn and clueless.* Adam thought her stubborn and clueless. Holly stewed over that for a good long time, but eventually she had to admit he might be onto something with the stubborn thing. After all, being stubborn as hell had pretty much directed her life. It was why she'd gone after Adam in the first place. Why she'd gone off to New York and married the first man to give her an ounce of attention. Why she'd let people think she was happy when she wasn't.

It was why she was here on this mountain with Adam rather than letting him go without her.

So, yeah. She'd give him the stubborn thing.

But clueless? Her gut was churning up pretty good over that one. If she hadn't needed him for navigating the now muddy, treacherous route, she'd like to show him clueless—with a boot up his very fine ass.

An hour later, the sky was as dark as gunmetal. The promised storm was nearly on them. She felt her chest tighten as she thought about her father, possibly hurt.

Or worse.

Another call to his cell got her nothing.

When Adam stopped and turned off the engine, silence reigned, except for the wind rattling the rain from the trees to the saturated ground. "Where are we?" she asked.

He pulled out his phone and checked for service. Some areas were complete dead zones, but in most they could get a few bars. He must have been able to do that now because he brought up a map, showing her their location. "We're about a mile northeast of Diamond Ridge."

She eyed the sky again. "It's pretty bad out."

"Not yet it's not."

She was glad he thought so. It was getting colder, but his easy confidence helped keep her panic at bay.

Because her father was out in this . . . somewhere.

"Donald would've been able to get farther in his ATV than this," Adam said. "The weather was good on the day he left. But any ATV tracks will be washed away by now." He turned to her. "Ready?"

*For what?* "Sure."

He got out and she realized he meant they were going to hike in that last mile. Milo jumped out, too, sitting at attention, staring up at Adam, who gave him some hand signal. At the sight of it, Milo took off, bounding over the terrain like a rabbit.

"Where's he going?" she asked.

"To search. He'll let me know if he sees signs anyone's been through this way, or if he finds someone."

Or a body.

Adam didn't say it. He didn't have to. He tossed her a pair of warm, thick gloves while he affixed two pairs of snowshoes to his backpack before gingerly pulling it on.

"Your shoulder," she said.

"I've hiked with far worse injuries," he said, brushing off her concern, gesturing for her to grab her pack.

She did and then stared at the trail ahead, which appeared to go straight up, vanishing into thin air. "It's a lot steeper from this side."

"It's an optical illusion."

She glanced up into his face. Damned if he wasn't the most annoyingly compelling man she'd ever met. His force of personality was so strong that she couldn't begin to fight her attraction to it. His hood hid much of his face from view except for his strong jaw and the stubble there that she wanted to rub up against like a cat. "Really? An optical illusion?"

"Nah." He stepped in front of her and began walking. "It's definitely steeper from this side. I just didn't want you to psych yourself out." He kept going, striding forward with purpose, not even bothering to look back to see if she was following.

"Hey," she said.

Adam wasn't a man to give in to such an indulgence as sighing, but she'd have sworn he did just that as he turned back to her. "You can wait at the ATV. I'll go see if he's up there."

"He's going to be," she said, moving toward him. "And I told you, I'm going with you."

And so they walked. They passed the mute evidence of a fire from several years back. The standing dead were bleached skeletal tree stumps intermixed with the living forest of younger pines and firs attempting to reclaim the area. She knew that plenty of big game wandered up here, living among the lakes and hidden bogs. "What if we run into the wolves?"

"I'm armed," was all Adam said.

Of course he was.

She entertained herself by staring at his ass. As far as scenery went, it was extremely watchable. She had no idea how he could look so sexy just walking. It was really intimidating, actually. She tried to find her own sexy, but that was hard in hiking books and Adam's oversized jacket over the top of hers.

After a few minutes, it began raining again, and Adam's ass, amazing as it was, could no longer distract her. "It's coming down good now."

Adam stopped and turned to her. He wasn't even breathing hard, the ass. "Need a break?"

"No." She'd take a break when she was dead. Which at this pace might be by dinnertime. "We keep going."

But after another few minutes, she was having her doubts whether she'd be with him at the end or not. She'd been doing a lot of sitting on her ass working at a desk lately. Too much. She needed to get back to some serious cardio. Not that she'd admit this since Adam's long legs were eating up the distance with no trouble, though she suspected he was holding back a little bit on her account.

Milo reappeared every few minutes, checking in with Adam, the two of them interacting as if they were one.

"Anything?" she asked. "He catching anyone's trail?"

"Deer. Wolves. Elk." He shook his head. "Nothing human. Holly—"

"No," she said, knowing what he was going to say. If her dad had come through here, there'd be signs. "Don't tell me he's not here."

He gave her a steady look and didn't tell her that. "You need water?"

"I'm fine."

He turned to Milo next, carefully checking the dog's paws, giving him water. Then they kept going, and Holly had an even harder time finding herself sexy in the mud-and-ice combo. Hard to be confident while feeling like a drowned rat.

Not that she cared about being sexy for Adam, not in the slightest.

Ten minutes later, they got to Diamond Ridge, the day camp area.

It was empty.

Milo ran through it, nose down, sniffing, searching, before coming back to Adam and sitting calmly.

"Nothing," Adam said. "No sign of anyone."

They searched for themselves, but Milo was right. Her dad wasn't here. She felt Adam's gaze on her, and met it. "Then he's at Mount Eagle," she said. "Or . . ."

"Or?"

"Maybe the caves at Kaniksu."

Something flickered in his eyes, coming and going too fast to name. "The caves?"

"At Kaniksu, yes. He's recently started going there, too."

He drew in a deep breath and nodded. "Call him again," he said, waiting until she did just that.

She did, and got her dad's voice mail message. "His phone's still off."

Or dead.

"Let's move," he said, bringing her thoughts back to something productive.

"Mount Eagle or Kaniksu?" she asked his back.

Adam dropped his chin to his chest and muttered something she didn't catch before lifting his head. "Mount Eagle first."

She nodded, and he gestured her ahead of him. "After you," he said.

As she led the way back to where they'd left the ATV, she wondered if he was watching *her* ass this time.

At the ATV, Adam pulled out lunch. He had bagels, on which he squeezed peanut butter from a tube, then sprinkled raisins on top. He handed her one, meeting her startled gaze. "What?" he asked.

"Nothing," she said. "Except this seems so . . . domestic of you."

"It's carbs, protein, and sugars," he said as if she'd insulted him. "Body fuel."

"It is," she agreed. "It's also a little cute, at least compared to the bag of beef jerky I packed."

He was far too good to scowl or frown at *cute*, but she could tell he was doing both on the inside. She watched him give Milo water and a doggy biscuit, his hand fondly ruffling the dog's fur.

In response, Milo set his big head on Adam's thigh and gazed up at him adoringly.

"He's pretty darn cute, too," Holly said.

Adam slid her a look. "What is it with you and cute?"

She wasn't sure. *Hormones?* "There's nothing wrong with cute, you know."

"We're *not* cute."

Okay, that was probably true about Adam ninety-nine percent of the time. To the best of her recollection, there was very little cute about him. Sexy, yes. Cute . . . *no*. But then he gave Milo a full body rub that had the dog practically purring, and she had to revise. Maybe he had more than one percent cute in him.

"He was neglected before I got him," Adam said, still stroking Milo. "He gets separation anxiety if he can't sleep near me. He goes to Dell's when I'm traveling and eats up Jade's shoes like bonbons."

"Aw, he misses you."

"More like Dell's a sap and lets him do whatever he wants."

"Where did you get him?" Holly asked.

"When I first got stateside, my counselor wanted me to get a dog. It's part of the therapy. I was working with dogs as a liaison between breeders and trainers and was in Arizona when I saw Milo for the first time. He was one of eight. I was supposed to take the entire litter. But the breeder refused to give me Milo, saying he was a liability. Apparently

he'd failed all early training attempts. The breeder was calling him Frat Boy, because Milo was always just looking for
a good time. Said he was no good, would never amount to
anything, and the possibility of him being an S&R dog was
absolutely nil. He wouldn't let me take him with the others
because he was afraid I'd demand my money back down
the road. Milo was slated for the Humane Society. Death
row, of course."

As if he could understand the words, Milo leaned up and
licked Adam's chin, and Holly felt twin tugs of amusement
and something far deeper and harder to breathe past. "So
how did you end up with him?" Holly asked.

"I said I'd make a deal for all eight or no deal at all." He
slung an arm around Milo, who leaned into him. "And the
breeder was right. He was a complete Frat Boy."

"And you what, dog-whispered him?"

Adam shook his head with a low laugh. "I'm not a dog
whisperer. That implies some sort of extraordinary ability.
I have a method with a curriculum. That's all."

"So you saved his life and kept him as your own."

"Well, I couldn't very well pawn him off on anyone."

Milo gazed adoringly into Adam's eyes, his own bright,
his tongue lolling out of his mouth, which appeared to be
tipped up into a smile.

Adam shook his head at the dog, but he smiled.

The guy didn't fool Holly for one hot minute. He'd always been far more into animals than people, a product of
growing up knowing that you weren't wanted or particularly valued, she supposed. That he'd managed to grow up
at all and not be a statistic was amazing, but that he was
also a man to admire, even more so.

And if she was admitting that, she also had to admit he
had a lot of really great qualities. Sure, he had more than his
fair share of faults as well; he was intensely private and
didn't like to share himself, not to mention doggedly aggressive and bullheaded . . . But on the other side of all that,

he put others' needs and safety ahead of his own, always. He was smart as hell, fiercely loyal, driven to succeed, and he had a deceptive playful side that she hadn't seen in a long time but was catching glimpses of now with Milo. She popped her last bite of bagel in her mouth. "Want to know what I think?"

"No."

She added obnoxious to his list of faults. "I think beneath that badass layer of testosterone and Neanderthal tendencies, you're just a big old softie."

He slid her a patented steely look. "Testosterone and Neanderthal tendencies?"

She shrugged and reached for her water. "If the shoe fits . . ."

He shook his head, but his eyes might have gleamed with the slightest bit of amusement as he did. "There's a fault with your logic."

"Yeah? What's that?"

"I'm not soft. Anywhere."

She choked on her water, which only got worse when he leaned in to pat her on the back. While she gasped for air and sputtered, he took the water and capped it for her. Then he held it back out to her, steady.

Definitely amused.

She snatched the bottle from his fingers, firmly ignoring the zap of attraction as she touched him, deciding it was static electricity. Unsure, and just a little shaken, she stood. "We need to get going."

They headed to Mount Eagle, and thanks to the weather, it took nearly all of their remaining daylight hours, and the trek didn't have a happy ending. The abandoned old ranger station that her father used as a hunting base when he was up here was just that—abandoned.

No one had been here in weeks, maybe longer.

Adam let out a breath and turned to Holly.

The wind was whipping, the snow falling lightly now.

He had his hood up, reflective glasses on, hands shoved in his pocket. With the daylight fading fast, leaving in its wake the hovering glow of dusk, he could have graced the cover of any magazine.

He took her breath. Oh God, she was stupid enough to let him take her breath.

"Hey," Adam said, frowning as he dropped his pack and moved to her. "You okay?"

When would he get it—she was always okay. Although she did feel a little dizzy . . .

Adam tugged her pack off, keeping his hands on her arms.

Milo came close and whined softly, nudging his warm, wet nose into the palm of her hand.

"We moved fast," Adam said, ducking a little to look into her eyes. "Really fast, at altitude. Sit a minute—"

"No." She shook her head and patted Milo on the head. "I'm fine."

"Uh-huh. Be fine sitting down." Adam pushed her to a rock in front of the shell of the ranger station and hunkered before her, hands on her thighs now, holding her in place, studying her face.

"It's nothing," she said, tipping her head up. A few snowflakes landed on her heated face. "I just got dizzy for a minute."

"Stay still."

Staying still was a great idea. Being this close to Adam, not so much. In fact, it was a really, *really* bad idea. The worst idea she'd had since . . . since that morning when she'd sneaked onto his ATV instead of finding another way to get here.

She looked off into the fading light rather than directly into his eyes. Looking directly into Adam's eyes was always a problem. It caused a condition known as lust, which in turn caused its own condition.

*Stupidity.*

She really hated this helpless attraction she had for him, especially since it wasn't reciprocated. Never again. She was never again going to love a man who didn't love her. From inside her pocket, her phone vibrated. Surprised that she even had reception up here, she pulled it out to find two texts, the first from Derek that was short and to the point.

Need to see you.

Ha. So he'd finally deigned to notice she was gone. He could "need to see her" all he wanted. She was over him and his needs.

Delete.

The second text was from Kate.

You okay?

This was debatable, but Holly typed back that she was fine, though there'd been no sign of her father yet.

Kate responded immediately.

Spending the night with the big, bad, stoic hottie?

Holly choked out a laugh. Adam leaned in and read the text before she could delete it. He went brows up and looked at her.

She shook her head. "Kate thinks she's funny."

"'Hottie'?"

"Yes, it's what people who look like you are called."

"Thought I was cute," Adam said.

"I'm rethinking that."

Still hunkered before her, balanced on the balls of his feet, he rubbed a hand over his jaw. Once again, the stubble there made a rough noise that scraped at her insides low in her belly.

And lower.

"We're not sleeping together," she blurted out.

"I know."

She felt . . . let down. How dumb was that? But damn, it would have been nice for him to reveal even the slightest bit of disappointment. Instead, he was back to his silent, badass self. He eyed the skyline, the line of his mouth grim.

He was dusted in snowflakes, not that he seemed to notice or care.

When he turned to her, she got sucked in by his gaze and had to fight the most insane urge not to fist his jacket and pull him close. For comfort.

For more.

The thought caused an inner heat barely doused by the cool flakes falling on them. But she couldn't go there, couldn't think about Adam like that, not with her dad still missing.

Actually, she shouldn't think about Adam like that, ever. "So . . . to the caves?"

He turned away. "In the morning."

Oh boy. "You mean—"

"It's time to stop for the night."

Something low in her belly quivered. Anxiety, absolutely. But also something else, something that had nothing to do with her missing dad. "I don't think that's a good idea."

"We're going to find him." His voice said there was no other acceptable option. "Just not until daylight."

She stared out into the night, thinking of all the reasons why her dad hadn't been in touch with her, not a single one of them good. She swallowed hard against the building fear and nodded. They were stopping for the night.

It was going to be a long one.

# Eight

Adam gathered wood for a fire, keeping an eye on Holly. She was sitting on a log, hands clenched, staring down at her feet as if she wasn't quite sure how they'd gotten her here.

She was cold, wet, and tired. He knew because he was those things, too. But discomfort was something he had learned to simply endure, and his own was insignificant compared to the discomfort and other various emotions pouring off the unusually silent woman in front of him.

The best thing he could do for them both was get the fire going, put food in their bellies, and make sure they got some sleep. It would also keep his mind off the fact that they were going to Kaniksu tomorrow.

The fucking caves.

He shook that off for now, he had no choice. They couldn't both lose it at the same time. Not that he intended to lose it at all.

The fire only took a moment. Another to access the food he'd brought and push some of it on her. Water, too. The altitude could be a real killer if they didn't stay hydrated. He was good at this part, at surviving. Even when others didn't. What he wasn't good at was emotions, and Holly was emitting them as fast and furious as the falling snow-flakes. He sure as hell wasn't in the mood to face yet another of his failures, but there she sat, his biggest one.

Needing him.

He, a man who could barely commit to a dental appointment much less another human being.

And yet he couldn't fail her.

Not again.

He concentrated on Milo for a minute, getting him watered and fed. Checking his paws again, making sure everything was okay. When he'd finished bustling around like a damn housewife, he sat across the fire from Holly. Across was best. Far enough away that he wouldn't be tempted to touch. Distance was the key here.

She appeared to be holding it together, but the cracks were showing. She was trying to be tough, trying to hold her own, and she was breaking his heart.

She lifted her head and stared at him with those gorgeous eyes. As always, her face and body language told him everything he needed to know about what she was thinking and feeling. She was upset, scared, unsettled, and . . . depending on him. There'd been a time where he'd have done anything to have her look at him like he was her everything. That time had passed. "It's going to be okay," he said, hoping to God that was true.

She nodded. Then shook her head. She put her hand to her chest. "I really thought we'd have found him by now."

Aw, hell. He rose and moved to her side.

"I'm okay," she said, breathless. "I think I'm just having a very mild, very overdue anxiety attack. Ignore me."

Yeah, right. He reached out to pull her in, but a quick glance at her face confirmed how much of a mistake that would be. Smoothly he adapted and tossed another log into the fire instead.

A wolf howled and was joined by a few others, and Holly tensed, and then scooted closer while still managing not to actually touch him.

"The fire will keep them back," he said.

"I know." But her eyes darted to the forest beyond.

"You're not breathing."

"I am so." She proved this by attempting to drag in a breath, which had her body brushing his. A quick tactile memory hit him, the feel of her warm skin and the soft weight of her breasts in the palm of his hand. The taste of her pebbled nipple as he sucked her in his mouth. The sound of her ragged, aroused breathing in his ear . . .

The ragged breathing wasn't a memory. She was going to hyperventilate. "Sometimes when people get anxious, they breathe too shallowly, from the upper chest. It's a natural response to stress. But your body responds with an increase in blood pressure, and then even more stress hormones are released, so it's counterproductive."

"I'm not anxious," she said.

She was sitting ramrod straight so she didn't accidentally touch him. Respecting the space bubble, he kept his hands to himself. "Yeah, I can see that."

She managed to roll her eyes, so she couldn't be too far gone. "Okay," she said. "So maybe I'm a little anxious."

"Breathe deeper," he said, and then, as had been done for him while in the midst of a knockout, drag-down anxiety attack of his own, he showed by example, inhaling deeply.

She attempted to do the same, the air catching in her lungs.

"Again," he said.

She was cold and shivering. *Fuck distance*, he thought, and slipped an arm around her to impart some of his body heat.

She made a soft sound that he couldn't even begin to interpret. Gratitude? Relief? Sorrow? He was completely out of practice in translating women sounds. "More deep breathing," he said, and set a hand on her stomach. "Let your belly go soft and relaxed, and breathe from your lower abs."

The wind picked up. She shivered again and he tightened his arm on her. Surprising him, she turned to face him and burrowed in.

Well, hell. He opened his jacket and pulled her in even closer. They were silent for long moments, until finally, he felt her relax.

"How did you learn that breathing thing?" she murmured.

"The hard way." He paused. "In therapy, after I got back."

"What else did you learn?"

He let out a mirthless laugh. "Patience."

"Patience?" She gave him a wry grin. "I think I'm speechless."

His mouth quirked. "I know. Miracles never cease."

She stared into the fire and sighed, the sound filled with self-disgust. "I'm tougher than this."

He shook his head. "Somehow it doesn't matter how tough you are. You can be tough as hell and still be leveled flat without warning."

She looked at him. "What do you do when you're leveled flat?"

"You make a plan, you move on that plan, and you keep breathing."

"I like the breathing part." She drew in a couple of deep breaths. "Some sugar would be even better."

He pulled a candy bar from his pocket.

She snatched it so fast he nearly lost his fingers.

Taking two bites in quick succession, she moaned in sheer pleasure.

Adam stared at her, knowing she had no idea how sensual the sound was or what it could do to a man.

She glanced at him, then took a longer look and blushed. "Sorry. Guess I really needed a fix."

"I can see that," he said, voice a little thick. "Good?"

"Amazing," she said, and licked her lips and then her fingers. When she caught him watching that with rapt attention, she stopped. Then the only sound, other than the crackling flames and whistling wind, was Holly swallowing hard.

To give them both a badly needed moment, he ran a finger over the gold chain at her neck, lifting the small, dainty charm.

"It's the Chinese symbol for strength," she said softly.

"You don't need a symbol for that. You've always been strong."

She shook her head. "Not always. It's from Derek."

And she'd kept it. He absorbed the pang of . . . jealousy? That didn't make much sense. Adam had left her. It was none of his business how much she'd loved someone else that she'd kept a piece of him around her neck.

"He forgot my birthday," she said. "My twenty-first. I guess I'd thought it would be a big deal . . ."

*It* should *have been a big fucking deal,* he thought.

"That's when I first started to know it wasn't going to work, that I wasn't important enough. But he tried to make it up to me, gave me money to buy myself a present. I'd seen the necklace in an upscale jewelry store . . ." She shrugged as if embarrassed. "I keep it because it's a reminder of what my life once was," she said softly, "and why I should be glad that I moved on."

Adam could see the fire reflected in her eyes, and much more, and wondered at how much this one woman could make him feel. Letting out a breath, he laced his fingers in hers, squeezing her hand. "I'm proud of you, Holly."

"For what?"

"For moving on. For being strong. For becoming a pretty damn incredible woman."

Her eyes never left his. "Not so incredible, really."

"You do what you think is right, always. Not what's easy, but what's right. You came out here after your father when no one else would."

She looked at him for a long moment. "You never talk much about your father."

No, he didn't. He tried not to think about him too much, either. "Not much to tell."

"There's got to be something," she insisted.

"He was Texan, and his first love was football. Women were his second love. He lived big and loud and was by all accounts a decent guy, up until he died in a car wreck."

"You were young," she said.

"Five."

"That must have destroyed your mom," she said.

"I don't know, to be honest. She's not big on emotions and feelings. Or at least on sharing them." He slid her a look. "Yeah, yeah, I inherited that from her."

She smiled. "You do okay when you want to. You ever see her? Your mom?"

He shrugged. "Some."

"She lives about an hour outside of Sunshine, right?"

"Yeah." In a double-wide, which was all she'd let Dell and Adam do for her. It was no secret that Nila had given up custody of her boys, leaving them to face the foster system. Guilt kept her from accepting their help now. "Dell sees her more than I do," he said. "He drives out there every other week and works a few hours, giving vet care to those who need it."

"That's sweet."

"That's Dell. I don't go out there unless I have to."

"Have to?"

"Once in a while something on her trailer breaks and I go fix it."

"When you have to," she said.

"Yeah."

"How's that not as sweet as what Dell does?"

Jesus. "Didn't we do this already? I'm not sweet, Holly."

"No, you said you weren't cute."

He wasn't either of those things, and she knew it.

"When's the last time you saw her?" she asked.

"A while ago. We had a disagreement."

"About?"

"Water." He and Dell had wanted to put some money into her well, to get her better-quality water, but she absolutely refused their help. Adam had done it, anyway, started the process to make the improvements, and Nila had called off the job. She'd made a rare appearance in town, at the animal center in fact, to tell him that his money wasn't welcome. He'd looked into her dark eyes and known it was nothing less than one hundred percent pride. That she regretted not ever spending money on her sons, and in light of how things had gone down, she didn't have a right to their money now. Adam didn't give a shit about any of that. He liked to think he didn't give a shit about her at all.

But he did. And all he'd wanted was to make sure she had some clean water, dammit.

But there was one thing Nila could do better than her sons. She could out-stubborn them. Adam told Holly the story in as few words as possible and she snuggled in a little bit more. "I don't know," she said softly. "Sounds to me like you have a little sweet in you, after all."

He tilted his head down to give her a look.

"You do," she insisted.

"I *don't*."

"You're here with me," she reminded him. "Because I asked."

His arms tightened. "I'm here because I want to be."

She ducked her face into the crook of his neck, but not before he saw the sheen in her eyes. He gave her a moment because the last thing he wanted was tears. He felt helpless against her tears.

"Adam?"

"Yeah?"

"Tell me again that we're going to find him." Her lips brushed his skin with each word, so that he barely was able to suppress a full body shiver.

"We're going to find him," he said.

She nodded, her frozen nose bumping into his ear. Snowflakes dusted her hair and shoulders. He found his hands sliding beneath the jacket, moving slowly up and down her back, warming, soothing.

Wanting . . .

She lifted her head and looked at him, then his mouth.

And like Pavlov's dog, his body stirred.

"Adam?" she whispered.

The sound of his name in her low, sensuous voice was doing him in. This time he had to clear his throat. "Yeah?"

She licked her dry lips, just a quick dart of her tongue, and he nearly groaned. "We're a bad idea. Right?"

"The worst." But here was the thing. Some of his worst ideas had turned into really great ones. Sure, he'd been burned by most of them, but there was something in the way she was looking at him.

It was an invite that he couldn't refuse. Cupping her jaw, he leaned in and covered her mouth with his. When she gasped in pleasure, he took full advantage, stroking her tongue with his in a deep, hot, wet kiss. No niceties. It had been a damn long time since he'd kissed her. Years. Something in him reared up and itched to remind her that once upon a time they'd been damn good together.

She murmured his name in the sexiest, softest murmur and dug her fingers into his biceps, squirming to get closer. Closer worked for him, and he let himself do what he'd been thinking about doing for hours—he touched. He touched whatever he could reach, letting his hands roam her glorious body, losing himself in her soft warmth.

She moaned into his mouth but slowly pulled back. Breathing unevenly, she shook her head. "That's not the bad-idea part."

"No?" Good. He leaned in to kiss her again but she put a hand to his chest. "I meant, the last time, it took . . . it took me a long time to get over you leaving like you did. No looking back. No letters. Nothing." She paused. "I got that you had to go, that the judge made you, but . . ."

The judge hadn't made him. That had been a necessary lie, so she wouldn't realize he was walking away from her by choice. He hadn't been able to make himself do that to her. Not loving this little walk down Guilt Row, he drew a deep breath. The way he'd left—no loose ends—had been the only way he'd known to handle the situation. It had been hell. His own doing, of course. He'd always been his own worst enemy. But even back then he'd owned up to his mistakes. He'd made a plan—get out of Sunshine and make something of himself—and he'd executed the plan.

Besides, she'd been made for better things than being with him. Far better. Life with him would've been a one-way ticket to Loser-ville.

Getting out of Sunshine had been good for him. The military had taught him discipline, how to make things happen, in a good way, and she had to know that. He'd trained. He'd fought. He'd learned.

What she didn't know was that he'd done it all with a good part of his heart back in Sunshine. "How long could it have taken?" he heard himself ask. "You were married less than a year later."

Her gaze whipped to his, and she flattened her hands on his chest, giving a good shove.

Still holding on to her, he didn't budge.

She made a noise of frustration and pushed again. "Let go."

He lifted his hands.

She stood up, crossing her arms over herself as she turned away. "It was more than a year."

Not much.

"Maybe we should try to get to Kaniksu right now," she said quietly.

Clearly, they were done with this conversation. Worked for him just fine—except now she wanted to try to get to caves. At night. His biggest nightmare, of course. "You want to move across twenty miles of rugged, isolated terrain in the dark."

"Fine. Stupid idea." She looked around at the fire, at the dilapidated ranger station that was little more than a three-sided hut, at the million acres of remote, isolated, rugged forestland surrounding them. "Could really use some more sugar," she said.

He started to rise to go to his pack, but she put out her hand. "No!" She shook her head. "God, no. Don't you dare bring out any more. My jeans are too tight as it is."

Not from where he was sitting . . .

She yawned and then sighed. "Do you really have more candy bars?"

"I've got a lot of things."

"Like?"

"Spare clothes and gear, topo map, compass, water, knife, first-aid kit, rope, rations . . ." *Condoms . . .*

"You're practically a Boy Scout."

Yeah, not exactly. He watched her fight another yawn and gestured to the shelter. "Go to sleep, Holly."

She pulled her sleeping bag from her pack and headed inside the shelter.

Adam gestured to Milo, and the dog followed her, sitting in the opened doorway where he would act as dubious guard dog. Adam stayed at the fire's edge, figuring that was the safest place for him. The air was still now and very cold. There were no sounds except the crackle and pop of the fire, and his own thoughts. It was damn rare that he allowed himself the luxury of what-ifs, but he was slammed with them now. What if he'd not broken up with her? What if he'd kept in touch? What if he'd told her how he felt? Would she still feel the same about him now as she had then, or would she have eventually dumped his sorry ass?

And the biggest question of them all—would they still be here, right here, caught up in the tangle of memories and emotions he no longer had the capacity for?

From where he sat, he could hear her tossing and turning. He knew without looking over there that she was cold. He grabbed his sleeping bag, and moved to her. "Get up a second."

"I'm not taking your sleeping bag, too," she said.

"Not taking. Sharing."

She sat up slowly, warily, watching as he unzipped his bag and then pulled hers off her body. She'd kicked off her boots but other than that remained fully dressed. He unzipped her bag, too, and then laid his flat, with hers on top.

Holly stared at the makeshift bed as if it were a poised rattlesnake, then unzipped her jacket—his, actually. He forgot to breathe, torn between wanting her to keep going and stopping her.

She wriggled out of the jacket, then carefully rolled it up. She set it in the middle of the opened sleeping bag like it was the border crossing of Baghdad—except maybe even more guarded.

"No crossing the line," she said.

He met her gaze. "Are you worried about me or you?"

She crossed her arms. "I'm not *that* attracted to you."

He toed the jacket. "You don't need this—you've already drawn the line in the sand. I think I can control myself." He was ninety-nine percent sure.

Okay, seventy-five.

Pointedly leaving the jacket in place, she slid between the opened sleeping bags and lay down, facing away from him.

He stared at her stiff spine and then found himself smiling. "I get it. You're not worried about me. You're worried about you. *You* can't control yourself."

She let out a derisive snort that didn't fool him for one moment. But the humor passed quickly because with *neither* of them trustworthy, he couldn't lie down.

"Where are you going?" she asked when he moved to the doorway again.

"To bank the fire." And to take a minute. A long one. He needed to think. It had taken her a while to get over him? Well, it had taken him a while, too. But he *had* gotten over her. He'd gotten over everything.

And she could do much better than being with a guy who now chose to feel nothing at all.

## Nine

H olly watched through the open wall of the hut as Adam poked at the flames. He wore multiple layers, including his down jacket, so she could only imagine the muscles of his back bunching and working, but her heart still skipped a beat, anyway.

Ridiculous. She'd given away far too much of herself to this man. Then. Now.

No more.

She sat up, arms clasped around her knees, concentrating on breathing evenly. Was he going to sleep out there? Then he'd be the cold one, and she wouldn't be able to relax worrying about him.

*Holly, Holly, Holly,* she chided herself. *You're not worried about him being cold so much as him not coming back in here.*

As if sensing her gaze, he rose and turned to her. It was snowing again, she realized, as he stepped under the dubious protection of their shelter, approaching in his usual silent way.

There'd been a time when just watching him had upped her pulse rate, when one look from him could melt her clothes away. Remembering that, what they'd had, yearnings assaulted her, no matter that she didn't want to feel them. He had a back-off demeanor now, which contrasted with the way he touched her as if she meant something to him. It confused her.

Hurt her.

And worse, she had no one but herself to blame. His words, when he'd chosen to give her any, had made things clear. He had no interest in a relationship of any kind. This was about finding her father.

That was all.

The fire's glow reflected off the fine sheen of melting snow covering his hair, face, and arms. The light played off the angles of his face as he came to a stop at the foot of their "bed." He unzipped his jacket, spreading it out on his pack to dry overnight. Next, he pulled off his sweatshirt. Beneath, he wore a thin long-sleeved shirt that clung to his every muscle. Using those muscles, he bent and untied his boots.

A sound involuntarily escaped her, and he glanced up.

She shook her head. Nothing. Nothing at all. In fact, she was just sitting here . . .

He kicked off the boots and rose. She wondered if he was going to lose anything else. Her body voted for the jeans, and at just the thought, she shivered.

"Cold?" he asked.

No. She was actually having quite the hot flash—not something she planned on admitting.

Adam checked on Milo, curled up by their packs. He stroked and praised the dog, then dropped to his knees at Holly's side. Little droplets of melted snow flew off of him, a few hitting her, sizzling on her heated skin.

"Sorry, I'm all wet," he said.

Yeah. And he wasn't the only one, she thought wildly as the fragrance of damp Adam drifted over her.

Heaven.

He stretched out on his side of the bedding, and when he came too close to the boundary of the United States of Holly, she adjusted the folded jacket.

He slid her a look.

She didn't care. She was taking no chances with herself. She would never survive a sexual encounter with him. And there would be a sexual encounter if they touched in the night. She could feel it. She—

A sound escaped him, one that seemed to be a low laugh. Startled, her gaze jerked up to his.

Yeah, he was definitely laughing, the bastard, chuckling low in his throat. Momentarily stunned at the smile on his face, the kind that included his eyes and affected her heart rate, she blinked.

"You're thinking so loud I smell something burning," he said.

"This really isn't very funny."

"You're right." He sat up in the middle of his designated area and folded up his discarded sweatshirt. Flashing her another rare smile, he placed it down as his pillow, and lay on his back, feet casually crossed, arms up behind his head. His shirt molded to every line of sinew on him.

She stared at him, eaten up with jealousy once again, this time over his "pillow."

"Problem?" he asked.

Oh, hell no would she admit that she wanted to share his pillow. "Not as long as you stay on your side."

He turned to face her, propping up his head with a hand. "You're such a liar." He was still smiling when he leaned over her, bracing his other hand on the ground at her far hip to give her a quick, hot kiss on the lips.

She gaped up at him in shock. Actually, she nearly moaned. "What was that?"

Still holding himself over her, he'd gone still, staring at her mouth as he slowly shook his head.

"Adam—"

"Shh a second," he said, and just looked at her. Then he lowered his head again. He started with small, brushing kisses, but it wasn't enough and she opened her mouth, touching her tongue to his lower lip.

A low sound escaped deep in his throat and he kissed her until her toes curled in her boots.

She had one hand in his hair, the other on his chest. Beneath her fingers, she could feel his heart pumping. The realization that she had every bit as much power over him as he had on her was heady. Closing her eyes, she let herself live in the moment, soaking up his taste, his touch, his scent, the heat that radiated off his body, all combining to rob her of the ability to think, to do anything but feel. And oh boy, the things she was feeling. He was deliciously hard, everywhere, and her hands were roaming south when he broke the kiss and rested his forehead against hers. After a minute, he lifted his head, shaking it as if befuddled.

Then he kissed the tip of her nose and . . . lay down.

While she continued to stare at him, he made himself comfortable, flat on his back again, all long-limbed, easy grace. And then he closed his eyes, his breathing immediately slowing and evening out, his body relaxed.

She stared at him, boring holes into him with her eyes. Because how could he relax? She couldn't relax, not with her body humming with a tension she didn't want to name, and her heart flapping ineffectively against her ribs. And then there were the other reactions, the ones she hadn't had in mixed company in a very long time.

Adam's hands were clasped on his flat stomach, his feet crossed. And if he breathed any slower, she'd have to check him for a pulse. He was clearly already deeply asleep, and this was as irritating as everything else about him.

"Lie down," he said, a quiet demand that had her nearly leaping out of her own skin.

She rolled her eyes at him, which was a waste because

his eyes were still closed, but she did lie down. She tried flat on her back, but there was a rock beneath her butt. And she was cold. She wished she hadn't been so adamant about the barrier. In hindsight, that might have been cutting her own nose off to spite her face.

Not to mention proving that she was every bit as stubborn as he thought.

Frustrated, she flopped onto her right side, facing away from him. But that rock that had bit into her butt was now hurting her hip. She flopped over to her left side and—

Adam reached out, yanked the jacket out from between them, slid a muscled arm around her waist and hauled her in so that she was spooned to him, her back to his front.

Heat infused her. His heat, which radiated out from his body to hers. "This isn't okay," she said.

"You still cold?"

Her head was pillowed on his bicep. His arm was wrapped around her, holding her closely, his hand opened wide and sitting disturbingly low on her belly. The backs of her thighs were plastered to the front of his and . . . and all their other parts were perfectly lined up. This made her parts very happy. And that wasn't all. She could feel that his parts were happy, too.

"Holly."

"No," she managed. "I'm not still cold." She was on fire . . .

"Good. Go to sleep."

Was he kidding? How was she supposed to sleep when all she wanted to do was turn over and . . . No. Don't go there. She sighed and regrouped, thinking about . . . mmm, if she wriggled just a little bit she could feel his muscles go all taut. Goodness, the man was locked and loaded. She squeezed her eyes shut and wracked her brain for a new train of thought in order to keep from rolling over and jumping his bones.

Her dad was still missing.

Yes, that did it. That swiped the sexual thoughts from her more effectively than a bucket of ice water would have. They were doing all they could to find him. Adam was doing all he could. And he'd made sure she was safe and fed and warm while he was at it.

It had been a long time since she'd let anyone take care of her, and she'd have thought it would be unsettling and uncomfortable. And while she'd like to think she could have handled this by herself, she knew she couldn't have.

Adam had come through for her, and he'd done so without any hesitation at all. In fact, the whole day had gone by and he'd only asked her one thing. It had been a question, a personal one, too personal to answer at the time. "Pride," she whispered.

Adam stirred slightly. "What?"

"Earlier you asked why I didn't tell anyone about my marriage falling apart. It was pride. Stupid pride."

He let out a surprised breath, disturbing the hair at her temple. "Why are you telling me this now?"

Good question. "I guess I just want you to understand. I didn't run off and get married to get back at you. I did it for even more stupid reasons than that."

"The pride thing," he said.

"Yeah." She sighed and admitted the rest. "My dad and Grif didn't want me to get married in the first place, so I couldn't tell them when it went bad. It was easy enough to keep it to myself, seeing as I lived so far away. But then, before I knew it, it'd become this huge secret."

"They didn't want you to get married for a good reason," Adam said. The arm he had wrapped around her tightened. "He was your college professor. Someone should've kicked his ass for even looking at you that way."

So he knew more of her past than she'd thought. "I was his teaching assistant, not his student, not technically. And to be honest, I wasn't really even an official teaching assistant. I was an errand girl, nothing more. As for why I let him in, he was very different from the men I'd known."

"No shit. He needed an AARP card."

She choked out a laugh. Derek was only eight years older than she. "Stop it."

"He had no business touching you."

They both left off the fact that at one time, most of Sunshine would have felt the same way about Adam touching her.

"And what do you mean he was different from the men you'd known?" he asked.

"The men I knew were all big and rugged and . . . tough. Alpha. Always so freaking alpha. Derek wasn't. He was . . . well, to be honest, he was sweet and gentle and approachable." At least at first. "He listened to me. He liked the things I liked. Reading. Going to art galleries and museums."

Adam didn't say a word to this, but she felt his censure just the same. "He was a whole new world," she said.

"Yeah? Then what went wrong?"

Why had she started this again? She couldn't remember. All she knew was that she wished she'd just kept her mouth shut and gone to sleep.


Adam waited, but it was pretty clear that Holly was taking a page from his own book and not planning on answering. It was a good strategy, but she had him curious now. "Holly."

"He was so different," she repeated softly. "And I . . . wasn't really prepared."

Okay, he wasn't going to like this story, he could tell. *Wasn't prepared for what?* "What did he do?"

"Just about everything that my father and Grif warned me about." She was twisting and untwisting her fingers together and he lifted his hand from her belly to settle it over both of hers.

"It's nothing you haven't heard before," she said. "It's a classic cliché, really. Apparently, old habits are hard to break, and he was still very attached to his students. Especially the female ones."

Son of a bitch. He'd cheated on her. Fucking idiot. "Ah, Holly."

"I know, pathetic, right? I just honestly believed that I was the only one, that I was special. But it's okay. It was a long time ago. I've learned a lot, and I've grown up."

"And yet," Adam said, coming back to the one point that was bugging the shit out of him about this whole thing, "you didn't tell anyone. You didn't seek help from your family or . . ." *Me.*

And why should she have come to him? He'd dumped her cruelly. But he couldn't help but wonder whether, despite her confession, she was holding back on just exactly how hellish her marriage had been.

"Are you kidding?" she asked with a mirthless laugh. "I couldn't ask for help. My dad and Grif had been so dead set against me getting married so young and then living so far away. I couldn't go to them. I had to handle it alone."

"You were *nineteen*."

"A grown-up," she insisted. "I'd gotten myself into that mess. I got myself out. I didn't need help, not from anyone. Especially my hotheaded brother and father."

Adam knew exactly how pissed off Grif had been about Holly rushing into marriage. He also knew Grif and Donald had flown out to New York several times to try to talk her out of it. And he'd known then—and now—that talking Holly out of anything she wanted to do never worked.

"They even tried to pay Derek off," Holly said. "That was probably my dad's idea. I don't know why Derek didn't go for that deal." She shook her head. "But you can see why I couldn't tell Grif or my dad when, a year later, I caught

Derek in our condo with his colleague's TA, testing the stability of our foyer table."

Adam winced. "Tell me you then tested out the stability of your boot to his family jewels."

She snorted out a soft laugh. "I threw his laptop out the window."

"Not bad."

"It was a third-story window," she said. "And it hit his precious car."

Adam felt a grin split his face. "Not bad at all."

She lifted her shoulder. "It was good, solid anger therapy."

Adam had gone through anger therapy, both officially and unofficially. Official anger therapy had taken place in his therapist's office in Coeur d'Alene, where he'd been given tools with which to work through his issues. They'd helped some. Maybe even a lot. But unofficial anger therapy had been a bigger help. Unofficial therapy had been Dell taking Adam to the top of Fallen Lakes, where they'd taken turns screaming at the top of their lungs into the canyon below.

Adam gave that therapy a big thumbs-up. He was feeling a little bit like he could use a visit out to Fallen Lakes right about now, in fact. "And neither Grif nor your dad ever suspected your marriage was in trouble?"

"Grif kept asking me if Derek had done anything he needed to get beaten up over," Holly said. "But . . ." She shook her head.

And he got it. They'd backed her into a corner, to a place she couldn't get out of without eating her own pride. She was lucky she hadn't choked on it. He buried his face in her hair, wishing he'd been there for her.

"So you see, right? I got myself into that situation, and—"

"And Reids don't quit," he finished for her. "Your father always says that."

She nodded.

"I get all of that," he said. "But Jesus, Holly, I don't think he meant for you to take it to heart in that context. You do realize that you don't *have* to be as stubborn as he is."

"I'm not. I'm not at all like him."

This wrenched a soft laugh from him. Because Holly and Donald? Two peas in a pod. Grif was the third pea. But Adam was smart enough not to admit that to a single one of them.

"I'm not," she repeated, sounding insulted as hell. "He's ornery, and when he thinks he's right, he won't budge an inch. He's ridiculously opinionated and *always* knows best. That's not me."

"Uh-huh," Adam said, trying to keep the sarcastic inflection from his voice, but he must have failed because she reached back and smacked him in the arm.

He let out another laugh and just barely ducked her second smack. Catching her hand in his, he tucked it against her chest. "Your dad is smart as hell," he said. "And incredibly intuitive. He's got the biggest heart of anyone I know. He'd give away his last buck. And you, Holly, are the apple that didn't fall far from the tree."

She played tug-of-war for her hand back and lost. "Fine," she said, sounding a whole lot less hostile. "Maybe we've got *some* things in common." She paused. "But I don't know about giving away my last buck."

He let go of her hand to slip his just beneath her sweatshirt, his fingers brushing the creamy, soft skin of her stomach. "Once you gave me everything you had."

"Yes, well . . ." Her voice was soft now, and thick. With memories? "I'm smarter these days."

They were both supposedly smarter now, which was a very good thing. Back in those days, there'd been no history between them, no rolled-up jacket as a barrier, no boundaries at all.

He'd given her everything he had, which admittedly

hadn't been jack shit. He wasn't sure anything would be different now, though he honestly hadn't given much thought to trying. He was still working on being okay with being among the living, when so many others he'd once known weren't. He'd mostly accomplished this by burying himself in work, spreading himself too thin so that he'd fall into an exhausted sleep at night.

Tonight wasn't going to be one of those nights.

Tonight he was going to lie here, wide awake, fighting not memories of war and destruction and loss but memories of a better time.

The best time of his life . . .

He thought about that for a minute and realized he wanted, *needed*, her to understand him. Unable to help himself, he let his fingers dance across her abs and felt her muscles quiver. "I told you I wasn't coming back because I didn't want you to wait for me."

"I know. You've said." She tried to roll away, but his arm tightened on her again, holding her still.

"You know that if I'd stayed," he said, "I'd have kept screwing up my life. I needed to get out of Sunshine, Holly. I needed to become a part of something and learn some discipline."

"I understood that. You *had* to go."

He grimaced at that, which luckily she didn't see.

She loosened her grip on his forearms and gentled her touch, stroking his skin, her words making him feel like an even bigger asshole. "Seems like maybe you got more than you bargained for," she said quietly.

He let out a low sound of agreement, then spoke the sentiment he'd held on to for too long. "I just couldn't have lived with myself, if I'd stayed and dragged you down with me."

There was a beat of silence. Then she fought to free herself and he let her this time. She rolled over to face him and he expected . . . hell, he wasn't sure what he expected.

Appreciation for what he'd done for her, maybe? Certainly a softening toward him. Warmth and affection. Maybe even more . . .

Instead her eyes were flashing the heat of anger and he'd have sworn sparks were shooting out of her scalp. "Look at you," she said, voice tight. "Making decisions for me. Guess that doesn't make you any different than any other man I've ever had in my life, does it?" She shifted back away from him, accidentally kneeing him in the groin.

Or maybe not so accidentally.

"And you shouldn't have worried," she said while he sucked in a careful breath. "Because in case you hadn't noticed, I managed to drag myself down all on my own just fine."

"Holly—"

"I'm tired," she said flatly, turning away from him now, giving him her back and a very cold shoulder. "I'm going to sleep."

He tightened his mouth to keep it from running away with his good sense. "Fine."

*"Fine."* She sat up and replaced the jacket barrier, making a point of patting it into place before plopping back down.

They both settled and went still. The only sound was their breathing, which seemed far too loud. Long moments went by during which he counted the soft flakes falling out of the sky and lightly fluttering down just outside the opened doorway.

"Adam?" she whispered after a long moment.

He sighed. He didn't want questions or a visit down memory lane. He wanted solitude and decompression. That's what he'd always wanted. Except . . . Except in this moment, he didn't know what he wanted. She confused the shit out of him, twisting him up, scrambling his brain. He had no idea why he even tried to control his feelings around her. Habit, he decided. He always maintained control, in every aspect of his life. It's what had gotten him through.

His therapist had warned him that part of the process was learning to let go of that control. Easier said than done.

Not buying his possum act, Holly rolled over to face him, giving him a little jostle. "Adam." She was peering at him in the dark, trying to see him.

Into him.

Usually just having her look at him the way that she did made every bad thing in his life dissolve into nothing. Now it made him unsettled. They were in far too close proximity for his walls to come tumbling down tonight.

*Retreat . . .*

Too bad there was nowhere to retreat to. Which meant he had no choice but to man up. "Yeah?"

She came up on an elbow and he braced himself. She wanted to understand him, the changes in him. He got that. But she couldn't. She could never understand the places he'd been, the darkness he'd lived.

Her expression held uncertainty.

He should reach out to her, touch her, assure her. But he didn't trust himself to do that, knowing all too well how easily he could lose himself in the physical attraction between them. He could bury himself deep inside her, finding a desperately needed release. But he would never allow himself to use her that way.

"I have a question."

Great. "Okay."

She drew a deep breath. "Why did you really let me come with you today?"

# Ten

Holly held her breath for Adam's answer. She wasn't even sure he *would* answer. She didn't know about him, but being this close was bringing back memories of other times. Better times. Times when they'd gone camping and been alone. But never with a barrier between them.

He spoke, his voice low and a little husky, as if he were filled with the same memories as she. "You weren't going to ever forgive me if I left you back in Sunshine."

"And you care why?"

Another pause. "I owe your father," he said carefully. "And I owe you, too."

Holly tried to read his face. Carefully blank. He was good at that. Hell, who was she kidding, he was the *master* at that. She knew he'd learned long ago that nothing good came of sharing his deepest, innermost thoughts, and that alone was enough to break her heart. There'd been a time where she would have given up her soul in order to allow his to be shared, but she'd long ago stopped believing she could get him to believe in her, in them, enough to let her in.

Why that still hurt, she had no idea. "You owe me nothing," she said. "And my dad—"

"Believed in me when few others did," he cut in. "He gave me a job when I was seventeen. And then after that drag-racing wreck, he helped me pay for an attorney."

"The charges didn't stick," she started, but he shook his head

"They'd stuck in my head," he said very softly.

She knew this. She knew all too well how much guilt and horror and regret he'd carried. But she also knew that even if that cop hadn't died, Adam had never intended to be with her forever. The accident might have been the catalyst for him to leave, but he'd have left her regardless. "Adam—"

"Go to sleep, Holly. Tomorrow we'll find your dad."

Hoping that was true, she closed her eyes . . . and then came awake some time later to find that she'd completely disregarded her own decree. She'd rolled right over the bunched-up jacket and onto Adam's half of the bedding.

And that wasn't the worst part. She'd vacuum-sealed herself up against the delicious heat radiating off his body. Carefully, without moving a single inch, she took stock. Adam was flat on his back, innocent—which did not help her. Because she knew him, at least she *had* known him, and there wasn't much innocence to him. There never had been.

But he was innocent now. It was she who'd climbed all over him.

He was asleep, his silky dark hair falling across his forehead, his body relaxed as she so rarely saw it. She lay there in the crook of his arm, one knee thrown across his legs, her hand settled disturbingly low on his belly, her position speaking of a deep, abiding trust. Trust in this man.

Taking in a breath and holding it, she began to slowly back off of him, but at her movement his muscles rippled like a big cat. His arms came up, pinning her in place, one big hand curled around her shoulders, the other sliding down her back to her butt, gripping a cheek with startling possessiveness. His breathing didn't change, remaining slow and steady. The tortoise. Except he was more like a cheetah, wild and wily and sneaky as hell. She found his gaze locked on her in the barely there light. "Sorry," she said, and tried to extract herself delicately.

He tightened his grip to stop her. He wasn't smiling, but instead looked very serious. Pausing as if to gather himself, he flipped them so that his hard body covered hers. His mouth skimmed her cheek on its slow path to her mouth, giving her plenty of time to say no, but the word got lost in the translation from her brain to her lips. Instead, her body was screaming, *Yes, yes, yes.* "Adam."

"You were feeling me up in my sleep."

"No, I . . ."

He turned his head and his lips brushed the inside of her arm. Which, she realized, was wrapped tight around him, along with her other one.

She was holding on to him.

He nipped the skin he'd just kissed and she felt herself go damp. Dammit. "Okay, yes," she said. "But I didn't mean to."

He dropped his head low enough to glide that oh-so-talented mouth along her jaw, down her throat, against the hollow of her collarbone. "We've both done a lot of things that we didn't mean to," he murmured.

She wanted to concentrate on his words, but his mouth was giving her an entire body shiver. "Don't," she whispered, clutching at him so he couldn't escape. She closed her eyes. "Don't toy with me."

Above her, he went still. "Is that what you think I'm doing?" His breath was warm against her skin, and he dipped to taste, stirring up all kinds of fire within her. He met her gaze, his own dark and heated as he slid a hand down her leg, pulling it up, around his hip, which grinded into her.

He was hard. His mouth was warm, firm . . . perfect. Both familiar and yet completely new and exciting.

"Does that feel like I'm playing a game, Holly?"

Before she could respond, he traced a sensual line from her throat to her ear with his lips, teasing the outer shell before lightly sinking his teeth into the lobe.

She sucked in a breath and tightened her grip on him. Bringing up her other leg, she cradled his hips within hers, and her inner 'ho rejoiced.

*Just this once*, her body begged.

*You'll regret it later*, her brain reminded her.

During this tug-of-war between her hormones and few remaining working brain cells, Adam's fingers drew hypnotizing circles along her body and she helplessly arched up into him. Her body was winning the war. "Adam—"

His hand caressed along her cheek and wove its way into her hair at the back of her neck. Tilting her head up, he waited until she met his eyes, the air crackling with tension. "Are we going to stop?" he asked, voice thrillingly strained, chasing another shiver up her spine.

"No," she whispered. *God, no.*

He held her gaze for a long beat while he seemed to wrestle with his own inner battle. Finally he leaned forward and brushed his lips to hers.

Her low moan gave him the access he needed and he deepened the kiss, his tongue stroking hers. She squirmed and wriggled, trying to get even closer. He rolled over her, never breaking the kiss as he cupped the back of her head, his thumbs stroking her throat.

She slid her hands beneath his shirt and over the smooth skin of his back, feeling the carefully leashed power of him beneath her fingertips. She wanted to unleash that power. She wanted that more than she wanted her next breath.

All this time, all these years, she'd never forgotten how he'd made her feel. And she'd wondered, had she done the same to him? Did he remember her touch as much as she remembered his? The truth was, she wanted him to. Wanted to remind him of how it had been. She wanted him to lose control with her, wanted him to wrestle hers away as well while he was at it.

She couldn't remember the last time she'd lost herself in passion and desire. She and Derek hadn't been together in a very long time. There'd been a few men since, and it had been nice . . . but she wanted much more than nice. She wanted to completely let go, and she knew Adam could do that. Make her let go.

Her hands went south next, into the back of his jeans to the best buns she'd ever had the pleasure of gripping. When she pulled him into her, his mouth came down on hers— hungry and edgy and demanding. Surely one kiss couldn't be all that, but this one was.

And she loved it.

Thrived on it.

She tugged at his shirt and he reared up to yank it off. "Careful of your shoulder," she managed.

"What shoulder," he said, and then went to work on her clothes.

"No, really," she said. "You need to—"

He slid her sweatshirt up and her bra cups down, kissing and suckling his way from collarbone to breast.

"Um . . ." She struggled to hold a thought. "Careful not to strain your stitches—"

"Holly?"

"Yeah?"

"Shut up." He pulled a nipple into his mouth and his big warm hand slid between her legs, and she completely forgot about his injury. *Too many clothes*, she thought dizzily. And either the man had the gift of reading her mind or he remembered her body with sharpshooter precision, because he had her completely naked before she could blink.

A man on a mission.

But with the feeling of something cold and wet in her armpit, she squeaked. Adam lifted his head. "Milo, bed."

Milo sighed at not being invited to the party and ambled back to his spot by the backpacks.

"He thought he was missing something good," Adam said.

"He is." Holly shoved his jeans down. Adam kicked them the rest of the way off and braced himself above her. He was hard against her inner thigh and she couldn't wait another minute. "Please," she whispered.

He made a low, innately male sound and dropped his forehead to hers. "Condom."

She went blank. "Oh my God." Had she actually, really almost forgotten protection? "You'd better have a condom. *Tell me you have a condom!*"

"I have a condom." Rising, he strode buck naked—and glorious—to his backpack, returning with a foil packet.

"Okay," she said on a sigh of relief. "We can be friends."

But though he slipped back beneath the sleeping bag, he didn't make a move.

"Are we stopping?" she asked, mirroring his earlier words. "Because I don't want to."

His thumb traced her lower lip, and then he bent and sucked on it. "No. Not stopping." He tore open the foil.

She took the condom from him, rolling it down his length while he watched. By the time it was on, they were both breathing unevenly again. Holly looked up into his face, feeling the flicker of unexpected nerves. For all of her adult life, she'd measured her sexual experiences against Adam. What if he didn't live up to the memory? Then he slid inside her, and she gasped, helplessly rocking up into him because it was everything she remembered.

And more.

He stretched and filled her so perfectly that she couldn't figure out how she'd ever lived without this.

Without him.

Except she hadn't chosen to live without him. *He'd* chosen that for her, all on his own, without giving her a say. At that thought, reality might have intruded, pulled her out of the moment, except . . .

Except, braced above her, buried deep, Adam had gone perfectly still, eyes locked on hers, his usual stoic expression wiped clean, replaced with sheer unadulterated pleasure and *need*.

For her.

It was rare to see him so unguarded. Rare and . . . beautiful. "Adam," she said, staggered by the emotion that swamped her.

"I know." Bending low, he kissed her slowly, until she moved restlessly against him, wanting to feel him move in and out of her, needing that more than she could remember needing anything.

But Adam was right about one thing: somewhere along the way he'd learned patience. Lots of it. When she arched up for more, he merely held her still, gently nibbling her lip as she tried harder, clutching at him, crying out from the heat building between them.

Soothing her with a wordless murmur, he finally began to move, filling her to bursting, and she nearly climbed up his body trying to get even closer, closer than was physically possible. Wrapping her legs around his hips, she did her best to ride him from the bottom, but he kept up his torturous pace, driving her right to the edge before slowing again.

"Now who's . . . playing?" she managed to grate out.

"Still not playing." His voice was thrillingly low and rough as he thrust again.

And again.

She could feel it now, the tease of an impending orgasm. Her toes curled, her inner muscles pulsed around him. Every inch of her was poised on the very edge and she didn't know if she could survive it. "Please," she begged against his lips. "Adam, *please* . . ."

He groaned and broke the kiss to give her what she wanted. His head fell back, eyes closed, face tight with hunger and desire as he moved over her.

They were both frantic now, but then his hand on her hip shifted so he could stroke a thumb over her center with gentle, deadly precision.

She exploded.

He followed right behind her, his eyes closed against the intensity, pushing so deep inside her, that for that one glorious moment they were one. There was only their rough, ragged breathing mingling with the late-night wind and rustling trees.

And Milo's left-out, put-upon sigh.

Holly didn't want to move. She didn't want to shake off the delicious cloud of satisfaction and comfort. Not to mention she was warm for the first time since she'd gotten out of her own bed yesterday morning. Her body was still giving off little aftershocks of desire that made Adam groan, and he shifted as if to move off her.

Needing his weight, loving the feel of his hands still gripping her tight, she clutched at him, then realized he probably wasn't experiencing the same need to remain close that she was, so she reluctantly let him go.

He rolled off her, dealt with the condom, then came back, pulling her in, pressing his lips to her temple. "Sleep."

Even in the dark, she could tell that the hard edge that had been there earlier, the hard edge that was always there whenever they had to deal with each other these days, was gone.

The softer version of Adam was still with her.

She liked seeing behind the tough-guy veneer and wondered what it meant that she was seeing the real man.

And how long he'd stay.

## Eleven

A dam woke instantly, heart still pounding. Not a full-on nightmare, thank God. He didn't do that whole leap-up-screaming thing so much anymore, just occasionally woke in a pounding rush, the air stuck in his throat.

Like now. And he knew why, too. Today, they were going to the Kaniksu Caves to look for Donald.

Just thinking about it had him breaking out in a sweat. Forcing himself to relax, he felt Holly curl around him, and just like that, the icy tightness in his chest began to ease. He continued to will his strung out body to calm one muscle at a time, allowing himself the rare luxury of a woman's welcoming warmth and softness. *Holly's* welcoming warmth. The female scent of her skin was both arousing and comforting, and gradually the pressure in his lungs eased. Turning his head, he buried his face in her hair for a moment, just breathing her in.

Then he felt a warm, wet nose in his ear. Opening his eyes, he met Milo's.

Dawn's first pink light was just creeping in. Adam

pushed the dog back a few feet and then looked down at the warm, sexy female in his arms. Her perfect little ass was spooned up against him. They were both naked, but basic chemistry had kept them warm. Hell, they could have kept all of Idaho warm with the heat they'd generated all night.

Holly's skin was scented with her usual enticing sexiness, though she also smelled a lot like him. It was erotic and . . . disturbingly intimate. He carefully rolled to his back.

Holly murmured something, flopped over, and scooted in to once again plaster herself to him.

Not him, he corrected. His heat. She was a heat-seeking missile. Her hair looked like an explosion in a mattress factory, flowing wildly over his arm and chest, tickling his nose. Before he'd even realized what he was doing, he stroked it back from her face.

In her sleep she scowled, an expression he was well used to. There hadn't been much to smile about between them.

Until last night, anyway.

At that uncomfortable thought, he began the tricky extraction process, pulling back, trying to disentangle himself from her. Not easy when she now had a grip on him with *both* fists, her thighs tight around one of his. Her breasts were pillowed against his chest, and when he shifted, her nipples puckered tight. He knew it was just a physical response to stimulation or maybe from the cold air around them, but it didn't stop his mouth from watering with the need to take a taste.

He resisted, barely, and only because he was already feeling like the biggest asshole on the planet for letting this happen between them.

It *shouldn't* have happened. Holly was hopes and dreams. She was . . . *forever*. Adam no longer had hopes and dreams; he was working on just getting through the moment. And forever? Forever was an *f*-word. He managed to move back another inch, and she actually made a soft little mewling protest that was both the sexiest and sweetest sound he'd ever heard.

Aside from the sounds she'd made last night.

All those years ago, she'd always responded to him with open eagerness. It had never failed to excite him then.

Seemed nothing much had changed now, either.

Of course, in those days she hadn't had anyone to compare him to in the sack, and that had been a rush all on its own. But even without that element, she'd been different from other women. She'd roused a protective, possessive nature in him that he'd never felt before. Of course he'd been young, stupid, and completely ruled by his dick.

He had no idea what his excuse was now.

He gently pulled his legs free from hers and came up on his knees, getting his first good look at her in the ambient early dawn light. Creamy skin, warm, gorgeous curves, and . . . patches of whisker burns on her throat, breasts, and between her legs.

*You are a complete asshole*, he thought, and spread the sleeping bag over her, forcing himself up.

He pulled on his clothes and boots and moved outside where the icy cold air slapped him in the face.

So did his moral compass.

Overnight, the snowfall had coated the land with enough powder to give depth to its features. He could see for miles, a broad sweep of spiky, naked trees and vast, rambling land, beautiful in its simplicity. He eyed the sky. Dark and tumultuous. They'd be lucky to make it another hour without more snow. It was the sort of morning that called for crawling back into the bed that held a warm, sexy woman waiting for him.

But that wouldn't fly.

He glanced back at her, where she lay curled up in his sleeping bag, only her blond hair showing.

God, how he loved the smell of a woman's hair. Not something he'd given much thought to in . . . well, years.

He'd been busy with other things like consecutive tours of being dropped into places that didn't even officially exist, backing up the good guys, losing half his unit because of bad intel, and then falling into a deep, dark pit of despair and guilt for being alive, all of which tended to chase away thoughts of the ladies. He drew a deep breath and had to shrug that off for now. Therapy 101—sitting on the guilt was unproductive.

Not that *that* had ever stopped him.

But he had other issues at the moment. Namely the caves.

He and Milo did their business. His shoulder was bothering him so he pulled off his shirt again, and then disregarding both the icy air and Dell's strict instructions, he removed the bandage as well. Everything seemed okay. He tried to replace it himself but couldn't quite manage that on his own. He was twisting around and doing his best when he found Holly standing in the ranger station doorway, looking only half awake and completely befuddled.

She'd wrapped herself in his sleeping bag, which slipped off her shoulder, revealing black lace. He didn't often give much thought to a woman's underwear. Mostly he liked it skimpy and on the floor, but that had been shortsighted of him because this little peekaboo hint was really nice, too.

Realizing he was staring, she turned and vanished into the shelter, then reappeared a moment later in her clothes. She was still looking a little blown away at the fact that overnight their landscape had turned into a winter wonderland.

Taking in her sleepy-eyed stupor, it was impossible not to feel a small surge of satisfaction for having rendered her so completely befuddled. "You okay?" he asked.

Her cheeks flushed, but she nodded, and he wondered if she was thinking about just how *very* okay she'd seemed only a few hours ago—while panting out his name in that sexy, breathy little whisper.

But whatever she was thinking, she wasn't sharing. And she didn't move from the doorway, either, instead staying far out of arm's reach, which meant she was wary.

Or smart as hell.

He tried to look into her eyes, but she was looking off to the right, at the long fingers of fog rolling in on the early morning air.

"Should we talk about it?" he asked, hoping like hell that she would say no. Talking wasn't high on his list of favorite things to do.

She shook her head and began to gather up her hair in that way women had, quickly piling it on her head, tying it there with an elastic band she pulled from her wrist. She moved to him, hand out for the new bandage. He held it up, along with a tube of Neosporin, and her fingers brushed over his shoulder as she turned him. Even this minor contact made him hard.

"Didn't Dell tell you not to touch?" she asked.

"Yeah."

"Didn't he also say if you did, he'd put a dog cone on you?"

"Yeah." He scowled. "So?"

"So, do you want to wear a cone around your neck?"

"He'd have to catch me first," he said.

She snorted, finishing with the antibiotic ointment. "Is Dell fast?"

"Yes. But I'm faster."

She replaced the bandage. "It looks good, Adam."

"Thanks." He craned his neck and met her gaze. "You're a lot hotter than my last doctor."

She gave him a look. "I'm the hottest anything you've ever had."

When he laughed, she smiled in response, and then looked around. "It snowed."

"Yeah. We were too busy to notice." The memory of what they'd been too busy doing made him even harder.

Holly's gaze dropped to his mouth and softened, giving him both a rush of lust and something else.

Unease.

Because he knew that look. It was the look of a woman who'd found something she wanted. Oh Christ. The repercussions of last night were going to hit right here and now.

His own doing.

He pulled on his shirt, and then his sweatshirt and jacket. Stalling techniques, of course, while he tried to decide how best to give her the bum's rush out of here without analyzing last night too closely.

She turned to him, eyes serious, unhappy, and his gut tightened. Hell. He couldn't do it, couldn't ignore this. Not with her. "I'm going to ask you again," he said quietly. "Are you okay? Do we have a problem?"

"No," she said. "Of course not. My father's missing—his phone is *still* off, by the way; I checked before I got dressed—and I just slept with one of the biggest mistakes of my life—a mistake who thinks *I'm* the mistake—but no, there's no problem."

"Okay, now I see," he muttered, stepping toward her. "I *knew* we needed to talk about this."

"Look, forget it. Let's just get a damn move on. It's what you do, right? When the going gets tough, you get going."

He opened his mouth, because that's *not* how it had gone down—*at all*—and she knew it, but he caught the flash of misery on her face before she turned away, so he held his tongue. "Holly."

"Great," she said, tossing up her hands. "Here it comes."

"Here comes what?"

"Your morning-after speech," she said. "I tried to avoid it, but some things I guess there's just no avoiding. So go ahead, Adam. Get it out before it chokes you."

He drew in a slow, deep breath. "Last night—"

"Wait." She jabbed a finger at him again. "I should warn

you—even though *I* just said last night was a mistake, if *you* say it, I *will* hurt you. Because I was lying, Adam. And don't think I can't hurt you. I've been taking kickboxing. I have moves, you know. Badass moves."

"Holly." He grabbed the hand she was waving around. "Nothing with you has ever been a mistake."

"But?" she asked. "Because there's most definitely a *but* coming, I can feel it."

He met her gaze. "But I don't want what you want."

She narrowed her eyes. "And what do you think I want?"

"A committed relationship."

She sucked in a breath. "And what about you? What do you want?"

"It doesn't matter what I want," he said. "It's not what you deserve, believe me. But I don't want to hurt you."

She nodded once, like she understood, then shook her head. When he opened his mouth, she glared up at him so he shut it again and gave her a moment.

"So . . . you feel nothing for me?" she asked.

Christ, she slayed him. "I feel entirely too much for you," he corrected. "But it's not enough. You deserve it all, Holly."

She blinked, clearly startled by this. "You mean another marriage?" she finally asked. "A white picket fence?" She let out a low laugh that held no amusement. "I've had those things. I don't want them again."

"You may not want them now, but when the times comes and you change your mind, you need to be with someone who wants those things, too. I'm not that guy, Holly."

"I don't like it when people tell me what I want, Adam." She turned away, looking toward the woods. "You have no idea what I want."

That was undoubtedly true, and it also proved his point. He knew nothing about being in a relationship day in and day out with a woman. He could satisfy her physically, but no matter if he wanted to be the One for her or not, he'd let her down because he couldn't keep her satisfied emotionally.

"And, anyway, this isn't even about me," she said. "It's about you. *You* don't want to have to be vulnerable to *me*. To anyone. You don't want to open up to me."

"I've opened up and shared more with you than just about anyone else," he said.

"But you've still held back. You think you have to be perfect or some other such idiocy. But you're forgetting, I already know you're not perfect."

Direct hit. And they both knew she was no longer talking about last night. "I didn't want to hurt you," he said.

"You made a blanket decision about us without me. That's what hurt me."

"Yes, I did that," he agreed. And he'd do the same thing again. "Come on, Holly, you know that back then a life with me was a guaranteed life of hurt." He'd done her a favor by breaking things off before heading into the military. He'd always looked back on it just like that, telling himself she'd be happier without him.

Which meant that he had no right to feel anything for her now. He'd had his chance, and he'd made the choice to walk away. He'd refused to alter his life to fit her into it. He hadn't been willing to add the complication. He wanted things as simple as possible.

Holly was a lot of things, but simple wasn't one of them. Then or now.

"So what was last night, then?" she asked.

Well, hell.

"You don't even know, do you," she said in disbelief.

No, he didn't. He didn't have a clue.

"Really?" she said when he remained silent. "You're going to go with the whole Dark, Tortured, Silent persona? Fine. That's fine, Adam. Stick with what you're good at. Because you *are* good at that. You're the master at that.

Sucking people in with your quiet, sexy charm, allowing them to think that they're special to you, that you're letting them in, all the while you're keeping them at arm's length and not letting them in at all."

He rubbed his jaw and studied her, wondering if she was always so damn prickly in the mornings. Another question that would be better kept to himself. He knew better than to get dragged into a fight with her on a mountaintop with a possible storm coming and her father missing and her emotions so high. Maybe he could tease her to break the mood. "Last night," he said. "When we—"

She closed her eyes. "Yeah, what about it?"

"You came, right?"

"Oh my God." Her eyes flew open and she gave him a narrow-eyed look. "You think I faked the orgasm?"

"*Three* orgasms," he pointed out, giving himself away. He'd known she'd come. He'd known exactly when and for how long, and he'd be reliving the moments for a long time to come.

Realizing he was pulling her leg, she blushed. "I wouldn't fake."

"Good to know," he said. "But you seem pretty cranky for someone who got some, so . . ."

"Okay," she said, backing away. "Fun as this awkward morning-after is, I'm going to . . ." She gestured to the woods.

"Wait." He pulled a small canister of pepper spray from his backpack. "Take this with you."

"For all the rapists that hang out here?"

"For the bears and other curious four-legged predators."

Nodding, she clutched the canister, turned on her heels, and headed toward the woods.

"Don't go far," he said to her stiff spine. "It's easy to get turned around—"

"Contrary to my latest stupidest decision—which was

sleeping with you by the way," she clarified helpfully, "I'm not a complete moron."

"I meant because of the snow. We only got a few inches, but it's deceiving." He shoved the first-aid kit into his pack. "I'll come with—"

"Follow me and die."

He went still. "Okay, but just remember, everything looks the same right now with the low light—"

She waved a dismissive hand and kept going, vanishing into the woods.

"Milo," Adam said, watching the spot where she'd vanished.

The dog bounded over.

"Seek," he said, and pointed.

Milo went trotting after Holly. If she wouldn't listen to reason, then she could have a babysitter while finding herself a tree.

But a few seconds later he heard her say "no," quite clearly, obviously to the dog. She must have also given him the stern finger point, because a chastened Milo came slinking out of the woods.

"It's okay," Adam told him. "Good job." He took a moment to call Dell and check in.

"Long night?" Dell asked casually.

"Don't start."

"I'm going to assume that since you're still breathing, Holly didn't kill you. You two find some . . . common ground?"

"I'm calling for my messages, Dell."

"Look, just say yay or nay cuz Jade keeps texting me, wanting to know if I've heard from you yet."

"Well, now you can tell her you've heard from me."

"So, are you confirming or denying?" Dell pressed.

"Jesus."

"Hey," Dell said. "It's not for me. It's for Jade. She's

convinced you're still into the guilt thing." He paused. "You're not, right? You're . . . okay?"

Adam resisted the urge to bash his head against the tree. "Should I assume there's nothing critical?"

"Depends on your definition of critical. Reno kicked me in the ass a little while ago. That horse has no manners."

"Tell him I owe him a whole apple," Adam said, and disconnected. He called Brady next, who told him that Donald still hadn't shown up or reported in.

"Not good," Adam said, because he knew what this meant—a trip to the fucking caves. Yay.

"You okay out there?" Brady asked, as always able to pick up on Adam's stress.

"Why wouldn't I be?"

"I don't know. You tell me."

Adam paused. "Fucking Dell," he said, and Brady laughed softly.

"Yeah, I'm right here next to him," Brady said. "So it's true, then. You and Holly."

"Dell doesn't know what he's talking about."

"So it's *not* true."

Adam drew in a deep breath, visions of last night haunting him. Holly beneath him, arms and legs wrapped so tight around him that he couldn't tell where he ended and she began . . .

At the long pause, Brady laughed again. "Good luck. And trust me, you'll need it."

Adam paused. "Did you need luck? With Lilah?" The question shocked him. If he could have taken it back, he would have, in a heartbeat.

There was a beat of silence that told him that Brady was shocked by the unexpected reveal of vulnerability as well, and if he laughed, Adam was going to have to kill him.

But Brady didn't laugh. "Hell, man," he finally said. "I needed a lot more than luck. I needed divine intervention to land that woman, and I *still* almost screwed it up."

Brady was just about the toughest son of a bitch Adam had ever known. And yet somehow he'd managed to land the sweetest woman on the face of the earth. They'd gotten married last month, a beautiful, emotional ceremony with a reception that had the entire town partying all night long. Still, Adam never got over his surprise while watching them together. Lilah would needle Brady, get on his case about something, anything. Food, work, his overprotectiveness . . . She'd keep after him until he'd start to get pissed, and then she'd go toe-to-toe with him. The kitten up against the lion. Adam had never seen anyone do that to Brady before, but Lilah had no fear of Brady. She'd throw her arms around the guy's neck and kiss him, and he'd grin down at her like a teenager. Even now, to this day, when Adam was with Brady when his cell phone rang with Lilah's ringtone, Brady would get that same big-ass grin on his face.

"*Don't* screw it up," Brady said.

With nothing else to say, Adam disconnected. He spent a few minutes packing everything up, with the exception of the two granola bars, apples, and water he'd taken out for their breakfast.

Still no Holly.

He paced the clearing, stopping every few seconds to peer into the woods where she'd vanished. "Holly."

Nothing.

Dammit. "I'm coming in, Holly." He did *not* want to surprise her. He'd armed her, for one thing. And getting Maced sucked. Besides that, he understood wanting privacy for whatever complicated morning routine a woman might try to go through out here. But if she was out there sulking, trying to punish him, then that was another thing altogether. He'd told her the truth last night, he wasn't playing games. "Holly."

Still nothing.

He gave her another sixty seconds, which was sixty seconds too long in his book because everything inside him was saying he needed to go after her *now*. He did realize that his instincts when it came to women were completely screwed up, but all his life his gut feelings were all he'd ever had. Even when things had gone FUBAR on his last mission, it hadn't been his instincts that had failed him. He whistled for Milo and then once again pointed where Holly had vanished. "Seek."

Adam followed the dog, immediately picking up Holly's boot prints in the snow. Milo had run ahead. Adam could no longer hear the dog, but then he heard the "tell," three short, quick barks in a row, signaling Milo had made his find.

Adam trailed after both Holly's booted prints and the dog's paw prints, coming into another clearing. There he found both his dog and woman sitting on a fallen log. He paused, not sure what the hell to say to her.

Holly was sitting, legs bent, arms around her shins, head down on her knees. He could see the tension in every line of her body, tension that he was going to hope like hell was temper and not tears.

Temper was always infinitely preferable to tears.

Milo stood at Holly's side, alert, eyes on Adam as he approached. "Good boy."

Milo happily relaxed and plopped down to the snow.

"Holly."

She lifted her head and looked at him. And for the first time since he'd last seen his therapist and had been forced to discuss feelings he didn't want to discuss, he felt that same old familiar lick of panic.

# Twelve

Holly took one look at Adam's expression and dropped her head back to her knees. Nope, she still wasn't ready to see him. "I told you I needed a minute," she said.

"No, you said you'd kill me if I followed you."

He didn't sound bothered by this, which somehow made her want to smack him. But she had bigger issues. First of all, she'd slept in her contacts, which always made her eyes sore and swollen. Dumb move. She'd just been forced to take them out and was as good as blind without them. And okay, so there hadn't been a whole lot of "sleeping" going on last night, but her eyes were definitely suffering the consequences—unlike the rest of her body, which was actually still operating on a low-level hum of excitement. She couldn't help it, every movement reminded her that she'd used muscles long out of practice.

That wasn't the only thing she'd been out of practice at. Having a man inside her, moving over her, murmuring sweet erotic nothings in her ear as he took her places she couldn't get on solo expeditions . . .

But he already regretted it, and that really chapped her ass.

And hurt her heart.

"I was willing to give you a minute," he said. "But you were gone much longer than that."

She jumped when she felt the warmth of his thigh as he sat next to her. The man moved like smoke. "Okay, so I needed a few minutes," she said, keeping her face averted.

"Are you crying?" He sounded worried. Going to war hadn't worried him. Facing down wolves hadn't worried him. Traveling into the storm hadn't worried him.

But tears apparently did. She sighed. "No."

Not that she'd admit it, anyway.

He let out a long, slow, relieved breath that made her grind her teeth. "Thank Christ," he murmured.

With a sound of exasperation aimed at the both of them, she rose to her feet, and then remembered the problem. Without her contacts, she couldn't see a thing. Dammit! She sat down again.

"Hey," Adam said with surprising gentleness. Crouching before her, balancing on the balls of his feet, he put his hands on her arms. She sensed his careful scrutiny, but thanks to being both near and farsighted, all of which added up to being as blind as a bat in daylight, she couldn't see his expression clearly.

Probably not a bad thing.

"Just having trouble seeing," she said.

"You wearing your contacts?"

For a guy who liked to pretend they barely knew each other—at least until last night—he sure remembered a hell of a lot about her. "I had to take them out," she admitted.

He let out a breath. "You have your glasses with you?"

"Maybe in my pack."

"Maybe?"

"Hopefully."

"Shit, Holly."

Which translated into *Dumb move, Reid.* Since she already knew this, she nudged him out of her way—or maybe it was more of a rude push—and rose. "It's no big deal. We can still do this." She pulled out her cell and hit Red's number.

"There's no news," Adam said. "I already checked."

Holly locked eyes with him as Red picked up. But Adam was right. No news. She slipped the phone back in her pocket and felt her chest tighten at the implications.

"It's only day four," Adam said.

And it wasn't unusual for her dad to be gone five days. Not that this made her feel any better. Maybe the wolves had stalked him, too. Or a bear. Or maybe he'd had a stroke. Anything could have happened out here. "Let's go," she managed, and started walking. *That's key,* she thought. *Keep moving.*

A hand grabbed the back of her sweatshirt and redirected her one hundred and eighty degrees.

"Right." She looked in the direction he'd pointed her in and realized that everything was . . . white. Without her contacts she had no depth perception, no sense of up or down, or right or left. It was like being in a terrifying cloud of nothingness.

This didn't help the clamp on her heart. She whirled around, panic a hot, hard ball in her throat, but two strong arms came around her.

She clutched at Adam, fisting her hands in his jacket, pressing her face into his chest.

He didn't say a word, for which she was grateful. He just held her, stroking a hand up and down her back while she took in his heartbeat, slow and steady. It had a calming effect on her, and she had to resist burrowing in even closer.

"You breathing?" he asked.

"Working on it." She let out a shaky breath. "That anxiety is some nasty stuff," she said, much more lightly than she felt.

She didn't fool him.

"Remember," he said quietly, "you've also got to have a plan and then move on it."

She knew how hard won this knowledge was for him. And he was right. "The plan is to find him," she said.

"So let's do that."

Yes. She was still getting used to the fact that Adam was crucial to the plan. She'd worried about giving him the ability to hurt her.

Again.

But the only person who could give him that power was herself. And she was older and dubiously wiser now. Besides, with the exception of their one big misstep last night, he'd clearly moved on.

He had a talent for that, and she was doing her best to learn it as well. "So what comes after the plan?"

He slid her a look. "Reframing your thoughts. Panic is often triggered by negativity."

"So . . . think positive?" she asked doubtfully. Nothing was ever that simple.

"Like a Hallmark card," he confirmed.

"Is that why you keep telling me it's going to be okay?"

"No, I keep telling you it's going to be okay because it *is* going to be okay."

"What about last night?" she asked. "Was that a way to reframe my thoughts into something positive?"

He laughed softly and shook his head. "Don't confuse being positive with hot-as-hell sex."

She couldn't believe it, but she laughed, too. "Well, you can see how I got mixed up, right? Because as it turns out, hot-as-hell sex is pretty damn positive, at least in the moment." Some of her smile faded as she realized that's exactly what he meant. In the moment. What they'd shared last night was a moment in time.

Nothing more. She pulled free.

"Holly—"

"Let's just go." It didn't help that he had to practically lead her out of the woods.

But at least she found her glasses in her pack and could see again. They ate breakfast, and when she was done, she looked up and found Adam watching her, expression hooded. "What?" she asked.

"Anyone ever tell you that with your hair up and those glasses on, you're a walking hot-librarian fantasy?"

Something low in her belly quivered. "I'm going to forget you said that."

He flashed her a small smile, and of course she didn't forget it at all.

They walked in silence back to the ATV. Halfway there, her cell beeped with an incoming text from Kate. One word.

Well?

Holly rolled her eyes and was typing *LATER* when Adam read over her shoulder. "Hey!" she said, trying to hide the phone.

He leveled her with a look. "You kissing and telling, Holly?"

She felt herself flush. "No!"

He just looked at her.

"I'm not! Kate's just butting her nose in. It's what friends do."

"And brothers," she thought he muttered.

At the ATV, Adam got their gear stowed and Milo settled before sliding behind the wheel. He handed Holly the binoculars. "Watch for signs while I drive."

She brought the binoculars to her eyes. "Signs of what?"

"Smoke, a newly made trail. Anything."

That was all well and good but looking through the binoculars while the vehicle was moving made her feel nauseous. "Let's switch," she said after a while. "I'll drive, you keep a watch out."

He shook his head and kept driving.

"Why?" she asked. "Because I'm a girl?"

"No, because you *drive* like a girl. No, scratch that. That's insulting."

"Yes," she said. "Thank you. It *is* insulting."

"Because you drive like a *granny.*"

"What? I drive perfectly fine."

"Yes, for an eighty-year-old granny," he said.

She choked. "And how do you know that?"

"I've been behind you on the highway with an entire lineup of other people all stuck because you were going like fifty-five."

"Which is the speed limit!"

"Sixty-five on state highways," he said. "Seventy-five on interstate highways, which is where you were." He paused. "Driving like a granny."

"I do *not* drive like a . . . Oh, forget it." She went back to the binoculars, but she found she couldn't let it go. "I'll have you know, I actually got a speeding ticket last year."

"For driving under the speed limit?" he asked.

"No!" She might have smacked him, but she saw the twitch around his mouth. She was amusing him. She hated being amusing. At least in this context. "I want to drive, Adam."

He grimaced.

And kept driving.

"I've been driving since I was fourteen," she said. "That's how old I was when I stole my dad's Bronco and took it for a joyride."

"Yeah, I've heard this story from Grif." He slid her a glance. "You had it in low instead of drive, and you dropped the engine out on Highway 47."

"One tiny little mistake," she said.

He grimaced again.

"Seriously." She held out the binoculars. "You're the tracker. Pull over."

"Christ." But to her utter shock, he pulled over. "You've got to baby it in the turns," he said, not moving from the driver's seat. "Don't slide into the ditch."

"I'm not going to slide into the ditch."

"And the clutch is a little sticky, so you have to—"

"I know how to do it." She slid over the console against him. Refusing to give any thought to how her body loved the contact with his big, warm, strong one, she gave him a shove out the driver's door.

Adam came around the front of the Ranger and gave her a long look as he slid into the passenger's seat she'd just vacated. "Be careful," he said.

"Be careful? Or drive the damn posted speed limit?"

He actually sighed and belted himself in. Then he reached into the backseat and buckled in a confused Milo as well.

She rolled her eyes and eased on the gas pedal and got them moving.

He was right, of course. She had to baby the thing in the turns, and the clutch was sticky. The road was slippery, the curves tight. She was concentrating on keeping them in the center of the one-lane road when she felt the weight of his stare. *"What?"*

"Nothing."

"It's something, Adam. Spit it out."

"I'm just wondering if you're going to ever get out of second gear. Or if your plan is to drop this engine, too."

She grated her teeth. How was it that everything always looked so easy when he did it? The fact was, it was lightly snowing again, and the road felt . . . narrow. She kept eyeing the ditches on either side, which were lower than the road and filled with a mix of snow and ice.

Total hazards. "Yes, I'm going to get out of second gear," she said.

"In this century?"

She gave the ATV a little more gas and navigated into third gear, just as they came upon a tight hairpin turn. The Ranger slid. All four tires lost traction, sending them sideways.

Into the ditch.

# Thirteen

The ATV didn't flip. It didn't do much of anything except tilt violently to the right and stop short enough that Holly nearly ate the steering wheel. She turned and quickly assessed Adam without meeting his eyes, then whipped around to look at Milo, who was okay but seeming a little confused as to how he'd ended up fighting the seat belt. "You okay?" she asked Adam.

"Are *you*?"

"Well, yes. But your steering doesn't respond properly."

Adam pulled off his sunglasses and stared at her, then whipped around to look at his dog, who'd resettled himself in his seat, utterly unconcerned at their predicament. He probably had a lot of experience with being in rough situations, this being barely a ripple.

"The steering doesn't respond properly," Adam repeated slowly, turning his gaze back to Holly.

"That's right." She tapped the steering wheel, as if she needed to demonstrate the piece of the Ranger she was talking about.

Adam shook his head and muttered something beneath his breath, which she missed. She didn't ask him to repeat it.

He gave her another indeterminable look, then slid out of the vehicle and took in the situation, hands on hips.

She got out as well. The two right wheels were low in the ditch, sucked into the snow, mud, and ice. It wasn't looking good. "Probably you need to have that steering looked at," she said.

He let out another long breath and brushed past her, burying his head in the storage compartment in the back, muttering again, something about insane granny drivers.

"I can hear you," she said.

"Good, because I was talking right to you."

Snowflakes drifted down as he set to work with a shovel. "Do you need help?" she asked.

He raised his head and gave her a long look.

Right. She'd helped enough.

He began shoveling at the back wheel, the muscles of his arms and shoulders working like a finely oiled machine.

"Careful of your shoulder," she said.

He didn't respond. After a minute, he straightened again. "Okay, get behind the wheel and hit it. Steer into the slide."

"Now?"

He shoved back his hood and hat to run his fingers through his hair. Coming from Adam, this was an extreme sign of agitation. "Well, I don't mean next week."

"Okay." She started to get in but stopped and turned back to him. "I'm really sorry I put your baby in a ditch."

"Uh-huh." He put his hat back on. "Hit it," he said again. "And steer—"

"Into the slide," she finished for him with a nod. "Got it." She settled herself in the driver's seat and glanced at Milo, who was still sitting in the backseat, calm as you please. "We're going into the slide," she told him, and put the Ranger in gear to go for it.

The engine whined and revved, the wheels spun, and a combination of snow and ice and dirt spewed out the back.

Milo, who'd stuck his head out the side to watch the wheels spin, licked some snow and mud off his nose.

Adam straightened and met Holly's gaze in the rearview mirror. A mixture of snow and mud dripped off his hat, ear, nose . . .

"Oh," she gasped. "I'm so sorry."

He swiped his forearm over his face and gave her another narrow-eyed look. "Again."

"But—"

"Again. *Less* gas."

She'd been trying to keep her cool, but at this she completely lost it. "Less gas! More gas! Don't drive like a granny!" She tossed up her hands. "Which one?"

Adam stood there, looking as if he needed to practice his breathing technique. "*Less* gas," he said again.

"Okay, but for the record, *you're* the one who said hit it." She eased onto the gas this time. The tires started to slide but Holly felt a surge, as if someone was giving the Ranger a push.

Someone was.

Adam.

He was behind the ATV, feet planted wide, putting his whole body into it as he muscled the Ranger out of the ditch. The wheels found purchase in the gravel and caught, and she drove back onto the road and stopped.

Adam strode up to the driver's side door and opened it.

"Guess my turn is over," she said.

He hauled her out.

Yeah. Her turn was over.

Then he backed her into the side of the Ranger, caging her in with his arms. He was covered in mud and snow, and she squished back as far as she could against the vehicle. "You're dirty."

"Very," he said.

Something unfurled in her gut and she was pretty sure it was arousal. "And wet."

"Uh-huh." He was still looking serious, but Holly could see the smile twitching at the corners of his mouth, and everything about her heated. His face was close to hers, but his sunglasses were back on, blocking his eyes.

"Are we playing?" she whispered.

"What did I tell you about playing?"

She wracked her brain. Hard to do with his big, hard body up against hers. And he was hard.

Everywhere.

And suddenly he wasn't the only one . . . wet. She opened her mouth to say something, she had no idea what, but he tucked a strand of hair behind her ear and trailed a fingertip down her cheek. Before she could finish process-ing that, he leaned down and kissed her. And not a warm little peck, either. A real long, wet, heated kiss that involved a lot of tongue and involuntary hard breathing on both their parts. When he broke the kiss and stepped back, she nearly slid to the ground. "What was that?"

"Not a damn clue," he said, still holding her face. "You make me crazy."

Okay. Good to know.

"Get in the Ranger, Holly."

She nodded, locked her knees, walked around to the pas-senger's side, and got into the Ranger.

He slid behind the wheel. He waited for her to get her seat belt on, and then drove in silence at a higher speed than she'd managed before, while keeping them perfectly in control. Of course. Because he was good at control. Real good.

And yet, she seemed to test that control. She had no idea why that thought made her feel better, but it did.

At the base of Kaniksu, they got out of the Ranger.

"We're walking from here?" she asked.

"No." He was looking down at the trail. There was a

fine dusting of snow across it but nothing obvious that she could see. But his attention was definitely caught by something.

Milo was nose to the snow, snuffling.

Adam turned back to her. "Someone's been through here, but that doesn't mean it's him—"

"It is." Or so she hoped.

They got back into the ATV. The road was covered in a few inches of light, dusty snow, with thick ice beneath from the previous rain, making the going treacherously slippery. A quarter of a mile before the caves, they had to park and walk in. Halfway there, Holly felt dampness inside her right boot. "Crap."

Adam looked over at her.

She sighed. "My boot. It's leaking."

"Your feet are wet?"

"Just one. But I'm not cold, we can keep moving."

With a shake of his head, he dropped his pack, pushed her down on a snow-covered rock, and squatted before her. "Take it off."

At those three words, uttered low and demanding, her nipples tightened as if he was talking directly to them. She pulled off her boot and he handed her a dry sock. While she wrestled that on, he pulled out a roll of something silver.

"Duct tape?" she asked.

"The magic fix-all."

And indeed, he wrapped it around the loose seam on her boot, and it was good as new.

In the meantime, Milo had definitely gotten on someone's trail. He was nose down, snuffling, completely focused. Holly followed his and Adam's trail, leaving them to do their thing. Watching them was . . . She shook her head and rubbed her chest, where there was an odd ache. Nerves, certainly. But a sorrow, too. She'd have never gotten this far without Adam's help, but being with him like this was harder than she'd thought.

She didn't want to fall for him again, but how could she not?

He'd come out here for her. He'd dropped everything to do this, simply because she'd asked. He'd shared his food, his equipment . . . his body. She smiled to herself at that and looked at him. He was moving along at a pace that she knew was for her benefit, not his. He had his pack on his shoulders, which was much heavier than hers, hoodie up, reflective sunglasses on, every movement a study in genetic, testosterone-filled masculine glory.

And he had no idea that she was walking behind him, waxing poetic to herself about him. The guy who'd once destroyed her. But . . .

He'd changed. Grown up from the wild hellion he'd once been. Everything that had come up, he'd handled, fixed, or resolved with quick, easy efficiency.

It was shockingly appealing. Lost in her thoughts, she was startled when he stopped so suddenly she plowed into him. Looking up, she realized they'd come around the last turn and faced the caves.

Tilting her head back, she took in the towering, building-sized rocks that had drifted down in the last ice age, forming a maze of open caverns.

Adam was standing still, staring at them as well. Holly dropped her pack and searched it for her flashlight. When she had it in hand, she turned to Adam with a hopeful smile that died in her throat.

The color was gone from his face and his entire body radiated tension. "Adam?" she asked, heart dropping. Had he seen a bad sign from Milo? She didn't know what the signal from dog to owner was when they found a dead body, and fear seized her. "Oh God."

"No," he said. "It's not that."

She looked at him, startled by his distant tone. It was very unlike him to not reach out and reassure her, but he was definitely not reaching out. If anything, he was completely blank-faced, and as mentally withdrawn from her as was possible. "What is it?" she whispered.

He shook his head as if tossing off a bad memory and then pulled out his flashlight. Expressionless, he started inside. "Stay close," was all he said.

Fucking caves, Adam thought. Of course it had come down to the fucking caves. His gut clenched tight, and with wooden feet he stepped to the ancient, three-story-tall rock formations and nearly suffocated—not from lack of air, there was plenty of air—but from the memories. Memories of another set of caves, on another continent, in another time.

*Dark.*

*The thundering boom of mortar.*

*Flash of a firefight.*

*Screams . . .*

Jesus. He took a deep breath and forced his feet to take another step.

"Adam?"

Ignoring the concern in Holly's voice, as well as the hand she set on his arm, he moved forward. Because that's what he'd learned to do.

Move forward.

Except sometimes it felt like all he was really doing was spinning his wheels. No matter how much he tried.

And then it happened. Three steps into the cave, his feet refused to go another step. Just flat-out refused.

The urge to turn and run out of there nearly overpowered him, and that pissed him off. It was just a few stupid rocks stacked on top of one another. Hell, he'd spent half his childhood hiding out here. He knew these caves as well as he knew the back of his own hand, so he refused to acknowledge the bells clanging in his head and the way his vision was flashing like IEDs going off around him. But he was sweating now, and yep, right on cue, a stabbing pain arrowed into his chest.

And then another.

He pressed his hand to it, hard, but it didn't help. It wasn't a heart attack. He knew this. But the pain still sucked the breath from his lungs and replaced it with a ball of bitter panic. Utterly out of control, he dropped to his knees rather than pass out. "Oh Christ," he whispered, because here it came. He set his hands onto the ground and let his head hang, eyes closed, as he tried to ride it out while his brain screwed with him.

"Adam."

He squeezed his eyes tighter but the images slapped at him, replacing his vision completely. Choking dust. Burning lungs. The stench of blood and fear.

And death.

"Adam. Come on, up you go." Pulling hands. "That's it, I've got you."

He opened his eyes, realizing that Holly had gotten him to his feet and outside the cave by sheer force. Pretty impressive given that he outweighed her by eighty pounds.

"Breathe, Adam." She crouched in front of him and tugged off his backpack, putting her cool hand to the back of his sweaty neck. "Bigger breaths," she said matter-of-factly. "Deeper."

Jesus. She was using his own techniques on him. Closing his eyes again, he dropped his head to his knees and concentrated on imitating her breathing. It was all he could do.

"Here." She thrust a bottle of water at him. "Slow sips."

He slid her a look as he drank, then moved to get up.

She didn't attempt to try to keep him down but merely got up with him and slipped her hand in his. "We walking, then?" she asked.

The royal *we* should have irritated the hell out of him, but he had other problems. There was the horror he felt that he'd let her see him like this. Shame that he wasn't in control. And then there was the fire still in his chest, and his heart was palpitating against his ribs so hard he was surprised they didn't shatter. He couldn't catch a damn breath, and while a moment ago he'd been flashing hot and sweating like a pig, he was now freezing-ass cold and shaking with it.

And having trouble remembering a single damn thing he'd been taught to stop this nightmare.

*Walk*, he thought. *Breathe*. So he did a few laps around a stand of trees, he and his parade. Milo. Holly. He could feel her calm, quiet presence at his side. She was still holding his hand, hers warm and steady in his icy one.

When he'd first come home from Afghanistan, he'd walled himself off from the world. His work made that easy. He'd slipped into a routine. He'd closed off his mind to feelings and emotions, because if he didn't allow himself to feel, then he wouldn't be vulnerable to loss.

His brothers had helped him feel comfortable. So had Lilah. And Jade. And if they'd treated him with a certain care, he pretended not to notice. And eventually he'd made his way back to the living. He'd been there awhile now and had thought this was behind him.

*Liar.* If that had really been true, he'd have long ago put himself on active S&R duty instead of incident command. Still, for the most part he'd managed to function at nearly one hundred percent, though his therapist had warned him that there'd be the occasional setback.

And there had been. It was a stark reminder of why he wasn't in a place to let anyone into his life. Why he wasn't ready for a real relationship. He couldn't do it to someone he cared about. Especially someone like Holly, a person he'd already hurt. "I'm not losing it," he said. "At least not completely. You don't have to walk with me."

"I know," she said. But she kept walking with him, Miss Total Control all of a sudden. She was shockingly calm and efficient, if not more than a little grim-faced, no doubt from having to get him out of the caves since he hadn't been able to manage it on his own.

Yeah, he really hated that.

Finally he let out a long, shuddery breath and stopped, leaning back against one of the tall, sturdy pine trees, eyes closed. When Holly didn't speak, he opened his eyes again and looked at her.

She gave him a small smile, but didn't offer any empty platitudes like "It's going to be okay" or "You're looking better now," for which he was eternally grateful. He hated useless, unnecessary conversation, and he hated to be patted on the head like a child and to be made promises that couldn't be kept. And he *really* hated being made to feel stupid, although he was doing a bang-up job of that all on his own.

He was also grateful that she didn't try to get him to talk about it. Thanks to therapy, he could, but he didn't like to, and he sure as hell didn't want to do it now, when every time he closed his eyes he was still flashing back. "I fucking hate caves."

She nodded. "I'm getting that loud and clear."

"I'm okay now."

She slid him a sideways look from beneath her sideswept bangs. She wasn't wearing any makeup, and her full lips pursed for a minute as she studied him carefully. "Really?"

"Yeah."

"*Really* really?"

"No." He blew out a breath. "But I'm getting there."

"Why don't you stay here a few minutes? I'll just go check the rest of the caves and—"

"No. I'm going with you, Holly."

She gave him a long look, but she didn't argue, once

again earning his undying gratitude. "Okay," she said. "But let's give it a minute first." That said she slid down the tree until she was sitting at the base. Since she was still holding his hand, he was pulled down along with her.

They were silent for a little while. Perfectly fine with him. It was cold enough and late enough in the season that there were no birds, no insects. Just the eerie, beautiful quiet of the remote landscape. "I didn't expect that," he finally admitted.

"What, you thought you were impervious to a freak-out?"

He turned his head and met her gaze. "Excuse me?"

"Don't even try to tell me that wasn't a complete freak-out," she said. "A most spectacular one, too."

He let out a low laugh. "Aren't you supposed to be kind to the mentally ill person?"

She held his gaze, all kidding aside now. "You're not mentally ill, Adam. You're human."

## Fourteen

Though Holly was anxious to look through the caves for her dad, she was more anxious about Adam at the moment. If she hadn't seen his panic attack up close and personal, she'd never have believed it possible for him to lose control so completely.

But he'd gotten it together pretty fast, much faster than she could have accomplished. It was amazing, and awe-inspiring. She felt other things, too. Far more complicated things. Affection, for one. It was hard to watch a big, bad, tough man like Adam fall apart and put himself back together again without wanting to hug him. And yeah, she really wanted to hug him—which would be essentially the same thing as hugging a lit fuse.

Go figure. Apparently he wasn't the only one of the two of them with a crazy streak.

As she watched, he settled himself back to normal. Normal being a cool, calm exterior that revealed nothing of the inner man. He lifted her backpack for her, setting it on her shoulders. He did the same with his own and moved to the entrance of the caves.

And stopped.

She came up beside him. "You don't have to do this."

"Yeah, I do."

She stared up into his face. Grim determination. "How do you manage S&R with this sort of PTSD reaction to tight places?" she asked.

He paused, and she wasn't sure he was going to answer.

"I don't," he finally said. "Or I haven't been. I work the incident command, organizing the search teams from a central location."

"But the other night, on the rescue for that kid, you weren't at home base," she pointed out.

"No. By sheer dumb luck, Kel and I were scoping out training terrain when the call came in. The kid had been last seen on the east bank of the Black Forest River. His brother kept saying they'd been by the big rocks near the river caves. But the only rocks out that way are on the west side."

"By the caves out there," Holly said.

"Yeah. We just happened to be close by and were able to respond within minutes."

"So let me get this straight," she said. "You went after the boy, even knowing you might have to go in a cave?"

"Yeah, well, luckily I didn't have to, or we might still be out there."

She met his wry gaze. "You did something superhero-like," she said. "It was all over the news. You shimmied down a rock cliff where he was clinging and were able to hold on to him until Kel got to you with ropes."

"Yes, I grabbed him and held on, but I didn't have to go into the caves."

"Well, if that's all . . ." Turning to face him, she slid her hand up his chest and around the back of his neck, tugging his face down to hers. She brushed her lips over his and then lingered.

He pulled her in without hesitation, took her mouth with his, and gave her a long, hot, lingering kiss. "Not that I'm complaining," he said when they broke apart, "but what was that for?"

"An apology," she said.

"For?"

"When we first started out yesterday, I didn't like you."

His mouth quirked slightly. "I tell you one sob story and you feel sorry enough for me to change your mind?"

"Is that what you think?" she asked. "That I feel sorry for you?" Silly, proud man. She went up on tiptoes and kissed him again. Gentle.

And then not so gentle.

"I feel a lot of things for you, Adam," she said. "Too many, probably. But one thing I don't feel is sorry for you. Clear?"

He raised a brow at her bossy tone, and she was gratified to see a light of good humor in his eyes. "Crystal," he said.

Even knowing he was humoring her, she felt relieved. He was going to be okay. She'd make sure of it. "Ready?"

The very ghost of a smile crossed his lips and she felt even better. "For anything," he said.

And she believed it.

They moved just inside the entrance to the caves, the cool wind at their back. Holly took her cue from Adam, and when he stopped, so did she. She was just about to once again offer to go in on her own, when he spoke.

"He's not here."

She bit her lower lip and stared into the dark opening.

"It's not because I don't want to go in there," he said. "Which I don't, by the way. I'd rather have my nuts cut off with a rusty knife." He pointed to Milo, who was sitting relaxed at Adam's side. "Milo's telling me no one's in here."

Holly's stomach cramped. "But what if whoever's in there isn't alive?"

He paused, and she got the feeling he was choosing his words carefully. "Milo's also a cadaver dog."

Her stomach dropped. "Oh?"

"Dead or alive, he'd know."

She let out a slow breath and Adam slid his hand into hers. Surprised, she met his gaze. "We're going to find him," he promised again. "Just not here."

"Then where?"

He turned and looked out into the gray, foggy morning. "Where we should have checked first," he said. "The place he first showed me back when I was a stupid punk-ass, where he goes to disappear."

"Where's that?"

"Fallen Lakes."

"No," she said, shaking her head. "He won't be there. That's where Deanna dumped him."

He glanced at her, brow furrowed. "What?"

"Yeah, he took her up there last week. They had some big fight and . . ." She broke off at the look on Adam's face. "Oh my God."

Her dad had been mourning the loss of that relationship all week, not that Holly had been exactly sympathetic. It had been hard for her to be when she distinctly remembered him *not* mourning the loss of his marriage to her mom.

Yet he'd mourned his girlfriend, Deanna, quite possibly the only person he'd ever really let all the way past his tough cowboy exterior. And suddenly, it made perfect sense. "He is," she breathed. "He's at Fallen Lakes."

Adam nodded. "I'd bet on it."

She looked up into the sky. "Think the storm's going to hold back for us?"

"No. But we can still get there." He was looking at the screen of his phone, thumbing through his weather app. "If you're not driving, that is."

She didn't bother to roll her eyes. They headed back to the ATV in silence. Holly's mind was whirling. Two days ago she'd been happily hoarding resentment, regret, and a whole bunch of other repressed emotions for Adam. She'd been doing so assuming that he was that same person he'd been all those years ago.

And in some ways he was. He still could think faster on his feet than anyone she knew. He was strong of body and mind, and he never, ever backed down. But he wasn't the same wild, dangerous rebel she'd once been so desperately in love with, and so desperate to save. Clearly he still had his ghosts, but he'd grown into a flesh and bones man, and a good one.

And suddenly she had a new problem. She was seeing Adam, the real Adam, warts and all. No rose-colored glasses this time. And she liked this man.

A lot.

She could fall hard for him, if she let herself. Luckily she understood him now and knew he wouldn't want that. She shouldn't want it, either. After all, her parents' marriage had been smoke and mirrors. Hell, her own marriage had been smoke and mirrors. Her entire *life* had been smoke and mirrors.

A façade.

She was good at that, at building unrealistic expectations. But she was over it. She wasn't living that way anymore. Her eyes were wide open now, and staying that way. Life wasn't perfect and she knew now it never would be. She had faults, and she wanted to be with someone who revealed his faults right up front. No hidden agenda. Adam fit that bill. Could she allow herself to fall for him again, the man he was now?

Or maybe the more accurate question was . . . how could she not?

\* \* \*

Adam stopped the ATV about a mile out from the base of the trailhead to Fallen Lakes and turned to Holly.

She was still wearing his hat, strands of hair framing her face. She pushed her glasses farther up on her nose, and he decided today she looked more like a walking/talking girl-next-door fantasy than the hot librarian. He wisely kept this to himself and pointed to the small plume of smoke ahead, about three hundred feet up.

She stared at it. "Let's go."

He drove in, stopping at the trailhead, knowing exactly what they'd find at the top. A wide sweep of the entire mountain range and valleys below, a staggering view that made the world look like a painting, and could make a man forget his pain.

Adam would know. It was the spot where Dell had taken him for "anger therapy." Every Wednesday for a full year they'd come up here after his postcombat PTSD therapy. They'd sit on the very edge of the cliff, feet hanging off into space, a beer in hand, and yell at the top of their lungs.

"It's not a hunting spot," Holly said, looking up. And up.

"He's not hunting."

"And you really think it's him?"

He gestured to the ATV half hidden beneath a few trees, which had the familiar logo printed on the side: REID RANCHING.

Holly nodded, got out of the ATV, shouldered her backpack, and started walking. Fast.

Adam caught up with her and slowed her to a halt with a hand caught up in her straps, pulling her back up against him.

"What are you doing?"

"Slowing you down," he said.

"Are you kidding? He could be hurt. Why else would he not be answering his phone?"

"Same reason I never did when I was up there." When

she just looked at him, he let out a breath. "Sometimes a guy just needs to be alone."

"A guy?"

"*Anyone*. Look, just let me go up there first and see what's up."

She narrowed her gaze. "You want me to stay here while you go ahead."

"Yes."

"*No.*"

Christ. He should have known better. She acted first and thought later, always.

"What if he's hurt?" she asked. "Or . . . ?"

"A dead man can't make a fire, Holly."

"I'm going."

He looked into her eyes. Yep, the Reid stubbornness was blazing. "Just give me a few minutes," he said quietly. "*Please.*"

She sighed. "Fine."

"I'll make it quick."

"Hmm."

He didn't like the sound of that, but he took the trail with Milo, who was focused and alert. "Seek," he said, giving the dog permission to go ahead and find the target.

Milo barked once and was gone.

Adam followed at a brisk pace and a few minutes later heard the three short, sharp barks signaling that the dog had located his target. When Adam walked the last switchback on the trail, he came out on the plateau, looking out at a heart-stopping view. The air was thinner up here and definitely colder. The snow had fallen heavier, and it was not melting off. There was a two-person tent pitched against the rocks and a small pit fire crackling. Sitting in front of it, holding out a stick with two marshmallows on the end of it sat a beefy, weathered man in his sixties. Donald Reid, in a beach chair on the snow, his two six-month-old golden retrievers at his side.

A part of Adam recognized the relief. He'd been fairly confident Donald hadn't gotten himself into trouble. But the truth was, the guy *was* getting older—not that Reid would admit the weakness.

And yet another part of Adam, a bigger part, was pissed off. Donald wasn't a man used to thinking of others first. Hell, neither was Adam for that matter, but all he could see was Holly's face over the past few days, and the worry and fear that had never left it.

Donald should have—could have—saved her a lot of stress.

"Adam," Donald said in surprise, rising. He groaned and stretched his back, his bones creaking. Then he shook his head and sat back down. "Damn."

"You okay?"

"Hanging in there. What the hell are you doing up here, son?"

Donald was a self-made man, and as such was often cavalier and self-centered, but once upon a time he'd been nice to a punk-ass kid for no reason other than Adam had been friends with Grif. The cranky bastard meant a lot to Adam. "I'm here looking for you," Adam said.

Thing One and Thing Two had rushed toward Adam, respectfully sitting at his feet to receive their praise for being such wonderful specimens. Adam bent low and hugged them both. Then they bounded around together in a happy pack with Milo just as Holly's voice rang out across the clearing.

"Dad!"

Donald turned in surprise toward her. She was in the same spot Adam had stood a moment before, stark relief all over her face. "You're okay?" She came closer and looked him over. "You are." She let out a breath and then pushed him so that he fell back into his chair. "When you're okay and not dead, you *answer* your phone, do you hear me?"

"Of course I hear you. The people of China can hear you." He was frowning. "Why the hell wouldn't I be okay?"

"Gee, Dad, I don't know." Holly's pale features were quickly filling in with a ruddiness in her cheeks that Adam knew was caused by adrenaline and fury. "Maybe because you *didn't return a phone call or text* for days?"

Donald shrugged but didn't have the good grace to seem even slightly apologetic. "I lost my phone."

Holly looked horrified at this. "You lost your phone? What if something had happened to you out here?"

Donald was starting to look insulted. "Like what?"

Holly bent and poked him in the chest. Reid love. They didn't hug and kiss—they poked.

"Like anything!" Holly said.

"What are you talking about? I'm perfectly healthy at the moment."

"Perfectly healthy men don't just vanish into thin air," she said. "They have reasons for scaring their family half to death. Was this about the breakup? About Deanna leaving you?"

Donald's face went blank. "I barely even noticed that."

She pointed at him. "Don't do that. Don't underplay it. I know you loved her."

*"Loved,"* he stressed. "Past tense."

"Oh, so is that why you have 'I Will Survive' playing on repeat on your office computer?"

He scowled. "Hey, that's my private office—"

"Or why you demon-dialed Deanna for three straight days until she finally blocked your cell?"

"I didn't—"

"She called me, Dad. She tried calling you back and couldn't get you. She was worried about you."

Donald turned away. "I wanted to make sure she was okay, that's all."

"She's fine. She's out of town with Thomas Pines."

"Pines Ranch Thomas Pines? Her boss? Christ. What is he, twelve?"

"Dad." Holly dropped to her knees beside him. "This is what happens when you date women three decades younger than you."

"Hmph," Donald said, crossing his arms over his barrel chest.

A Reid standoff.

Adam knew they had a cantankerous affection for each other. He also knew that Donald would move heaven and earth to make his children happy, but he wanted them happy *his* way, according to his specs. He set boundaries and brooded when those boundaries were breached. He was stubborn and driven and . . . stubborn.

Grif and Holly were two peas in a pod that way.

"I can't believe you came all this way to look for me," Donald said.

"We came a lot farther than you even know," Holly said. "First we went to Diamond Ridge and Mount Eagle. And—"

"Both of those places suck and have ever since *Hunting* magazine posted that article declaring them part of the country's top-ten best-kept secrets. I don't go there anymore."

"Did not know that," Holly muttered. "And Kaniksu Caves?"

Donald slid a look in Adam's direction. "The caves?"

Jesus. Seemed he'd hid his neurosis from exactly no one.

"We were worried," Holly reiterated.

"Yeah, well, you shouldn't have come," Donald said. "Either of you."

"I thought you might be hurt!"

Donald sighed. "Look, it's nice that you worried. Really. And I'm glad you're here. But I don't understand. I go out all the time and you've never said a word. So what's this really about?"

Holly sucked in a breath, looking shaken. Like maybe she wasn't exactly sure. For the first time since they'd started this thing, she looked lost, and Adam felt his heart squeeze for her.

"It's about the fact that you can't just vanish anymore, Dad," she finally said. "You're getting—"

*"Careful,"* he said, pointing at her.

"Older."

Donald stood up and Adam stepped between them. "Okay, time out," he said, wanting to stop them before this got out of hand, because when things got out of hand between him and his brothers, fists tended to fly. He couldn't imagine it getting to that point between the Reids—they probably fought with a lot more class and used their words instead—but no sense in testing things. He pinched the bridge of his nose before turning to Holly. "Nice job on the staying, by the way."

Holly crossed her arms. "Did you know about this?"

"Do you really think I'd have dragged you all over hell and back if I had?"

"Right. Of course not," she said. "You wouldn't have spent an extra minute in my presence unless absolutely necessary, is that it?"

"No." *Jesus.* How did this become about him?

She was still breathing heavily from her walk up here. Actually, she'd had to have hauled ass to arrive as fast as she had. She must have yesed him, waited until he'd gone on, and then run like hell after him and Milo.

Sneaky.

But not surprising.

He'd have done the same. Which made her a woman after his own heart. Too bad his heart wasn't in operating order.

*And yet it had worked just fine last night . . .*

No, that had been a different part of his body entirely. Yeah, that was bad. Really bad. And damn. So good . . .

He still had no fucking idea what he thought he'd been doing. None. Zero. Nada. A point proved by Donald's next words.

"Have to admit, I'm surprised to see the two of you together." Donald divided a long, questioning look between them before settling on his daughter. "Though I am glad to see you finally got over your silly crush and can be friends with him."

*"Dad."*

"What?" Donald said. "It's not like it's a secret. Hell, how could it have been with the way you used to moon over the poor guy?"

The "poor guy" struggled not to grin.

Holly made a sound that managed to perfectly convey her thoughts, and moved close to her dad's fire, thrusting her hands out over the flames, carefully not looking at Adam, though her ears looked very hot.

And if he looked very carefully, there was also steam coming out of them.

Adam knew better than to stir a woman's temper, especially *this* woman's. Her fuse was long, but once it was lit, it went off like a firecracker. Still, he couldn't help himself. "You used to moon over me?" he asked.

# Fifteen

At the low, sexy voice in her ear, Holly closed her eyes but not before she gave him an elbow to the gut. Then she huddled closer to the fire, staring into the flames.

Adam flashed her a rare two-hundred-watt smile but backed up a step, giving her some room. Not, she was quite certain, because she'd actually hurt the big oaf but because he *wanted* to move. Adam didn't do anything he didn't want to do.

And just like that, unbidden, came a flash of what he'd wanted to do last night. Or rather, *who* he'd wanted to do.

Her.

She shivered before relegating the erotic images to the back of her mind, where she could pull them out later, when she was alone. Because right now her dad was watching her carefully, a small frown on his face. Though he was generally clueless to the workings of a woman's mind, he was clearly getting a vibe from her.

"You really thought something bad had happened to me," he said.

Holly sighed. "It could have."

"You need to worry more about yourself."

She slid him a look.

"You're across the country from your husband, who, by the way, never appears to call or check on you. What is he so busy doing that he doesn't have time for you?"

His new TA, no doubt. Worse, she was thrown off by her father's reference to her marriage. They *never* talked about her marriage. "We're talking about you," she reminded him. "This whole thing is about you."

"Well, now we're talking about *you*. You had to have that guy, remember? There was no talking you out of it. So what the hell good is he if he's not ever at your side?"

She shook her head, discombobulated. "In all this time, you've never asked about him." She felt Adam's gaze heavy on her. "Which means that this is nothing more than your latest distraction technique. But you can't distract me, Dad. You nearly killed me with worry."

Her father couldn't be distracted, either. "What the hell is going on with you, Holly? And don't say nothing. It's about Derek, right?"

She narrowed her eyes. "Why are you suddenly asking about him?"

"Call it a gut feeling."

She sighed. "Fine. He's no longer my husband. Happy?"

"Ecstatic. But what the hell?"

"I left him, Dad. I left him a long time ago."

"And you didn't think this was pertinent information?"

"You never asked. You never even talked about me being married. And as far as pertinent, it's no more pertinent than you and Mom giving lip service to being married when in reality you were separated almost all of my childhood."

He blinked. "At least we didn't traumatize you and Grif with fighting, like so many other couples do."

"You were three thousand miles apart. I don't think that proves much. Plus, it was all pretend. You both hid all your feelings. The calm front was just a façade." She crossed her arms and turned away. She wasn't doing this now. Not in front of Adam, who was watching their bickering session with carefully hooded eyes.

Donald rose and grimaced but then wavered. He paled and put a hand to his heart. Holly's heart stopped and she rushed over to him.

Adam got there first, pushing Donald back down to the chair with surprising gentleness, hunkering before him, looking into the older man's face.

"Dad," Holly said urgently. "What is it? What's wrong?"

"Nothing. I'm fine."

He wasn't fine. He looked clammy, sweaty. And he was breathing erratically. "Dad—"

"Don't fuss," he snapped, and waved her away.

Stung, Holly backed up, then watched in disbelief as Adam reached in and took her dad's pulse, getting a weak smile out of him in the process.

"The low blood pressure again?" Adam asked quietly.

"Yeah, the fucker."

Adam rifled through his pack and pulled out a bottle of sports water.

"Not thirsty," Donald said.

"Drink it. You're probably dehydrated and the electrolytes will help the hypotension." He unwrapped a snack bar. "And eat this."

"Those are disgusting."

"It's got salt in it. That will help, too."

Under Adam's watchful eye, Donald drank and then ate, and then drank some more.

"Better?" Adam asked.

"Yeah." Donald sighed and looked slightly sheepish. "I hate this shit."

"What shit?" Holly asked. "What's going on?"

Adam never took his eyes off Donald. "You need to tell her. She deserves to know."

"Deserves to know what?" Holly demanded, her gut tight. "Dad, tell me."

"I had a little problem a few months back. You were in New York. With your non-husband."

"I was procuring my divorce," she said tightly. "What kind of problem?"

He paused. "A heart attack problem."

Holly gaped at him. *"You had a heart attack and didn't tell me?"*

"It was a *little* one. A *very* little one. And I've completely recovered. It's just that some of the meds I'm on now to lower my blood pressure have some side effects, that's all."

"That's *all*?" she repeated, her voice cracking. "You had a heart attack and you didn't tell me? Did you tell Griffin?"

The guilty look on his face said it all. "Oh my God. You didn't tell either of us," she said, shaking her head in disbelief. "Dad. How could you?"

"Because you would have worried. You'd have nagged me about my eating habits, about the too-young girlfriend, about going out on hunting trips alone—"

"You think?" Devastated, she pushed her glasses up and pressed her fingertips to her eyes, drawing in a deep breath. She dropped her hands and tried to make him understand. "Dad, you can't do this anymore. You can't take off on your own like this."

"I'm telling you, I'm healthy as a horse."

"Except for the heart attack and the low blood pressure."

He waved that aside. "I'm taking my meds. Exercising. Doing everything I'm supposed to. I'm not going to change, Holly. Not even for you."

She looked at Adam, who wasn't giving much away, except for maybe regret. *He'd known.* She couldn't stop thinking about that. He'd known about the heart attack, which was undoubtedly why he'd come in the first place.

She drew in a deep breath and shook her head. She'd have to deal with him later; her father's health was far more important. "How are we going to do this?" she asked him. "Get him back?"

"I'll get myself back," Donald said indignantly.

"You'll be more comfortable in the Ranger," Adam said.

"And I'll drive his ATV," Holly said.

Donald shook his head. "You're not driving my ATV."

"And why the hell not?" Holly demanded.

"Because you drive like your grandmother."

Holly felt her own blood pressure rise, but it didn't start to boil until she met Adam's gaze. His dark eyes were warm and filled with humor, the ass. "Deal with it, Dad," she said. "Because *you're* not driving back. Now let's go." She didn't want to risk getting stuck up here for another night. She could handle no running water, not to mention the lack of a toilet or electrical outlet for her hair straightener. What she couldn't handle was another night with Adam—and now also her father—both of whom she was afraid she loved dearly in spite of their many, *many* faults. "Dad, tell me the truth—are you really okay, or should we call for help to get you out?"

Her dad laughed. "You've got the best S&R guy right here. I think he can handle me."

"*You* can handle you," Adam told him. "Hell, you can probably still outdo me."

Her dad smiled, pleased at that. But Holly met his gaze and saw the truth. That he *was* aware that he was getting older, that he'd had a health scare, and it had done just that—scared him. But he wasn't the sort of man to go out without a last fight. He always said he'd never be the sort of man to lie down and let old age catch him. "Okay," she said softly. "Let's go. But do me a favor and take it easy on your S&R guy. He'd just gotten back from a rescue when I dragged him out here. He's injured and probably exhausted."

Donald flicked a glance at Adam.

Adam shook his head. "I'm fine."

"Hear that?" Donald asked Holly. "He's fine."

Men. "He's got a bunch of stitches in his shoulder."

"That's nothing," Donald said.

Holly just stared at him, and her dad patted her leg. "Honey, after the things he's seen and done, these past few days have probably been a picnic in the park. Isn't that right, boy?"

Adam's mouth quirked slightly, as if the thought of being a boy was amusing to him. And hell, it probably was. Even when he'd been young, he'd never really had the luxury of being a child. As long as Holly had known him, he'd always had that air of tough readiness. But surely he wanted to get back as badly as she did. Even badasses needed rest.

Adam repacked his gear to add some of Donald's load to his, and then they left. Holly started down the trail ahead of them. Adam watched her go for a minute, then slid his gaze to Donald. Who was eyeballing him blandly. Like a rattler at rest. Or the father of a beautiful woman . . .

Yeah. There was nothing more dick shriveling than lusting after a woman and being caught at it by her father. No matter if the father was a man who'd been there for him more than once.

Saying nothing, Donald began walking, keeping the pace slow. Adam accommodated him, thinking maybe the guy was feeling more weak than he'd let on.

"What's up between you two?" Donald asked bluntly, not sounding old or particularly weak at all.

Adam thought about pleading the Fifth and not answering, but he respected Donald too much for that bullshit. "None of your business."

Donald stared at him for a long beat, then let out a bark of laughter that had Holly turning around to look back at them. She narrowed her gaze on them both, but then faced forward again, continuing on at the same pace.

Donald shook his head at Adam and kept walking. "You're not her type."

This was undoubtedly true, but for a little while last night he'd felt a whole hell of a lot like her type.

"She likes them older, sophisticated," Donald said. "The cerebral type. I told you this years ago. You don't listen."

Once again, Adam's gaze locked on Holly walking ahead. She had her ear buds in, iPod in hand, clearly over the both of them. "I listened," he said. He just hadn't necessarily agreed.

"Yeah, *after* you got yourself in trouble," Donald said. "If it hadn't been for that, I'd never have been able to talk you into getting the hell out of Dodge and into the military—where I knew you'd learn what you needed to learn."

"You mean how to be a functioning member of society instead of a drain on the system behind bars?" Adam asked.

"Well . . ." Donald rubbed his jaw ruefully. "Yes."

Fair enough. Adam had definitely been on a one-way track to the wrong side of the law. "It worked."

Again, Holly whipped around, eyes narrowed right in on Adam.

The minx hadn't been listening to music at all. She'd been far too busy eavesdropping. She glared at him and then stared at her father. "*You* talked him into going into the military?"

Adam grimaced. "Listen, we're going to lose daylight if we don't keep moving—"

Holly lifted a hand in the direction of his face, the universal sign for him to *Shut it*.

Adam shoved his hands in his pockets. This wasn't going to go well. For any of them.

Holly stalked back toward them. "What do you mean, *you* talked him into going into the military?" she demanded of her dad.

Well, shit.

"You remember the trouble the boy got himself into there at the end," Donald said.

"Yes," Holly said. "He was always in trouble. That was nothing new."

"Not like that last time," Donald said. "He could have ended up in jail."

"But he didn't."

"Because it was suggested that if he went into the military, it would be a better course of action."

"Suggested by you," Holly said, clarifying.

"Yes," Donald said.

Holly turned to Adam, emotion blazing from her eyes. He could have dealt with that—except for the hurt. Christ, so much hurt.

"So you didn't *have* to go into the military," she said. "The judge didn't make you. You chose to leave." Not a question but a statement.

It hadn't been the biggest lie he'd ever told her but definitely the harshest. "Yes," he said quietly. "I chose to leave."

She blinked once, then looked at her father again. "And you had a hand in it. It was your idea. *You* talked him into going into the military, which could have cost him his life."

"At the time I thought it was best."

Holly lifted a hand and rubbed it to her chest as if it ached. "You took him from me."

Donald's gaze never left her face. "Well, to be fair, I didn't know there was a you and him. If I'd known, I'd have sent him a lot farther. Like to fucking Mars."

Adam gave a wry smile. It was true. Donald was notoriously protective of his only daughter. When she'd run off to New York and gotten married at nineteen, it had nearly killed him. If Donald had been aware back then that Adam had taken his precious daughter and shown her a walk on the wild side—for an entire summer, in fact—it was questionable as to whether or not Adam would still be breathing.

But Holly wasn't amused. Not in the slightest. She

turned on her heel and kept walking. For about three seconds. Then she whirled back and blasted her father with another look. "I can't believe you interfered with my life that way."

"I believe it was the boy's life I interfered with," Donald said mildly.

Holly ignored this and faced Adam. "And you."

Yeah, him. The crux of her problem. Hell, let's face it, he was the crux of a lot of problems.

"You protected him all these years," she said, pointing at her dad, "by not telling me that it was *his* idea. Why?"

Fair enough question. "Because it was the right thing to do."

"You let me think the judge said you had to go."

"Because I didn't want you to think you could talk me out of it. I needed a clean break."

"From me."

"From everything," he said. "Going was the right thing to do. I wasn't about to let your dad take any blame or have you decide to waste your life waiting on me. I went because I needed to go, Holly."

She stared at him for a long beat, then tossed up her hands and stalked off, muttering something about stupid, stubborn, idiot, Neanderthal alphas who were too stupid, stubborn, and idiotic to know a damn thing about life.

## Sixteen

Holly drove her dad's ATV back to Sunshine, and she felt quite badass while she was doing it, too. It was hard to maintain a good mad while enjoying the hell out of herself, but she managed. For a while, anyway.

Her dad rode with Adam and all three dogs. They stopped at regular intervals, which she knew was for her sake. But she didn't need the extra care. She could take care of herself. Especially since the snow had stopped and the fire road was manageable.

By the time they got off the mountain, she wasn't mad at either man. Much. She really did understand why Adam had left for the military all those years ago. She also understood why her dad had encouraged him to. Adam had been right, he needed to go. It had changed his life, set him on a different path, one that worked for him.

She couldn't resent that, not even a little bit.

No, what she resented was the fact that neither of them had trusted her to be grown-up enough to handle the situation.

*Because you hadn't been . . .*

During one of their stops, she called Red and e-mailed Grif about finding their wayward father. The heart attack news would have to wait until she could tell him face-to-face, online. She also contacted Kel and Kate, just to fill them in. Kate responded with an immediate text.

You get lucky up there with your tracker?

Holly's return text was simple and to the point.

You need your hormone levels checked.

Back in Sunshine, Adam got out of his Ranger to walk her father inside the big old ranch house. Holly moved to her dad's other side and got a gruff "What did I tell you about hovering, girl?"

Holly clenched her teeth and backed off. Inside, the two men holed up in Donald's office for a few minutes, where apparently no vaginas were invited. She was reduced to pressing her ear to the door to eavesdrop but could hear nothing.

Were they even breathing in there?

She feigned an interest in the row of pictures along the hallway wall for another few minutes for the excuse to be standing there, but since the pictures were all of her father's favorite pets from over the years, she tired of that quickly. She tried an ear to the door again, and had just settled up against the wood when it was pulled open. She nearly fell but Adam caught her and pulled her out of the office with him as he shut the door behind them.

She jerked upright and out of his grip, and tried to look busy.

Adam wasn't fooled. "You catch all that, or do you need an instant replay?"

"No." She sighed. "The damn walls are too thick, I couldn't hear a thing."

Adam's amusement faded. Taking her hand, he led her down the hallway, then outside, away from prying eyes and ears. "I got him to agree to go back to the doctor for a full checkup," he said. "Just to make sure everything's okay. I think his blood pressure meds aren't a good mix with the antidepressants he's taking."

She unconsciously put a hand to her heart. "He's on meds for depression?"

"Yeah, and before you ask, no, I didn't know."

"Oh my God."

Stepping close, he wrapped his fingers around the wrist of the hand she was holding to her heart. She looked up into those eyes, warm and steady on hers, and actually felt some of her tension drain.

Of course, then an entirely different kind of tension filled her. She had no idea what it was about Adam that never failed to inspire confidence and a feeling of security. He could make it all better with one touch, which was just about the craziest thing. No one could make things all better. She freed her hand and slid it up his chest, tipping her face to his.

He stepped into her, holding her gaze for a long beat before lowering his head and brushing his lips to hers. When she sighed in pleasure, he took her mouth with his. No other word for it. He took, and she gave. Willingly. Gliding her arms up around his neck, entangling her fingers in his hair, she pressed closer. A groan sounded and she honestly wasn't sure which of them it came from.

When Adam pulled free, his voice was lower, huskier. "Let me know if you need anything."

She nodded, staggered by the intensity of their connection. It was different this time around. Deeper. Stronger.

Scarier.

She'd already decided on the ride home that she didn't need to put a label on whatever this was. She'd done that once, and it hadn't worked out for her. She didn't need him to acknowledge wanting her when it was right there for her to see. She didn't need him to put words to the fact that in spite of themselves, they had a relationship of sorts, whether it was friends, or friends with benefits, or more.

The bottom line was that he'd proved how much he cared about her with every action he made over the past few days. A conversation about it wouldn't make it any more real than what it was right now. "Thank you," she said softly.

"For the kiss?"

She smiled. "For finding him for me."

His gaze drifted down over her mouth again. "That wasn't all we found."

"No, it wasn't."

He held her gaze, then stepped back and shoved his hands into his pockets as if he didn't quite trust them. And that. That all by itself made her feel even better. Because she wasn't the only one fighting this thing. In fact, she wasn't planning on fighting it at all anymore.

But she understood that he would.

Too bad he didn't stand a chance . . .

"He's promised me full disclosure after his doctor appointment," Adam said.

It took her a moment to switch gears. "And what about me?" she asked. "Do I get full disclosure, too?"

Adam shrugged.

She narrowed her eyes. "You're kidding me. I don't?"

"He doesn't want you to worry."

"Well, he won't have to worry about me worrying, since I'm going to kill him."

Adam shook his head. "Do I need to go back in there with you and referee?"

"No."

He nodded and, with one last long look, left.

Holly headed inside and hauled open her dad's office door. He wasn't at his desk as she expected. He was on the couch, head back, staring up at the ceiling, Thing One and Thing Two at his feet. At the sight of her, the dogs bounced up and tried to slobber her to death. "Sit," she said.

Thing One leaned on her, leaving dog hair all over her jeans. Thing Two licked her hand. *"Sit,"* she repeated sternly.

Neither of them listened. "Obedience class isn't working."

"Adam says it's the owner who needs to be trained." He snapped a finger and the dogs obediently sat.

Holly sighed. Okay, so *she* needed obedience class.

"Listen," her dad said. "I don't want you to tell Grif about . . . you know."

"The heart attack?"

"Yeah. I don't want him worrying about me while he's over there."

"Dad, I told him you were missing and that I went out after you with Adam."

"Goddammit." He glared at her, eyes bloodshot, the lines in his face drawn. He seemed older than she could remember him looking, and her heart clenched.

"So, it's okay for you to keep a secret for years," he griped, "and yet you babble about me to the entire fucking world?"

"Maybe that's our problem. As a family, we don't talk much."

"Well, you picked a hell of a time to change the rules."

He was brooding, and sensing it, Thing One and Thing Two hopped up and surrounded him. Holly moved closer, too, because he looked sad sitting between the two happy pups. Too sad. Feeling grateful to have him home safe and sound, wanting him to know it, she leaned in and kissed his tight jaw. "We'll deal with it, Dad. Okay? We'll deal with it together."

He nodded, then paused. Clearly he wanted to say something, and since it was unlike him to hesitate over anything, ever, her gut tightened. "What?"

"I never asked about Derek, but that doesn't mean I didn't wonder. In fact, I'd guessed about you splitting up." This didn't surprise her. Her dad kept himself incredibly busy, but he was astute and as sharp as a tack. Not to mention nosy as hell. He liked to know what was going on with his people. "I contacted him and asked him directly. He confirmed that you'd filed for divorce. I didn't say anything to you about it because . . ."

She stared at him in shock, because this *did* surprise her, though it shouldn't have. "Because why, Dad? Why didn't you tell me that once again you'd interfered?"

He grimaced. Guilt? Probably not. Probably just bracing himself for the fight about it now that he'd confessed. "Because you didn't tell me yourself," he finally said. "I thought you didn't want me to know. And for the first time in your life, you've seemed . . ." He searched for words, and when they came, they weren't what Holly expected. "Sure of yourself," he said quietly. "And happy in your skin. I didn't want to take that away from you."

"Oh." Her throat felt tight, but she nodded. Because it was true. Being back here in Sunshine, running the business side of things for Reid Ranching *had* empowered her. "I see."

"Actually, no you don't." He scrubbed a hand over his face. "And damn, but I'm really bad at this." He dropped his hand and met her gaze. "All your life, Holly, you've hidden yourself, conforming to what you thought I wanted. Or your mom. And then that asshole you married to spite me. You hid yourself, and I let you. I was wrong. You needed to find your own way, and you've done that. You've become tough and strong. A true Reid. Damned if I was going to take that away from you."

"Oh, Dad." She nudged Thing One off the couch and plopped down in his spot. They sat there a moment, companionably quiet.

"He's a good man, Holly."

Head back, she craned her neck to look at him. "Who?"

"Adam."

Her heart knocked once against her ribs. "That was never in question."

"He's a good man," her dad repeated. "And if I had any hand in messing things up the first time, I'm sorry."

"It wasn't you." She'd wanted Adam to stay in Sunshine—but she'd wanted that for her, not taking into account his wants. She'd been immature and selfish. "You were there for him, guiding him when he needed it. You did what was right for him."

Which was more than she'd managed.

"I did. And I'll do what's right for him now, too," her dad said.

"Which is?"

"Give him my permission to date you."

Holly stared at him, not knowing whether to laugh or be horrified. "Dad, you do realize that we don't need your permission."

"Well, of course I realize that. But I want him for you."

Laughing won, she decided. "You spent the past decade trying to talk me out of Derek."

"Adam's a better man."

She agreed. "Adam's not ready for me."

Now her father laughed, too. "Since when has something like that ever stopped you?"

Adam spent his first day back out on Bear Lake evaluating a class of five trying to pass their S&R certs. He got home later than planned, missing dinner with Dell and Brady, both of whom had left him bitchy texts like a couple of women.

This suited Adam, who wasn't ready to be grilled. He still hadn't processed all that had happened in the past few days. Being in such close proximity with Holly had fried his brain circuit. At least that was the story he was going with, since he couldn't come up with any other reason for what had happened between them.

Being with her again had done something to him, cracked something open deep on the inside. He wasn't sure how or what, but he knew one thing.

He was feeling again, *way* too much.

Then there'd been the matter of the caves and his massive failure to handle himself there. Yeah, fun times. He was really enjoying obsessing over that . . .

He'd done his best to shove it all away, but that wasn't working out so well for him. And he knew better, anyway. Shoving the bad shit deep always backfired, because then he ended up at the mouth of a set of caves having a breakdown . . .

Christ.

Completely over himself, he got up early the next morning to take out his horse. Reno was a four-year-old American quarter horse and the other love of Adam's life besides his dog. Two years ago, Reno had been rescued from a traveling carnival looking like a bare sack of bones and skin, covered in sores from being beaten. With Dell's help, Adam had nursed him back to life. These days Reno was fit and happy—and demanding.

When Adam got close enough, Reno nickered in greeting and butted him in the chest, snorting with eagerness to get out. While Adam saddled him up, Reno frisked him for apple slices—which he found in Adam's jacket pocket. "You're an attention 'ho, you know that. Like a woman," Adam said, hearing the footsteps behind him. Knowing it was his brother, he didn't turn.

"Don't let *your* woman hear you say that," Dell said, leaning against a post.

Adam imitated Reno and ignored this. He hopped into the saddle and took off, leaving Dell to eat their dust.

*His woman.*

He didn't have a damn woman and didn't have room in his life for one, anyway. He didn't have time or inclination or need. He didn't have shit. He sure as hell didn't have a single thing to offer a woman.

*So why have you done nothing but think about her?*

He brushed that thought off the same way he'd brushed off his brother.

Or tried.

But it didn't take Dell long to saddle his horse and urge Kiki to catch up to Reno. Kiki had a thing for Reno. A competition thing. The two horses nickered at each other while Dell tipped his hat back and flashed a triumphant smile at Adam.

The brothers were as competitive as their horses.

"In a hurry, then?" Dell asked.

"Needed a ride."

"Thought maybe you'd already gotten one of those recently."

Adam shot his brother a long look, which Dell met evenly. "You seemed . . . relaxed, is all," Dell said.

Adam shook his head. "Is this why you're up at the crack of dawn? To bug the shit out of me? Where's Jade?"

"She's pissed off at me right now."

"Maybe you can pretend I'm pissed off at you, too."

Dell sighed. "You're no fun anymore."

Adam didn't respond to that, since it might very well be true. "Why's Jade pissed?"

"Because I asked her how she felt about diamond rings."

Adam stared at him. "You asked her to marry you?"

Dell shrugged. "Not yet."

"So how does she feel about diamond rings?"

"She says she's happy living in sin with me and doesn't see the reason to complicate things."

Adam looked at his brother, the guy who defined laid-back and easygoing, the guy who'd never wanted a relationship, much less a wedding ring. "You really want to marry her."

"More than anything." Dell leaned forward and gently patted Kiki's neck. "I'll wear her down. Eventually."

Adam smiled. "Going to be fun watching you try."

They rode hard out to Crescent Canyon and stared down at the valley below.

Dell dismounted and, holding Kiki's reins, walked to the edge. He looked down for a long moment, then tossed his head back and let out a yell. When he was done, he turned to Adam.

Adam dismounted Reno and joined his brother. Side by side, they stared down into the meadow, dotted with a mix of snow and mud. It was late enough in the year that everything was still brown from a late fall, and far too early for any hints of spring. And yet the meadow was quiet, serene. Beautiful.

"Do it," Dell said.

"I'm good."

"Do it or I'll push you off."

This wasn't true. Dell wouldn't push Adam off because then he'd have to run Belle Haven alone, and he was too lazy to handle it all by himself. Adam turned his gaze to the meadow. The deal was to think of the thing that you wanted to let go of. So he closed his eyes and knew exactly what he wanted to let go of—the memory of Holly having to get him out of the cave. Just thinking about it he felt himself start to sweat. He drew a deep breath and yelled at the top of his lungs until he had nothing left.

Still staring into the meadow, Dell reached out and clasped a hand on Adam's shoulder. They stood like that until Reno nudged Adam, searching his pockets for more apple slices.

Dell laughed when the horse found them. "You are such a softie," he said.

If Adam hadn't just yelled himself hoarse, losing all the tension in his entire body, he might have shown Dell just how much he *wasn't* a softie. But he was feeling much more relaxed now and not up to a tussle. They got back on their horses and rode to Belle Haven, arriving in plenty of time before Dell's patients.

Dell was a damn good veterinarian and extremely popular. Usually he was busy from morning until night, seeing anything from the animal kingdom that needed him. In general, his appointments ran the gamut from a rabbit with an abscess to a goat who'd let her curiosity get the best of her and had ended up with her head stuck inside a mailbox.

Adam had a busy day. He worked an S&R for a hiker who'd turned out to not be lost at all but hiding out from his pissed-off wife after he'd blown their savings at an online gambling site.

It was much later that afternoon when Brady and Twinkles, his rescued mutt, cornered Adam in the staff room. Brady was tall, broad-shouldered, and built for a fight. They'd certainly had plenty when they'd been teenagers, but they'd both mellowed in their old age. "How you doing?" Brady asked.

Adam shrugged, bent to scratch Twinkles behind the ears, and then searched their refrigerator for something to eat. For several years now, he'd not felt much, including hunger. He'd eaten in order to fuel his body, nothing more. But lately he'd been hungry. Famished, even. He found a big, fat turkey club sandwich. *Score*.

"Shoulder okay?"

Adam nodded as he dug into the sandwich. When he looked up, Dell was there, too, exchanging a long look with Brady. "What?"

"You're eating my sandwich," Dell said.

"Yeah." Adam took another huge bite. "It's good, too."

Normally Dell would call him an asshole, but he didn't. This was because both Dell and Brady had been treating him with kid gloves ever since he'd gotten back from Fallen Lakes—which, FYI, he hated. *Hated.*

"Poker night," Dell said. "My place."

They played bimonthly with Lilah and Cruz, her partner at the kennels. Poker night was taken very seriously. Adam had won big the past three times they'd all played, so he knew everyone would be out for his blood tonight. Normally this wasn't a problem. He was good at being unreadable. Few could outbluff him. It was a talent that had served him well through his teenage crime spree, and then the military. And now at kicking some poker ass.

But he wasn't in the mood to play. He shrugged, signaling maybe he'd be there, maybe not. And since Dell wasn't going to stop him, he ate more of the sandwich.

Dell glanced at it longingly but didn't say a word.

"What does that mean?" Brady asked Adam. "That shrug. You're coming, right?"

"Maybe. I'm tired."

Brady and Dell exchanged another look.

"What now?"

"You tell us what," Dell said, eyeing the sandwich, and if Adam wasn't mistaken, his brother's mouth was watering.

Adam took another big bite and shook his head. "Not a clue."

"Okay, can we stop with the bullshit?" Brady asked. "You went on a rescue."

Ah, so the kid-glove treatment was from the rescue out at Bear Lake, not related to Holly at all. "Yeah," he said. "I went on two rescues this week actually. So what? I do it *every* week."

Of course it wasn't every week that he also banged his co-rescuer on a mountaintop, but that was best kept to himself.

Twinkles eyed Adam's food and whined. Brady scooped the little guy up and cuddled him. Brady, the big badass, cuddling a damn dog. It'd be funny, if Adam could find the funny in anything right now.

"Here's the thing," Brady said. "You don't go on rescues."

"What the hell are you talking about?" Except Adam knew *exactly* what he was talking about because it was true. Adam hadn't been *on* a rescue, as in hands-on, since he'd gotten home from overseas, and they all knew it. How he'd actually thought this was some kind of secret, he had no clue. He ate some more of Dell's sandwich, which helped ease his pain in a big way. "Jade makes excellent sandwiches."

Dell sighed as Adam finished it. "How do you know that Jade made it?"

"Cuz you barely know where the kitchen is, much less how to use it." Adam opened a bottle of water and drank deeply. When the last drop was gone, he swiped his mouth and studied his two brothers, who were in turn studying him like a bug on a slide. "Jesus. You two need a life."

"Actually," Dell said slowly, as if speaking to the village idiot, "we have lives. We've been thinking that *you* need a life, but you appear to be getting one. Want to talk about it?"

Still with the fucking kid gloves. Adam shook his head and slid him a look, because, really, since when did they talk about feelings? Without a word he turned back to the refrigerator and eyed a plate with three chocolate cupcakes on it. Nice. He pulled it out and went to work on the first cupcake.

"Those are mine, too," Dell said.

Adam finished the first cupcake in two bites and when Dell didn't stop him, he went for another one. "Wouldn't want to upset the crazy person," Adam said. "Best to let him have the cupcakes."

Dell sighed again.

Adam licked the last of the chocolate off his fingers and handed over the empty plate before heading for the door.

"I think he's fine," Brady said to Dell.

"Could've told me that before I let him eat all my fucking food," Dell muttered.


Adam didn't go to poker.

Instead, he crawled into bed and slept like the living dead and woke sometime near dawn, just before whoever was coming up the loft steps got to his front door. The urge to reach for a weapon and point it at the intruder was still as strong as it had been two years ago but he no longer acted on it.

Brady let himself in and hit the light. "Don't shoot."

Adam shook his head and flopped back to the bed. "You're supposed to say that before you come in."

Brady laughed softly. "Trigger finger still twitchy, huh?"

Brady would know the feeling. He'd been army, Special Forces.

Adam closed his eyes.

"Ignoring me," Brady said. "Good plan." He dropped onto the bed, sprawling out on his back next to Adam. Tucking his hands behind his head, he crossed his feet, and studied the ceiling. "You're going to have to get a duster up there, man," he said idly, staring at the dust bunnies in the rafters. "Women don't want to look at that shit hanging down on them while they're concentrating."

"Your women have to concentrate?"

Brady grinned. As his wife, Lilah was the only woman in Brady's life now. She'd grown up with Adam and Dell, and Adam loved her like a sister—he absolutely did not want to think about what Lilah did to put that particular smile on Brady's face.

"Lilah has no complaints," Brady said.

Adam grimaced. "Why are you in my bed, then, if you've got Lilah in yours?"

"She's got a duck emergency."

"She finally decide to cook Abigail?" Adam asked, referring to the duck that Lilah watched at her kennels. Abigail was a menace, and half the town had been threatening to cook her for years, but Lilah loved that thing. Lilah loved everything. Even the idiot currently lying in his bed.

Brady looked pained. "Do yourself a favor and don't let Lilah hear you talk about cooking Abigail."

Adam just looked at him and Brady sighed. "Look, I know something happened to you when you went after Donald with Holly. What was it?"

If he let himself, Adam could still smell the caves. Smell his failure. Turning his head, he eyed the dust bunnies in the rafters.

"Okay, tell me this," Brady said. "Is something wrong, or are you feeling sorry for yourself for some reason?"

"I'm *good*."

Brady went still for a long beat. "Shit."

Adam nearly smiled. "I'm good" was code for "I'm not going to talk about it." It had been evoked years and years ago, when they'd been punk-ass kids. Adam had gone out and done something stupid. Shock. He'd had a run-in with a guy several years older than him, and Adam had actually gotten the best of the asshole. Said asshole had vowed revenge, and he'd gotten it a week later, when he and four of his friends had jumped Adam and beaten the shit out of him.

He probably should have gone to the hospital, but they'd been in a foster home, the best foster home Adam and Dell had ever landed in, run by a guy named Sol Anders. Sol had been a good man, the best any of the three boys had ever known, and they hadn't wanted to risk getting sent away.

So Adam had invoked the "I'm good" code. They'd managed to hide his injuries, and he'd recovered. Ever since, if any of them needed to be left alone, they said, "I'm good," and that was that.

But Brady was lying there looking like he'd just swallowed a bitter pill, though he held his tongue as he rose from the bed. "Whatever. I'll stop asking if you're okay, but you're on your own with Dell. You know he's as bad as a chick."

This was true.

Milo was on his own bed at the foot of Adam's, and Brady crouched in front of him. The yellow Lab rolled over on his back, exposing his junk and a big grin, a blatant invitation to pet him. Brady obliged, then rose. "Going running. You coming, or you too pussy?"

Milo understood the tone if not the words, and he bounded to his feet, totally game.

They both looked at Adam.

Like he could stay in bed now. He got up and, ignoring Brady's grin of satisfaction, pulled on his running clothes.

# Seventeen

H olly stood in the grocery store perusing the rows of
candy bars on display near the checkout. She needed
sugar. *Badly.*

Earlier today, flowers had been delivered to her office. A
beautiful vase of red roses.

No card.

There weren't a lot of possibilities. There was only one
man in her life, and he was in it fairly reluctantly. She
wouldn't have laid odds on Adam being the flower-sending
type, and the gesture threw her. Especially since he hadn't
made a move to call or see her since they'd left Fallen
Lakes.

Thinking about it had led her here for candy. She had a
Snickers in one hand and a 3 Musketeers in the other. She'd
been trying to make a decision between them and was leaning toward buying both when she felt a hand settle at the
base of her neck.

It could have been anyone, but she knew it was Adam by
the way her nipples went hard. She angled her head back.

Yep. *Adam*.

"The 3 Musketeers," he said. "Always the 3 Musketeers."

She would have liked to eat him up, or maybe put her hands all over him, but luckily her hands were full. She waved the Snickers. "But the Snickers has peanuts. That's protein. That makes it practically a meal."

He looked over the display. "I could make you forget the candy," he said so casually it took her a minute to absorb the meaning of the words.

There was no doubt that he could make her forget the candy. Adam Connelly could make her forget a lot of things. Too many things. "Thanks for the flowers, by the way."

His brown eyes met hers. "Flowers?"

"The roses that were delivered to my office earlier."

He cocked his head curiously. A genuine response.

"You didn't send them," she said.

"No."

She stared down at the candy in her hands, feeling incredibly silly. Of course he hadn't sent the roses. She'd known it wasn't his thing.

He tilted her chin up, his eyes regretful, and she shook her head. "It's no big deal," she said. "Forget it. What are you doing here?"

"Top secret mission." He nudged her around the corner of the aisle and out of sight of the checkout clerk. Opening his jacket, he revealed . . .

A kitten.

The little gray ball of fluff was tucked into his hoodie pocket, fast asleep. At the sudden exposure to the bright fluorescent lights, it blinked and yawned, and looked up at Adam with sleepy adoration. *"Mew."*

Adam's hand came up to cradle the weight, the thing barely filling his palm. His work-roughened fingers gently scratched under its chin, and its eyes closed in utter bliss at the touch.

Holly knew just how the kitten felt. She'd melted from one touch of those fingers, too.

"She's a belated wedding present to Lilah from Dell and me," he said. "I'm just getting some supplies."

Aw. That was possibly the sweetest thing Holly had ever heard.

"She's cute but a complete menace," Adam said. "She's going to drive Brady crazy." He flashed a badass grin, and Holly laughed. Okay, not so sweet. She should have known.

"Brady's a pretty tough guy," she said. An understatement, of course. "This doesn't concern you?"

"Nah. Lilah won't let him maim me. She likes my face."

So did Holly. "Where did you get the kitten?"

He nuzzled the little thing, his voice soft. "Found her abandoned on our doorstep this morning. That happens sometimes—people know Dell isn't going to turn an animal away."

"So how did you end up with her?"

"I got in first."

"Adam Connelly, one big softie," she said. "Who knew?"

"Yeah." He lifted the kitten up to his face. Man and feline studied each other. The kitten reached out and tried to bat his nose, making the man smile, his real smile, the one that reached all the way to his eyes. "She faced down Beans and Dell's damn parrot earlier," he said. "She's four ounces soaking wet and held her own. She's going to grow up a real fighter." Still holding the kitten, he filled a cart with supplies, and though it was ridiculous, there was something about watching the big, tough Adam Connelly cradle the thing against his chest that did her in.

He checked out and pulled Holly with him out the door.

"Wait," she said. "The candy." She *needed* that candy . . .

He didn't let go of her as he carefully and gently set the kitten in his truck. Then he not so gently pushed Holly up against the truck and kissed her, slipping a hand beneath her shirt at her waist, trailing his fingers along her spine. When she no longer remembered what she'd even gone to the store to buy, he lifted his head and gave her a steady gaze.

"Okay," she said shakily, still gripping his arms. "You're good. You should wrap that up and sell it."

"It wouldn't be fair to the other candy."

Adam spent the next day up north with Brady and Donald, hitting a string of Reid ranches. Adam had provided guard dogs earlier in the year and was doing a quick training session, checking up on the dogs and handlers.

Brady flew them in their chopper, and by the time they arrived back in Sunshine, it was just past six. Adam drove Donald out to his home ranch, and for a minute, Donald sat in the cab of Adam's truck, chin jutting toward the wing of the huge ranch house where the offices were held.

"Only one light left on," he pointed out. "Most of my staff knows the value of having their nights off for personal time."

Adam knew which light was on and who hadn't given herself a night off.

Holly.

Clueless, Donald slid out of Adam's truck. "I think I'll head into town for a drink," he said. "I'll be gone awhile." He cocked his head and studied Adam. "Long enough for any idiot to find his own way to an enjoyable evening."

Okay, maybe not so clueless . . . "What the hell are you up to?" Adam asked him, eyes narrowed.

"Who me? I'm an old man. I can't get up to much these days."

"Bullshit."

Donald smiled, clapped Adam on the shoulder, and then was gone.

Adam stayed in his truck a moment. "I'm not going in there," he told Milo, who was in the backseat.

Milo yawned and plopped down. In two seconds, he was snoring.

Adam let out a long breath, shouldered open the truck, and got out. Apparently he was going to be the idiot, after all.

He found Holly sitting behind her desk, head back, eyes closed. She was wearing a wraparound dress and heels, hair piled on top of her head, glasses perched on the tip of her nose. Forget the girl-next-door fantasy *and* the hot-librarian fantasy—she was currently rocking the secretary fantasy big-time. "Hey," he said.

She didn't move and he realized she had ear buds in. Whatever she was listening to had her utmost attention. She was utterly still, with a dreamy look on her face.

He moved into the office and she still didn't budge. In fact, she seemed to sigh in pleasure, vividly reminding him of what they'd been doing the last time he'd heard that sound come from her lips.

Then, as now, she'd been flushed and . . .

Aroused.

Fascinated, curious as hell, he came around her desk and perched a hip there, leaning in. The pulse at the base of her neck was fluttering, and her skin seemed dewy. "I have to know," he murmured, "what the hell you're listening to."

With a screech, she jumped up, her eyes flying open. She gaped at him, then tore the ear buds out of her ears. *"Adam."*

"Me," he said. "Didn't mean to scare you."

"I'm working. I—" She drew in a deep breath and smoothed the front of her dress.

Her nipples were hard.

"I'm really busy," she said.

"I can see that."

"I was just listening to an audio book," she said, sounding breathless. "For my book club. I'm behind on the book. I didn't hear you come."

No, but he had the feeling he'd almost heard *her* come. "You were listening to your book club read?" He knew that Jade and Lilah belonged to the same book club, and they'd both been complaining about this month's read, which was supposedly pretentious, boring, and had a sucky ending.

Her eyes slid to the iPod on her desk, still on play. "Um. Well, actually . . ."

He picked up a forgotten ear bud and pressed it to his ear.

A sultry, sexy female voice was narrating, her voice low and suggestive: "He worked his way to her nipple, giving the tight tip a long, leisurely lick before sucking it hard into his mouth. Satisfied with her shaky moan, he slid his hands to her hips, catching the sides of her panties, dragging them down her long, luscious legs. His lips followed, her hips jerking as he got close to the promised land . . ."

Adam grinned up at Holly. "I didn't know you guys read porn at your book club. No wonder Lilah's in it."

Holly made a grab for the ear bud, but he held it out of her reach.

"Fine," she said. "So it's not a sanctioned book club read."

"No?"

"No, the book club reads are boring."

Adam stuck the ear bud back into his ear and wasn't disappointed.

"She writhed beneath him," the sexy narrator continued, "while he deeply inhaled her rich scent. Bending low, he nuzzled her waxed mound and said . . . *Trust me.*"

Adam snorted and looked at Holly. "FYI—*never* trust a man who says, 'Trust me.'"

She snatched the iPod, practically climbing up his body to do so, not that he minded one little bit. "What are you doing here?" she snapped.

"Dropping off your dad." He stroked a damp tendril off her forehead. "You look like you need a man, Holly."

She raised her chin and looked him in the eye. "I've discovered I don't need a man to be happy."

"Is that right?"

"Yes," she said. "And besides, you've made it perfectly clear that you don't need me, either, so . . ." She moved to walk around him but he caught her wrist.

"You're right. I *don't* need you," he said. "I don't *need* anyone." He pulled the struggling, pissed-off woman in between his legs, waiting until her flashing eyes met his. "But I *want* you, Holly. Always have, always will."

She went still, staring at him as his cell phone rang, with the tone that told him it was an emergency. Still holding her gaze, he pulled his phone from his hip and glanced at the screen. Shit. Reluctantly, he let go of her.

She fisted her hand in his shirt. "Wait a minute. You're just going to say that and then leave me? In this state?"

He looked down at his own erection. "If it makes you feel better, you're not the only one." He pressed a hard, fast kiss to her very kissable mouth. "Have to go."

"But—"

He slid the ear bud back into her ear. "This seemed to be taking you where you need to go," he said. "Finish listening to it. I'm going to like thinking of you, here, getting off on it."

She blushed and bit down on her lower lip. He groaned and leaned in for one more kiss and then forced himself out the door.

The emergency call from Kel turned out to be a county-wide drill. A fucking drill. But it was mandatory, and it kept him out at Bear Lake for the rest of the long hours of the night: cold, icy, miserable.

Well, except for the one thought that warmed him every time it crossed his mind, which was constantly—Holly at her desk, hot and bothered, listening to that book.

\*   \*   \*

Two days later Holly was in the Reid Ranching offices, neck deep into quarterlies, when Grif called her on Skype. She answered with a huge smile, waiting as her brother's pixelated image swam into view. He was in army cammies and dark wraparound sunglasses that he pulled off at the sight of her.

As always, she studied him carefully, heart in her throat, but he looked good, she decided. Then again, he usually did. Unlike Holly, he'd taken the best from his ancestral gene pool: their dad's height, dark good looks, and quick smile and quicker wit, plus their mom's unusual gray eyes and ability to see right through any and all bullshit. He'd gone into the military about the same time as Adam, choosing army. It hadn't been trouble that Grif had been running from, though; it had been Sunshine itself—and ranching.

And their father.

This life here in the Idaho mountains might seem idyllic and slow and perfect to her, but the very thing she loved about it was exactly what Grif had never wanted. Unfortunately, as the only son of a ranching icon, he'd faced a lot of pressure to stay.

But he'd gone, and though he'd come back on leave whenever possible, he never remained in Sunshine for more than a week or two without going batshit crazy. Though Holly would never push him to stick around when he clearly didn't want to, she missed him. A lot.

"You're a sight for sore eyes," she said.

"Same goes." His usual fast smile faded. "Been trying to get you for a few days."

She'd missed his call yesterday. "Dad's okay."

"He had a fucking heart attack?"

Dammit. "You've talked to Adam."

"Yes, but only because he answers his phone." Grif blew out a breath. "I heard it from a friend of a friend who works at the hospital. When I couldn't get you, I called Adam—

who didn't want to tell me, either, by the way. You're all on my shit list."

She winced. "You called at three in the morning. I'm sorry, I had my ringer off."

"It was the only time I could get through. Tell me, Holly."

She sighed. She'd like to wring Adam's neck, except then she'd have to see him again. And after the other day and her most embarrassing moment, her current plan was to lie low. "Apparently he had a mild heart attack three months ago. I was in New York and you were . . . well, somewhere. He managed to hide it because his hospital stay was only a few days. He says he's been following doctor's orders and doing everything he's supposed to. But from what I can gather, Deanna dumped him because his mortality scared her."

"Or because it reminded her that he was an old son of a bitch."

"Or that," she said dryly. "In any case, he was suddenly alone, and depressed. Or was, anyway."

"Was?"

"Well, once we got him back, news sort of spread that he was a free agent. Now he's got both Mrs. Graham and Mrs. Rodriguez visiting all the time, cooking for him."

"Mrs. Graham, the hot forty-something redhead mayor?"

She laughed. "Yes."

Grif shook his head, looking both appalled and impressed. "Go, Dad."

"I guess . . ."

Grif let out a breath. "Now tell me about you."

"What about me?"

"Your divorce."

"Dammit! Adam has a big mouth."

"What is all this, Hol?"

"Well, let's see. You and Adam have been gossiping like a pair of little girls, so it must be middle school recess!"

He smiled and immediately looked younger, softer than the hardened soldier he'd turned himself into.

"It's not funny," she said, but seeing him smile made her smile, too.

Her office door opened and Kate strode in carrying two lunch boxes—one *Star Wars*, the other *Transformers*—and a drink carrier of two steaming coffees. "I've only got a half hour," she said, not looking up, concentrating on keeping the drinks balanced. "Kyle Wu dunked Emily Carter's ponytail into the finger paints this morning, taking her from blond to green in zero point two. So now I've got a parent conference at one thirty to get yelled at by Emily's dad. Good thing he's totally hot." She glanced over at Holly's opened laptop, caught sight of Grif, and jumped.

The coffees clattered together and spilled down her front. She sucked in a breath and dropped everything. "Oh, shit. Shit, shit, shit." She pulled her blouse away from her skin. "And *ow*."

Holly rushed forward. "Are you burned?"

Sucking in air through her teeth, Kate did the hot-coffee-on-her-chest dance, and then ripped her blouse off. She sighed in relief for the briefest of seconds before remembering Grif. Squeaking in embarrassment, she covered her boobs with her hands and ducked behind Holly's desk.

From her crouched position, Kate grimaced up at Holly and mouthed, *Oh. My. God. Did he see me?*

Holly shook her head no. A little white mercy lie between best friends, because of course Grif had seen her, from her pretty leopard print bra to her very full 36Ds bursting from the seams.

They were hard to miss.

"Hey, Kate," Grif said from the desk.

Kate dropped her head to her knees. "Hey, Grif."

Grif stretched his neck and tried to look down. "You okay?"

"Uh-huh."

"Sure? Because all I can see are your ears, which are twitching."

"Only one-third of the population can twitch their ears," she muttered, face still averted. "And only one-third of those people can twitch one ear at a time," Kate said. Still out of sight of Grif, she smacked herself in the head.

Grif laughed softly, amused by the stats Kate always spouted when she was nervous. "Good to know."

Kate ducked even lower and shot Holly a pleading save-me glance.

"Okay, well, I'm glad you called," Holly said to Grif. "It was good to talk to you. Be careful out there, it's a full moon tonight."

"And because of the earth's rotation, we're even closer to the moon and its pull," Kate said, lifting her head. "Also, Venus is the only planet that rotates clockwise." Then she covered her own mouth with her hand, closed her eyes, and shook her head.

Grif grinned. "Maybe you should stand up and let me look at you. And make sure you weren't burned."

Holly rolled her eyes. "Say good-bye, Grif."

"No, really, I'm a trained medic. I should check out—"

"Uh-huh. Love you." Holly shut her laptop.

Kate slowly rose, her very pretty breasts quivering. "Oh my God. Griffin Reid saw my boobs."

"You're no longer the invisible high school geek, you know. You're all grown-up and pretty."

"Pretty much a mess, you mean."

"I'm not kidding. If I was a guy, I'd totally want to do you."

Kate beamed. "Really?"

"Really! Honey, you're the swan now, why do you still get so nervous around guys?"

"I'm only hot without my clothes, and no one ever sees me without my clothes. Just my ob-gyn, and now Griffin Reid."

Holly handed her a wad of napkins, which Kate used to

mop up the coffee. "Would you stop referring to my brother by his full name? He's just a regular guy."

"Yeah, a really, *really* good-looking guy."

Holly grimaced. "Nice bra, by the way. And what happened with that online dating service you joined?" She pulled her sweater from the back of her chair and handed it to Kate to put on.

"All the guys I'd want to date live in Coeur d'Alene." She slipped into the sweater, looking far better in it than Holly had. "I don't have time to drive hours for my nookie."

"Seriously. Is that all you think about lately?"

"You don't get to ask me that. You got lucky this week."

"I . . . what?" Holly went still, the proverbial deer in the headlights. "How did you know? Who told you?"

"You. Just now."

Holly dropped into her chair. "That's a good trick."

"I'm a teacher. I know *all* the tricks. Well, except how to get *myself* some nookie." She picked up the lunch boxes and handed Holly one. "And I can't believe you were going to try to keep such vital information from me."

Holly searched for a different topic. "So how is it your fault that Kyle ruined Emily's hair?"

"Oh, it's not. But Emily's mom was a high school beauty queen and she pays big money for her blond hair every three weeks. Her daughter's a natural, and they'd just had their hair blown out and done up. Green wasn't in the cards. Nice change of subject, by the way."

"Dammit, you really are good."

"Don't you know it." Kate opened her lunch box.

The two of them met every week for lunch, taking turns providing the meal. On Holly's week, she'd run into town and pick something up, usually from the deli.

When it was Kate's turn, she cooked. Today's lunch was carefully and lovingly packed chicken enchiladas, and Holly's mouth watered at the scent. "You're a domestic goddess." She sank her teeth into her first bite and moaned as pleasure exploded across her taste buds.

"Yeah?" Kate asked.

"Oh my God, yeah. Now be quiet. My food and I need a moment."

Kate grinned and nodded. She was good with silence.

Sort of.

Okay, she was horrible with silence. She managed to hold it for one full minute—a record. "Tell me about the trip with Adam."

Holly pretended that Kate was really asking about the trip. "You know we found my dad."

"Yes, on day two. Which leaves one whole night unaccounted for." A teacher through and through, Kate paused, waiting for the correct answer. "I want details, Holly. Spill."

"You first," Holly said. "How was ballooning?"

Kate shook her head. "I didn't go."

This was a surprise. Kate had so been looking forward to it. "Why not?" She frowned. "Wait. By any chance, did Grif talk you out of it?"

Kate blushed. "Why would you think that?"

"Because he IMed me right before I left the other day, and he'd been keeping track of you." Holly watched, fascinated as Kate's blush reached the tips of her ears. "Kate, what's going on?"

She waved a hand in front of her mouth. "I used too much chili pepper. Yow, it's hot."

Holly grabbed a bottle of water and pushed it across the desk toward Kate, who grabbed it gratefully. "I mean between you and Grif. What's going on between you and Grif?"

Kate choked on the water.

Holly set down her fork and stared at her friend, torn between amusement and horror. Kate was as up-front and honest as they came. She didn't have a deceptive, manipulative,

evasive bone in her body. What she did have was a crush on
Holly's brother. Always had. But Holly thought she'd gotten
over it, since the last time Grif had come home, he'd plowed
his way through every single woman he knew.

Except for Kate.

"Tell me you're not pining away for him," Holly said.

Kate took a bite of enchilada and shook her head.

"Kate."

Kate took a second, huge bite of food so that she couldn't
talk.

Holly thunked her head to her desk. *"Kate."*

"Look, he's not even home or planning to be home anytime soon. And I'm doing the online dating thing. A guy's
going to turn up. Hopefully in the same country as me. One
who's not my best friend's brother. No worries, okay?"

"It's not about him being my brother. It's about you.
I love Grif, very much, but you need a *one*-woman type
of guy."

"No," Kate said. "I've decided I'm not going to limit my
options to one guy. I bought a wide selection of sexy linge-
rie, not just this one bra. And I intend to find a wide selection of men to go with." She looked at her watch. "Can I
keep the sweater for now? I've gotta go. Oh, and book club
tonight, don't forget."

"I'll be late. Thing One and Thing Two have training
class first."

"Since when do you take your dad's heathen puppies to
obedience training?"

"Since he paid for the classes but can't go. Like you
said, they're heathens. They can't miss a lesson."

"Uh-huh." Kate tucked her tongue into her cheek. "And
does your willingness to suddenly do this have anything to
do at all with the obedience class teacher?"

Holly busied herself with cleaning up. "I have no idea
what you're talking about."

"Yes, you do. And so do I. We teachers are hot."

"Aren't you late?" Holly asked desperately.

"Yes." But Kate didn't move. "Adam's the instructor, right? The guy you're apparently going to give another shot at breaking your heart?"

"I'm not going to let him do that. It's not like that this time."

"What is it like?"

Holly hadn't the foggiest . . .

"Holly," Kate said very gently, reaching for her hand. "Why go back to Hurt City? You've already been there."

"I'm just living in the moment," Holly said. "That's all."

"And the moment is telling you to go for the hottest man in town?" Kate asked. "Well, I guess that makes sense. Gotta aim high."

"And I'm not going to give him the power to hurt me," Holly said. Probably. "I'm not going to give anyone the power to hurt me, not ever again. I'm just trying to enjoy life."

Kate smiled at that. "Well, he certainly has a look about him that says he knows how to make a woman enjoy herself."

Holly couldn't stop the satisfied sigh that left her lips, making Kate laugh.

"I'm jealous," she said, standing, gathering the two lunch boxes. "It's been too long since I had that look on my face. Just be careful, okay? Promise me."

"Scout's honor," Holly said. "I'll be the Queen of Careful. Tonight's just about helping my dad."

Kate shook her head. "You're the worst liar on the planet, you know that? Every time you lie, you suck your lower lip in between your teeth. You need to work on that."

When Kate left, Holly brought up the camera function on her phone and looked at herself. "You are not falling for him again," she said, and caught herself sucking her bottom lip in between her teeth. "Dammit!"

*  *  *

Much later, Holly went in search of Thing One and Thing Two for their class. She found the dogs were with her dad, who was hitting golf balls into a tin can in his office.

The six-month-old puppies were sleeping, but when Holly walked in, they bounced up, ready for action. Seventy-plus pounds of action each barreled straight at her, tongues lolling, eyes bright with excitement, ears flopping without restraint.

She held up a hand. "Stop!"

To be fair, they did try. But the wood floors didn't provide any traction, and they slid, barreling straight into her, taking her out at the knees. She hit the floor, which apparently was an open invitation to play. She tried to get up twice and was knocked back down by sheer exuberance. Giving up, she lay on the floor. "Help."

Her dad laughed. "You volunteered for this . . ."

She rolled to her knees and got herself up. She was covered in dog hair and also some doggy drool. Eau-de-dog. "I could be in New York, working at some fancy bigwig corporation, you know, putting my pretty education to good use. I don't have to be back here being kissed to death by wayward puppies."

"True. But you made a choice. Sorry already?"

She let out a breath. "No." Not even a little bit. She'd discovered something about herself coming back here. She hadn't been cast in a plaster mold at birth—she was whomever she chose to be.

And right now, she liked the person she'd chosen. She liked being that person here in Sunshine. And after her two-day foray into the wilderness with the sexy, enigmatic blast from her past, she could even imagine herself sticking here for a long time.

She pictured what Adam's expression might be if he could hear her thoughts, and it made her smile. The big, bad, tough, edgy, dangerous-as-hell Adam Connelly didn't show much on the outside, but on the inside he'd be panicking big-time.

She'd like to see that, but it would have to wait.

Because she might be ready for Adam and whatever came with him, but he was most definitely not ready for her.

# Eighteen

A dam stood in the yard watching as his human and canine students began arriving for his dog obedience class. The group comprised mostly new dog owners and wayward puppies, so he was expecting the usual mayhem. Normally he prided himself on being the calm in the storm, but tonight Holly pulled up and his calm suddenly vanished.

She got out of her Jeep wearing her work clothes, which was a business suit that meant all business. Problem was she had legs longer than the legal limit and a body that fueled his every fantasy.

She stood with the rest of the class, a leash in each hand, doing her best to corral her father's dogs, and he had no idea what the hell she was doing here. He met her gaze.

She gave him a little smile.

"Your dad okay?" he asked.

"Yep." She nibbled on her lower lip. "Just giving him a break."

She was lying, and he had no idea why. But he didn't have much time to dwell on it. Liza Molan was at the front of the class with Babe, her golden retriever. Liza worked at the diner in town, and they'd gone out once about a year ago. He hadn't pursued more with her. He never pursued more. He'd made that clear up front, and she'd seemed good with it. But then she'd left that crazy "mastering" message with Jade, and now she was giving him the hungry eyes, assessing his level of interest.

It was zero.

Adam's gaze then shifted to Holly, who was still attempting to wrangle Thing One and Thing Two. Liza moved in front of him, blocking his view. "Hey there." She flashed another smile. "I so need your help here. Babe's always picking something up and chewing on it, and I can't seem to make her drop it for me."

Adam looked down at Babe. "Show me," he said.

"Well, sure," Liza said. "Right now for instance, she's chewing on a rock—"

But Babe had spit out the rock at Adam's quiet "show me."

Liza stared at Babe. Then at Adam. She laughed, pushing her hair out of her face. "Oh, right. You meant drop. You said show me, and she dropped it to show you what she has. Why won't she do that for me?"

"She's a retriever, a working breed," Adam said. "She needs to feel like she's busy. That takes a lot of time and attention."

Liza smiled and fluttered her lashes. "Most women need a lot of time and attention . . . I guess this is where the mastering comes in, right?" she asked hopefully.

There was a soft choking sound from Holly's direction, but when Adam looked over at her, she was bent over tying her boot, hair in her face.

Adam turned back to Liza, who leaned in close and put a hand on his arm, pressing her breasts into him. "So, about the mastering thing . . ."

Another snort sounded, but before Adam could respond

to either female, two dogs on the other side of the lineup went at each other. Never so happy for a dogfight in his life, he stepped in between the two fighters, grabbing their leashes, getting the situation under control far too quickly. Afterward, Holly was staring at him wide-eyed, looking like maybe she was impressed that he'd broken up the fight without bloodshed. He appreciated her admiration, but this was his job.

The good news was that Dell had come outside with Gertie, and Liza appeared to forget all about Adam.

Thank God for fickle women.

Adam got everyone started on practicing sit and stay, then moved to stand next to Dell.

They both eyed Gertie. The St. Bernard was lying down, too lazy to sit up. "You really going to try this again?" Adam asked. Gertie had dropped out of two previous obedience classes.

"Maybe the third time is the charm," Dell said.

Maybe, but doubtful. Because the problem wasn't Gertie. It was Dell, who loved Gertie just the way she was—lazy and slightly naughty. Shaking his head, Adam moved on, going over all the basics. Just as in Gertie's case, it wasn't about training the dogs. It was about training the dogs' handlers. It was about commitment and trust, both of which were crucial to success. Adam had ten weeks to get that through to people, to demonstrate to each owner exactly how to communicate with their dog to get them to respond.

"Training is a series of choices," he said. "You need to make the good choices really good and the bad choices completely undesirable." He eyed everyone struggling to control their dog. "As we stand here, your dogs should be sitting calm at your side."

"Sit. *Sit*." This from Gayle Little, who was yelling at her year-old black Lab, jerking on his leash. "I'll give you a doggy biscuit to sit. I'll give you the whole bag. Just sit!"

Adam moved to the pair. "Remember when we talked about making sure you're giving the right command?"

Gayle, fortyish, a businesswoman and mother of teenagers, blew out a frustrated breath. "I knew if I caved to the 'Oh please, can we have a puppy, Mom!' that I'd be the one to end up here," she said. "I'm not good at this. I've told him to sit a million times."

"It's not the words you use," Adam told her. "It's the tone. He can't hear the message you intend when you're yelling at him."

"He's not listening, no matter what my tone."

"Kids don't listen, either," Adam said, "but you have consequences for that, right? Like taking away privileges, using time-outs."

"Yes, of course, but I don't want to be mean to a dog."

"In the animal world, dogs correct each other without hesitation," Adam told her. "You've seen this: they'll snap in one instant and then play in the next. They don't punish one another; they correct. That's how you train effectively."

"So how do I correct?" Gayle asked.

"Don't scream your command. Say it and mean it. Your success will depend on how motivating you sound." He turned to the black Lab. "Sit," he said with calm authority.

The dog sat.

Gayle blew out a breath. "So, in other words, it's not him, it's me. Is that it?"

"You can do this," he said.

She smiled and shook her head. "Hell, Adam. I just realized, it's not my tone, it's *yours*. You speak, and I'd do anything you asked of me."

"Me too," Liza said quickly, nodding like a bobblehead. *"Anything."*

Adam felt Dell roll his eyes. He was also pretty sure Holly snorted again, but when he looked at her, she was concentrating on Donald's dogs.

He got the class back to work. He had them walk in a large circle, and each time they stopped, the dogs were to sit.

Holly was having trouble with this. Her dad's dogs kept getting tangled up in her legs.

"They're distracted," she said breathlessly, arms straining to hold the dogs.

This was because Thing One was staring at the cute little white springer spaniel next to him. "Distracted by tail," Holly said with some disgust. "Just like a man."

Hard to argue the truth. Adam stepped between Thing One and the spaniel.

Thing One's gaze rolled up Adam's legs to his face, and then he sat. Adam looked at Holly. "It's your job to keep his mind on the task."

"Uh-huh," she said dryly. "Is this where the . . . *mastering* comes into play?"

He slid her a look that she met evenly, with a daring quirk of her brow.

Under the guise of shifting the leashes back into her hands, he leaned in. "Are you asking for a private lesson?"

"If I get to be the master."

He gave her his best wicked smile. "Only the teacher gets to master."

She bit into her lower lip and slid a look to the building, specifically the loft where he slept at night. *Playing with fire,* he told himself, with only one possible outcome—someone was going to get burned.

Somehow he got through the rest of the class. When it was over and his pupils had all headed to their cars, Brady stepped outside. He intercepted Holly on the way to her Jeep.

"Worried?" Dell asked Adam, the two of them watching Brady and Holly from across the lot.

"Why would I be worried?" Adam asked.

"Because your woman is talking to your nosy brother, who's maybe spilling all your secrets."

"She's not my woman." Although ever since their trek, she'd been starring in all his late-night fantasies . . . "And I don't have any secrets."

"Uh-huh."

Okay, so he had plenty of secrets, and he *was* uneasy. He'd been so since they'd gotten back. Adam was a realist and always faced the facts head-on. The facts here were simple. He'd had some problems when he'd come home from his last tour. He'd also had enough counseling to know that his reactions to what he'd faced over there weren't unexpected. And he was better. But he still wasn't back in the game. He was still being a benchwarmer in his own life. From the outside looking in, it might appear that he was an active participant, but he wasn't. Not fully. He wasn't letting people in. If he could let anyone in, it would be Holly, but he honestly wasn't sure if he could.

The cave incident was a perfect example. He'd failed there, big-time. With an audience of one, no less. It was more than a little humiliating that after all this time he was still so fucked-up.

And now Holly knew it, too.

He had no idea if she was going to keep his little—big— secret, and that was more than a little unsettling. He headed toward her, complete with his shadow. "I don't need an escort," he said to Dell.

Dell kept walking with him.

Adam slid him a look. "Thought you said Brady was the nosy brother."

"It runs in the family."

Holly had put the dogs in the Jeep, and Brady was showing her something on his phone. A picture, it turned out, of Brady and her dad on horseback. Brady looked up as Adam approached. "Hey. Holly was just about to tell me why it took you three days to find Donald."

"Two days," Holly said, meeting Adam's gaze. "It only took two days."

"I could have gotten from here to Timbuktu and back in two days," Brady said. "Next time, you should take me. I'll fly you in the chopper."

"We had a lot of ground to explore," Holly said.

"Explore." Brady went brows up at this. "Is that the line he gave you? Did he take advantage of you? Because if he did, I could beat him up for you if you'd like."

"No!" She laughed, then took in Adam, who was doing his best to appear utterly uninterested. "You could really beat him up?" she asked Brady. "He's pretty tough."

Brady laughed.

Adam slid him a long look but Brady wasn't cowed. "I could totally take him," he said.

Yeah, over Adam's dead body.

Maybe.

"We really did have a lot of places to look," Holly said. "We hit Diamond Ridge and Mount Eagle first, and then the Kaniksu Caves—"

"The caves?" Brady turned to Adam, mocking gone. He knew how he'd managed to avoid any caves at all. And perfect, now both brothers were looking at him like he was a ticking time bomb.

"You got inside the caves?" Brady asked.

Jesus. This got better and better. "It's not a big deal," he said before Holly could say that no, in fact, he hadn't gotten all the way inside the caves before having a colossally fucking humiliating breakdown. Because he *should* have gotten inside that cave. It wasn't like they'd been in enemy territory, with bad intel and half the good guys already dead.

"And then from there, we went to Fallen Lakes." Holly reached out to squeeze Adam's hand. "I'd never have found my dad without him."

Brady was clearly surprised, and so was Dell. They were surprised because they'd been giving Adam the kid-glove treatment, and Holly hadn't bothered with kid gloves at all.

"Huh," Brady said, looking impressed. His gaze warmed considerably as he smiled at Holly.

She blinked, as if blinded by the sight, and Adam rolled his eyes. Brady had always had a way with the ladies. But then Holly turned to Adam and the look on her face was all for him, and the oddest thing happened. His chest loosened from a tension he hadn't even realized he'd been holding.

He could trust her, *really* trust her, the way he trusted Dell and Brady—when he didn't want to kill them, that is. The knowledge wasn't expected, but he wasn't quite sure it was welcome, either. He'd liked assuring himself that she was just a diversion. Nothing more.

But she kept being more.

He wanted to touch her. Not just for sex, though he wanted that, too, wanted to bury himself deep and lose himself in her again. God, how he wanted that, to put his hands on her and have her hands on him.

But he also just wanted her close. He wanted to hold her and not let go. And damned if that wasn't a thought. Maybe he *should* sleep with her again, work on clearing up this confusion with some down-and-dirty sex.

Except with Holly, it wasn't just sex. He shoved his fingers in his hair and tugged. This wasn't helping. He realized everyone was staring at him, but just then Jade stepped out the front door of the center and waved him over. *Thank God.* No more time to obsess or further embarrass himself, he had work. "Gotta go."

"Adam," Holly said.

He slowed, though he didn't want to, and looked down at the hand she'd placed on his arm. Dell and Brady moved off, giving them privacy. Privacy he was damn sure he wasn't prepared for, not with her.

"I'm hungry," she said. "Want to get dinner?"

He looked into her eyes and knew he had to be honest right now, or this would get as out of hand as it had the last time. "Dinner isn't what I'm hungry for, Holly."

Her mouth opened, then closed. He didn't know what she'd been about to say, but he knew that her response *should* have been a slap across his face. He certainly deserved it, if not for the other night on the mountain, then for all those years ago when he'd touched her and shouldn't have.

But as it turned out, Holly had no response at all—at least not one she was willing to share with him. She gave him nothing but a look that he refused himself the luxury of interpreting. With a nod, he walked away, telling himself he was doing them both a big favor, but especially her, one she'd thank him for eventually.

# Nineteen

olly knew damn well that Adam had tried to scare her off. But she was no young girl, and she was not easily scared off. In fact, nothing much scared her at all anymore.

Except hiding her feelings.

She watched Adam stride to the porch where Jade stood waiting for him. Gertie was lying at his feet in an exhausted heap on the front steps. Obedience class was hard work. At Adam's approach, she rolled onto her back, her tail beating the ground, dust rising. He crouched down, ruffling her fur, giving her a smacking kiss right between her eyes.

Gertie writhed in ecstasy, giving him as much emotion as a dog could possibly give.

Adam gave it back, honest and uninhibited, and from across the yard Holly melted a little, even as she sighed.

A hand settled on her shoulder. Dell's. "It's not you," he assured her.

"No?" She was pretty sure it *was* her.

"No," Dell said. "It's because Brady here dropped him on his head when we were teenagers."

Brady smiled fondly at the memory. "That's not why he's an idiot. It's because she's his cave."

"Huh?" Holly said, but Dell was nodding.

"Yeah," Dell said. "That's it exactly." He looked at Holly. "You're his cave. The thing he fears yet wants the most. You're going to have to make it safe for him to come inside."

Well, gee, if that was all. "And how do you propose I do that?" she asked.

"Turn on all the lights and send him invitation?" Brady suggested.

Dell shook his head. "Too subtle. You need to set a trap and drag the big lug inside."

Holly let out a low laugh. They loved Adam. That was beautifully clear. But they didn't have a clue. She just hoped she did.

She walked to her Jeep and then took a call from her office about some billing mishap. By the time she disconnected, she was the last one from the class left in the lot. Dusk was falling but she had no trouble seeing across the yard to the very serious basketball game going on. Three-on-three and she knew the players on the skins team.

Dell.

Brady.

And Adam.

The three of them looking so hot that she was momentarily frozen, unable to look away. Dell passed the ball to Brady, who flung it to Adam. Adam caught it and flew toward the basket, where he was rudely and harshly fouled, his opponent's hand chopping through the air, making an audible smack against his arm and hand. As if he didn't feel a thing, Adam executed a layup with panther grace. Clearly his shoulder wasn't bothering him in the slightest.

His opponent, one of Dell's vet techs, swore viciously.

Adam gave him a steely-eyed look but didn't retaliate for the foul or call him on it. "Game point," he said, and passed the ball to Brady, who swished in a sweet three-pointer. *Game*.

Sweating, filthy, the brothers grinned and high-fived each other in triumph.

And from inside the chilly interior of the Jeep, Holly got a hot flash. She shoved the vehicle in gear and drove off into the night.

Holly was a half hour late to book club. By the time she got there, the food had been devoured, dessert included. Dessert was the whole reason for going to book club, dammit.

Kate was sitting next to Lilah and Jade. There were at least ten other women there as well, all of them discussing the chosen book with an intensity that matched the death and gloom of the plot.

Holly hadn't enjoyed the book. She liked books with happy endings, and this one hadn't had anything close to an HEA. She sat in the chair next to Kate and pulled the book from her purse.

"You're glowing," Kate whispered. "Why are you glowing?"

"It's sweat," she whispered back. "Thing One and Thing Two are a pain in my ass."

"Sure it's not the instructor making you sweat?"

Holly hid her face behind the book.

Kate pushed the book down and took in Holly's expression, her smile fading. "Okay, now you're scaring me," she whispered. "This isn't just fun and games for you. *He's* not just fun and games for you."

Holly glanced around and found Lilah and Jade listening in unabashedly. Great. Holly flipped through the book, pretending to listen to the discussion going on around her. They were talking about the characters.

"It's all about the characters for me," Jade said, and looked at Holly.

Lilah nodded her agreement. "Character growth is everything."

"How about compassion?" Kate asked. "Loyalty? Heart? Because this . . . this *book* that we let into our lives"—she sent Holly a long glance—"needs to be compassionate. It needs to be loyal to a fault and have heart. Flawed is okay as long as it has heart."

"That's a big order," Lilah said. "But in this case, the . . . *book*," she said meaningfully, "flawed as it may be, can absolutely live up to expectations—if given a chance."

Holly looked at both Jade and Lilah, two very sharp women. Two very sharp women who loved Adam like a brother. "I don't mind flaws," she said carefully. "What book doesn't have flaws?"

"You're sure?" Kate asked. "*Sure* sure?"

Holly hugged the book to her chest and nodded, hoping like hell that was true, and that she knew what she was doing.

The next day Dell walked into Adam's office and deposited a ten-week-old black Lab puppy on his desk. A female, who lifted her head and blinked at Adam with sleepy dark eyes.

"You look familiar," he told her, scooping her up. "You're one of the Moorelands' puppies."

The Moorelands raised Labs and were clients of Dell's. And Adam's as well, since he'd trained nearly all their dogs.

"She's going to make a great watchdog," Dell said.

"Yeah?" Adam cuddled her close. She stuck out her pink tongue and licked his nose. "Looks like maybe she's more of a lover than a fighter."

"Well, she has to be trained, of course," Dell said.

Adam lifted his gaze to his brother, who was, for once,

giving nothing away. "You taking on another dog? Gert's gonna be jealous."

"Not me."

Ah. He saw where this was going now. "I've already got Milo."

"Not you, either." Dell dropped into a chair and slouched back, making himself comfortable. He smiled. His I've-been-meddling smile.

"Shit," Adam said, eyes narrowing. "What are you up to?"

"Nila's place was broken into last night."

Their mom lived in an unsecured trailer on acreage that yielded no crops or anything else of value. She had nothing to steal. "Was she hurt?"

"No. Pissed off but not hurt. Probably just some stupid teenagers, bored and looking for trouble." A touch of a smile crossed Dell's mouth at that.

They'd both been there.

"So you're giving her this killer to watch over the property?" Adam asked, laughing softly because the "killer" was already fast asleep, her head on his chest.

"Not me," Dell said. "I'm booked today."

Adam's laughed faded. "No."

"Why not?"

"For starters, Nila hasn't spoken to me in months."

"Yeah, not since she came here and threw your money back in your face. I know. Does it really matter, Adam? This has to be done." Dell stood up. "Oh, and bring your toolbox. She's got a lock that needs fixing and a leaky sink."

"Shit. She's not going to let me fix anything for her."

"Yeah, she will, because it doesn't require you putting out any money." Dell moved to the door. "I loaded some supplies for the puppy into your truck."

"I didn't say yes."

"You didn't say no, either."

"You're the one who goes out there and provides actual services," Adam said. "I have nothing to offer her, we have nothing to talk about."

"You know damn well what you have to offer. You can fix what needs fixing, and she won't have to pay for it. Bring her the damn dog, Adam. See your mother. Help her out. I'll give you a Boy Scout badge for it."

Adam flipped him off. Dell returned the gesture and left.

Adam looked at the sleeping puppy. "Well? You going to be a watchdog or what?"

She opened her eyes and licked his chin again and then set her head back on his chest. Trusting. Sweet. A real badass.

Adam shook his head and walked out to his truck, puppy in tow. Just outside of town, he came upon Holly on the side of the highway, kicking her tire.

Adam spent a moment wrestling with his conscience and then pulled over. "Stay," he said to the puppy, and got out.

Holly watched him come toward her. She'd stopped kicking her tire and was now leaning against the Jeep as if she was just out for a little sunbathe.

"Problem?" he asked.

"Nope."

He eyed her very flat tire and, unbelievably, the pair of pliers sticking out of it. "So that's what, a figment of my imagination?"

"Ran over the stupid thing. I mean, who does that?"

"You, apparently." Adam crouched down and studied the tire.

"It's dead."

"Yes," he said. "Very dead." He rose. "Spare?"

She shook her head. "It's flat, too. I've called Red. He's coming out, but he's going to be an hour or so."

Adam nodded. "I'll give you a ride."

She looked at him for a long moment. "I can tell you're

on a mission, and it's not a happy one. I can wait for Red, Adam."

He met her gaze. How the hell she managed to read him like she did, when no one else could, he hadn't the foggiest idea. "I'm not leaving you out here on the road like this."

"But—"

Jesus. "Just get in the damn truck, Holly."

Unbelievably, she smiled. "And you think you're not sweet." She sashayed toward his truck and hopped up into the shotgun position. He stood where he was for a moment, taking a deep breath. Then he ambled over and got in behind the wheel.

Holly was snuggling the puppy, who was practically beside herself in ecstasy. "She's the cutest thing I've ever seen," Holly said. "Where did you get her?"

"She's not mine. I'm delivering her." He put the truck in gear and looked over his shoulder to make a U-turn.

"Oh, please don't," Holly said.

"Don't what?"

"Don't go out of your way to take me home. I'll come with you to deliver her."

"No," he said.

Holly blinked, and he cursed himself for making the reveal. She was sharp as hell, and the wheels in her brain were whirling so fast there was almost smoke. There was no way he'd get rid of her now. "It's a forty-five-minute drive," he said.

"I don't mind."

She didn't mind. Perfect. Jaw tight, he drove. And drove. Out of town. Into the hills. Past the hills to a tiny dirt road to Nowhere, USA.

And stopped at the double-wide trailer that Nila called home.

The puppy was asleep in Holly's lap. Holly had gifted Adam with silence on the ride, but he could tell it was costing her. He gestured to the trailer. In the open doorway stood a tall, willowy woman in jeans and a long sweater. No shoes. In spite of it being winter, Nila rarely ever wore shoes, even though he'd made sure that she had some. "Nila," he said. "My mother."

"I thought she was mad at you."

"She is."

"The puppy's for her? You're bringing your mother a puppy to make up with her?"

Because that thought clearly had her going all soft in the eyes, he shook his head. "The puppy's from Dell, not me." He took the puppy from her hands, wrapped her inside his jacket, and opened the door. "Stay here."

"But—"

"Holly." Christ, this was hard enough. He couldn't do this with her here. "Please."

She stared at him for a long beat, and then nodded. "I'll stay," she said quietly, and reached out and squeezed his arm. Soothing him. "I promise."

Nodding, he shut the truck door and walked to the back and grabbed his toolbox before heading toward the trailer.

Nila watched his approach with dark eyes that gave nothing away. Like mother, like son.

"Adam," she said.

"Dell said you need some stuff fixed." He showed her the toolbox.

She nodded but continued to block him. Great. He met her gaze. "You still mad at me?"

"You going to try to give me money again?" she asked.

"Not today."

A very small smile curved her mouth, and she moved aside for him but then stopped him with a hand on his arm, gesturing to the wriggling mass beneath his jacket.

Adam pulled out the puppy and handed it to her.

The breath left her lungs in a soft "awww," and her gaze flew to his face. "Homeless?"

Adam lied without compulsion. "Yes. She needs a good home."

Nila hugged the thing in close, and Adam knew the puppy would be completely accepted.

In a way he never had been.

Shaking that off, he fixed her lock and sink in five minutes flat and then headed to the door. The puppy supplies had been moved from the back of his truck to the top step.

Holly, of course.

"Here's everything you'll need," he said to Nila. "She'll have to get her shots in a few weeks. Dell will take care of that. If there are any problems, call one of us. When she's a little older, I'll train her for you."

Nila gestured to the truck. "Who's that?"

Adam looked through the windshield at Holly, who smiled. His chest had been tight for the past two hours, too fucking tight, but her smile eased it somehow. "A client's daughter."

Nila looked at Holly for another moment and then at Adam. "She's more."

Adam didn't bother to ask how she knew. "You have enough supplies for several weeks. I'll send Dell with more."

"I'd like you to bring them to me."

Adam looked at her, seeing a warmth in her eyes that hadn't been there before. "Okay."

Nila nodded and turned to go inside. "Bring the woman with you. She makes you smile. You have a good one."

And then she shut the door.

Adam was still shaking his head when he slid into the truck.

"What?" Holly asked.

"She likes you."

"How about her son?"

"He likes you, too."

She smiled and then let him drive back in peace. When they got back to her Jeep, the tire was repaired. Holly leaned in and gave Adam a kiss. "Thanks," she said.

"For?"

"For letting me in. Did it hurt?"

He stared into her smiling eyes. "Only a little."

She laughed. "I'm growing on you."

"You're absolutely not."

"I so am." And then she was gone.

He watched her drive off into the sunset and had to shake his head. Because she was right. She was growing on him.

Big-time.


That night Holly sank into a hot bath. With a sigh, she set her head back and relaxed. She was supposed to be reading next month's book club book. Lilah had picked it, and she'd chosen a romance. Damn newlyweds. Lilah had told them all that she expected a full book report on the characterization of the hero, but she'd been looking at Holly when she'd said it.

Holly knew that Lilah was wondering, hoping, that she wasn't going to hurt Adam.

She wasn't.

She planned on being the best thing that had ever happened to him.

And he her . . .

God, she could still, if she closed her eyes, feel his hands on her body. Just the memory of the way he'd touched her was enough to arouse. She could still hear his low erotic whisper in her ear, feel the delicious roughness of his day-old beard when he'd scraped it over her inner thigh, see the look of pleasure on his face as he'd taken control and moved over her.

She wanted him again.

Still . . .

She drifted on that thought for a while, until from the tub's edge, her phone buzzed an incoming text from Derek.

I'm appealing the divorce. Need to see you.

Holly nearly dropped the phone into the tub. He was appealing the divorce? Since when? And what the hell was he talking about? He'd had his chance already, back when she'd filed and he'd ignored it. She'd had to petition the court for an uncontested divorce, and again he'd ignored it. Holly had met with the judge, who'd finally granted the divorce. So what was to appeal now? Grinding her teeth, she pounded out Derek's number.

He answered with, "Hey, wife."

"No," she said. "No, no, no, no. *Not* your wife."

"Technicality."

"We're *divorced*," she said. "You didn't show up for the hearing, but I did. I heard the judge decree it done. There's nothing to appeal. We're free of each other. You promised."

"Ah, but I never promised any such thing."

This was true. He hadn't. He hadn't said a damn word in all this time, just radio silence.

"I'm thinking we rushed this thing through," Derek said.

Holly was holding the phone so tight she was surprised it didn't shatter. "How is *years* of separation being hasty?"

"I don't know, Holly. It just is."

"I was gone for weeks before you even noticed."

"I'm noticing now. I miss you."

Bullshit, he missed her. "Call one of your students," she said.

"Yeah, that's just the thing," he said. "Single professors don't really have any business calling their students."

She almost drowned herself by accident trying to stand up in the slippery tub because she liked to stand up when she was yelling at someone. "Are you kidding me? *That's* why you're going to appeal? Because being married gave you an edge with the silly, floozy college coeds?" She stepped out of the tub and stood naked, trembling in fury as she dripped water all over her bathroom. "You are slime, Derek. Scum. The scourge of the earth—"

"Listen, sorry to interrupt this fascinating tirade on my character, but you do remember that you were once one of those silly, floozy coeds, right?"

She disconnected. And then, because she was out of control, she tossed her phone to the counter, where it slid across the granite and hit the tile floor. *Think,* she told herself. An appeal isn't the end of the world. No judge would grant him an appeal.

Probably.

Steaming, she yanked a towel off the rack and dried herself. She stormed into her closet and stared at the slim pickings. She needed to do laundry. Dammit. She grabbed the first thing she came to, a little black cocktail dress. Whatever. She shimmied into it and grabbed her keys. Maybe she'd once, very briefly, been a silly coed, back when she'd been desperate to belong, desperate to be loved, but no longer. She was a woman who'd gotten herself a life, one she actually liked.

She started out the door and then realized she was barefoot, so she shoved her feet into the mud boots by the door. Then she stalked to her Jeep and headed down the road, reminding herself that she was no longer desperate to belong or desperate to be loved. She'd grown up. It wasn't a mindless connection that she sought now. Nope, this time she knew *exactly* what she wanted.

And she was strong enough to go after it, too, settling for no less than absolutely everything.

Except . . . was that really true? Was she really getting everything she needed from Adam? Was she going to be able to accept what he could give her?

*Yes,* she told herself, ignoring the little clutch in her gut. *At least for now.* She was going to choose to be happy, and to that end, she pulled into the drugstore parking lot, belatedly realizing that she was wearing a cocktail dress, and . . . oh God.

Big, old, clumsy mud boots.

Too late now, she told herself. If she went back home, she'd never find the courage to come back out. So she wore her outfit with pride, right into the drugstore.

And then the liquor store.

Her third and last stop was Belle Haven. She parked and drew a deep breath. Then she got out of the Jeep and clomped in the boots toward the stairs.

A shadow stepped out from a side door. Tall, dark, built. He had Adam's dark eyes and mocha latte skin, the same tall, rough-and-tumble exterior that said he was up for anything, complete with the devastating Connelly smile.

Dell.

"Hey," he said. He stepped under the porch light and his smile faded. "You okay?"

She ran a hand over her hair, realizing she'd literally run out of the house. No makeup. Hair still up from her bath, damp tendrils hanging in her face. Fancy LBD.

And then there were the mud boots . . .

Dell ducked down a little, looking into her eyes. "Holly?"

"I'm fine. I'm just here to . . ." *Jump your brother's bones*.

He waited patiently, looking more fascinated with each passing second.

Holly closed her mouth.

Dell laughed softly and nodded toward the brown bag she was holding. "Whatcha got?"

She hugged the bag to herself. Oh, hell no! No way could he see what she had in the bag.

"Okay," Dell said easily, still amused. "So you don't want to talk. You'll be quite the pair. He's upstairs. Oh, and Holly?"

"Yeah?"

"Be gentle."

She felt the blush heat her face. "Excuse me?"

"You're going to light into him for something, right?"

"No, I—" She nibbled on her lower lip. Okay, that was probably less embarrassing than the truth. "Maybe."

Dell's smile softened as he looked at her for a long beat. "You know, you might be just what the doctor ordered tonight."

"Why, is something wrong?"

Dell hesitated, which was unlike him. Neither of the Connelly brothers were ones to mince words or hold back. "What's wrong?" she asked.

"There was a search and rescue tonight that turned into a search and recovery before an S&R team could be mobilized."

She knew what a recovery meant. They'd gone to get a body.

"They used Milo," Dell said. "He's young, but he's an excellent cadaver dog." He met her gaze. "It's tough on Adam still. Finding bodies. Sometimes the old demons get him."

Holly's heart clenched hard, and she nodded. She'd never been to war. She'd never rescued anyone. She'd never *failed* to rescue anyone. Hell, she'd never had to see a dead body and probably never would. Adam had done all of that and probably more than she could even imagine. He'd put his entire adult life on the line for others, and never once had she thought of what the consequences might be. "Is there anything I can do?"

Dell looked at her, appraisingly. "You care about him."

A question, not a statement.

"Always have," she said.

Dell cocked his head. "Always?"

That secret was so old she'd nearly forgotten it was a secret. She thought about denying it, but what was the point now? And besides, Dell was far too sharp and astute to believe her, anyway. *"Always."*

There was a beat of silence as he processed this, then he let out a long breath. "Guess I should have seen that one from a mile away. There always was something between you two."

A truer statement had never been uttered. "So what do I do?" she asked. "He's not exactly good at accepting help."

Dell tipped his head back and looked up at the silent loft. Then he met her gaze. "You know what I think? I think you're good at winging it. Just don't let him chase you away with that bad 'tude of his. It's all a front. Beneath, he's a pussycat."

"Do you really believe that?"

He laughed. "Undomesticated wildcat, maybe."

She sighed and walked up the stairs, heart pounding so loudly she didn't think it was even necessary to knock. Surely he could hear her coming.

But she did knock.

And he answered, wearing low-slung jeans and nothing else. He took one long, slow look at her, hands up high, braced on the doorjamb. Silent. Whatever he thought about her appearance, he was keeping it to himself. Fair enough. She'd certainly kept far too much to herself. *Talk,* she reminded herself. *You're here to talk.*

But her mind didn't get the message, couldn't get past the gotta-have-him signals her body was putting out. Crowding him, she plastered her body to his, talking the very last thing on her mind.

# Twenty

Adam stared into Holly's gaze and felt something shift in his center of gravity. It was a good thing he was holding on to the doorjamb above his head because, good Christ, she leveled him flat.

"Yesterday, at class, you said you weren't up for food," she said. "That food wasn't what you wanted."

His mouth went dry. He wasn't up for this, for battling wits or whatever she thought she was doing. What he *was* up for was a night alone. Being in such close contact with her on the mountain, and then again at the class, had stirred up emotions he didn't want stirred up.

Brady had accused him of feeling sorry for himself.

Adam didn't want that to be true, because that meant he was a fucking pussy, but he was starting to fear that it *was* true. Grif had made a career out of the military. Adam had always thought that he would, too. But he was still broken, as it turned out.

And that pissed him off.

He wanted to be alone to lick his wounds in private, but

hell if he could get any alone time. Between Brady and Dell, and now Holly, it was like living at Grand Central Station. "I'm not up for games, Holly."

"I know. But as was previously established, neither of us plays games." Her gaze ran over his body. She nibbled on her lower lip as she looked at him.

She was thinking of sex. And of course he was *always* thinking about sex, so they were perfectly in sync. He loved her body, loved being all over it, loved the reactions he got from it. From her. But even he knew this had *bad idea* written all over it.

She looked down at the bag she held and something in her expression narrowed his senses and made him curious enough to take the bag from her. He peeked inside and found a bottle of Jack Daniel's and a box of . . .

Condoms.

She cleared her throat and shifted her weight, and he tore his eyes off the condoms to look at her. Her cheeks were flushed, her eyes bright, pupils dilated. Yeah. She was absolutely thinking of sex.

Which meant he needed a shot of the whiskey. What stopped him from suggesting just that was his realization that she looked like needed it even worse than he did.

Something had driven her here, to this. To him. "What happened?"

"What makes you think something's happened?"

"Well," he said, his gaze raking over her, "for starters, you're wearing a fancy-ass dress with mud boots. Which, by the way, is sexy as hell."

"The dress?"

"The boots."

She looked down at herself. "Maybe I'm making a statement."

"Which is?"

"Some things aren't as they appear on the outside."

He cocked his head. "Like?"

"Like . . . an onion, for example. The layers have to be peeled away one at a time to see the real heart and soul of what's beneath, you know? Even a bruised onion, a damaged onion, is worth saving."

He just stared at her. "You're trying to tell me something."

"Yes! Listen, once upon a time, you were the bad influence, right?"

"Yes," he said slowly.

"Well, it's my turn now, at least for tonight."

This might have made him smile. If he didn't want to both fuck her and strangle her at the same time. And he did want both of those things—badly. Then she leaned in, her body brushing his, and he flashed back to the other night on the mountain. When he'd been with her, his entire world had shrunk, pinpointed to nothing but sensations. The feel of her hot and wet around him, the way her fingers and thighs held him tight, the sound of her voice.

The heat of her skin.

*It doesn't have to be just a memory.* Hell, her hands were on his chest right now and gliding lower. He caught them in his so he could think. His brothers seemed to think he was being a dumbass when it came to this, to her, that he should do the right thing and open up and let her in.

That she needed him every bit as much as he needed her.

He was still processing that, just as he wanted to know what had put the haunted shadows in her eyes. "What brought this on, Holly?"

She went still, then looked away.

He moved so she had no choice but to meet his gaze. "Tell me."

"Derek's appealing the divorce."

"Why?"

She shrugged. "Turns out, he likes the shield of being married. Gives him an in with all the cute coeds."

The fucker. "Where is he?"

"I don't know," she said, "but when I find him, I'm going to kick his ass."

"Yeah?" He wouldn't mind seeing that. "How about I hold him down for you?"

"Aw." This made her smile. "That's the sweetest thing anyone's ever offered to do for me."

He was a lot of things, but sweet most definitely wasn't one of them. "You got your attorney on this?"

"Not yet. Derek just told me."

And she'd obviously come straight to him. Adam didn't know what to make of that. Truth be told, he'd always been a little jealous of Holly's marriage. He could admit that now, at least to himself. Adam might not have been the right man for her, but he sure as hell wouldn't have cheated on her or treated her like shit. He'd have—

Saving him from that ridiculous train of thought, she gave him a little push and pressed the advantage, stepping over the threshold and shutting the door behind her. Snatching the brown bag of goodies back from him, she pulled out the bottle of Jack and tossed the condoms to the bed.

He arched a brow.

She broke eye contact and struggled to open the bottle. "Dammit," she muttered when she couldn't get it. "This never happens in the seduction scenes in the stupid movies."

If she'd come to seduce him, it wasn't going to require much effort on her part. Hell, who was he kidding, it would take *zero* effort on her part. He really needed to stop this, now, but instead, he was just staring at her, his mind racing.

His usual MO was to avoid feeling, at all costs, but whenever it came to Holly, that resolve seemed to fly right out the window. He was feeling so many things, he didn't know where to start. "You really shouldn't be here."

"Why not?"

*Yeah, ace. Why not?* "Earlier tonight, for starters."

"When you were rude?" She was bent over the bottle

now, which she'd shoved between her legs to get better leverage as she tried to open it.

"I wasn't rude," he said. *Abrupt, maybe,* he silently conceded. She was still fighting with the bottle, so he slid his hand between her legs and took it from her, absolutely not noticing how warm her inner thighs were or how they'd also warmed the bottle.

Much.

She sighed and straightened. "Thank you."

He didn't open the liquor. Instead, he set it on the coffee table.

She narrowed her eyes. "Problem?"

"Why did you protect me with the cave bullshit?"

She blinked. "Protect you?"

"You told Brady I went into the cave."

"You did go into the cave."

"No, *you* did."

"You were right there with me, Adam."

"For two feet, maybe. Before my complete mental breakdown."

She studied him a moment, and he hated that enough to turn his back on her. But not before he grabbed the bottle of Jack. She'd been right, the top was tight, but he managed to get it opened and tossed back a healthy shot. It burned a path clear to his gut to match the burn in his chest.

"You went in," she said softly behind him. "And you'd have gone in even farther if you'd had to, if my father had been in there. I know it."

He decided another shot was in order. And Jesus Christ, it burned more than the first. "You don't know that."

"I do." She took the bottle from him and tossed back her own shot, licking her lips afterward, as if she was trying to get a taste of him off the bottle.

It shouldn't have done anything for him, but it did.

She did.

"I don't need you to baby me," he said, struggling to stay on track. "I don't need to be protected."

"Of course not," she said. "Only a crazy person would try to baby or protect you." She took another shot, as always, matching him step for step. Then she set the bottle on the coffee table and put her hands on his arms, backing him to the couch. "You do it all, Adam. Always, no matter what."

"Stop."

"You stop." She gave him a little push and he went down to the cushions. Standing over him, she kicked off the boots. Then pulled off her sexy-as-hell dress.

Beneath she wore nothing but a sports bra and panties. Simple white.

"Um," she said, looking down at herself for a beat. "Pretend I'm in black silk."

He didn't have to pretend. She was gorgeous in the white cotton. Hell, she'd be gorgeous in a potato sack.

Reaching behind her, she grabbed the whiskey and drank again. She missed a drop, it slid down her throat and over her collarbone, heading south.

"Oops," she said, and leaned back, a movement that thrust out her breasts.

God, he loved her breasts. They were full, soft. Real. And, he knew from experience, extremely sensitive. But he was no longer a hormone- and testosterone-ruled teenager, driven by his sex drive—even if he did keep his eyes on the drop of whiskey . . . "This isn't going to work, Holly."

She glanced down at the obvious erection straining the front of his jeans and went brows up.

"Okay," he said, standing, having to put his hands on her hips as he did, to push her away.

Or at least that's what he meant to do, but his hands didn't get the message from his brain and they tightened on her. "I'm not good for you."

"I trust you, Adam."

"You shouldn't."

"Are you kidding me?" She gave him another shove.

"What the hell, Holly."

"What the hell is"—she punctuated this with yet another shove, even harder—"I needed help finding my dad. And did you say you couldn't be bothered? No. You were willing to do whatever it took. You were injured and exhausted, and you still dropped your own work and responsibilities without hesitation and took me all over hell and back. You were, *are*, the one man I can trust. With *anything*."

"No," he said, shaking his head. *Hell no*. "I'm not up for that level of blind trust."

She glowered at him and took another sip of the whiskey, until he removed it from her fingers. "Jesus," he said, "what's gotten into you tonight?"

"Well, not you," she said, and made him choke on his own long pull of the Jack.

She was flushed, her eyes glossy. Half-baked from the alcohol and gorgeous with it, she pointed a finger in his face. "You, Adam Connelly, are a big, stupid . . . *man*."

He choked back a laugh. "Is that the worst you've got?"

"No. I have lots more." She crawled into his lap and kissed him.

He let her do it, kissing her as she wanted, catching her tongue with his like he wanted, rubbing up against her when he needed. He felt her tremble and held her close, letting go of his will to resist her, allowing his hunger for her to take over and pour out of him.

But then she shocked the hell out of him by gripping his arms and giving him a helluva shake for a willowy, partially drunk woman.

"You have it all wrong," she said.

"What part?"

"The *not-coming-into-my-cave* part."

He blinked. "Huh?"

She made a face and waved a hand. "No wait. Can't say it like that, I'll scare you away again."

He had a feeling he was going to have to kill his brothers, but before he could move, she was in his face, her own deep and intent. He looked into her shiny blue eyes and saw . . . everything.

It was staggering.

"Who did I go to for help?" she asked. "*You*. Who has everyone always gone to? *You*." She tossed up her hands. "Do you think it's because you're cute or something?"

He opened his mouth at that but she stabbed a finger into his chest again. Since that was starting to hurt, he grabbed her hand.

"Come on, Adam," she said. "Even Thing One and Thing Two know the truth. When *anyone* needs someone to count on, you're the one. You're not magical, you're no superhero, but you're enough. *More* than enough. And . . ."

It took him a moment to find his voice through a throat that was thick with things he didn't want to put a name to. "And . . . ?"

"And . . ." She cupped his face and stared at him some more. Then she shook her head. "You know what? You're not ready for this conversation." And with that, she climbed off his lap and headed for the door.

## Twenty-one

H olly got to Adam's door just as he grabbed her, whipped her around, and pressed her back to the wood. She stared up at the tall, built, hot man holding her pinned, and shivered in anticipation. "Adam—"

"Hell no are you leaving now."

She melted and cupped his jaw. "I wasn't leaving." And then, instead of fighting him as he'd clearly expected, she pressed up against him, nuzzling her face into his throat. "I was just making sure the door was locked."

He went still at that revelation, still as the night, so she reached behind her and locked the door herself. Then she reversed their positions, pressing *him* to the wood, sliding her hands up his chest and into his hair.

He closed his eyes, as if just the touch was too much to take, and that one small tell squeezed her heart. Letting her thumbs trace his beautiful jawline, rough with at least a day's growth, she sighed with pleasure. No, he wasn't a superhero, but he was, she'd begun to fear, the man for her.

The only man for her.

Gliding her fingers into his hair, she tugged him down and kissed him. He got right with the program, no hesitation, taking over in his alpha way. This was no tentative kiss. It was demanding, full of pent-up passion and tension and years and years of emotion all tied into one.

She loved it.

She loved everything about it, and she was desperately afraid she loved everything about him as well. She'd loved the teen he'd been, the one who hadn't left her for the military, or another woman, or for shits and giggles. He'd left her because he'd had to go to make something of himself.

He'd done that, in spades.

Clearly, he wasn't sure if he'd succeeded, if he was good enough. But he was. That was something she could fight, and she would. She'd fight for him. For them. "Adam?"

"Yeah?"

"There's something more I want to say. Okay?"

His laugh was soft, ruffling the hair along her heated temple. "Since when have I ever been able to stop you from doing what you wanted?"

It was all the invite she was going to get. "You always do whatever it takes to make things right," she said quietly, using her hands on his face to tilt it down so that he was looking right into her eyes. No missing the point, not this time. She wanted him to know exactly how she felt, wanted him to get the meaning of every word. "You'd have gone to the ends of the earth to save my dad, and I want you to know you're the bravest man I've ever known."

"Holly," he said, sounding staggered as he dropped his forehead to hers.

"It's true, Adam. You're a hero to me. You always were. Even when you left me, which you did out of some misguided, stupid attempt to protect me from *you*, of all people, you big, stupid man."

"You're repeating yourself." But his arms came around her and he remained quiet. He was listening. He wasn't necessarily buying what she was saying, but he was listening.

Usually it was the other way around. Usually he drove their conversations. Their fights. Their . . . everything. They were in uncharted waters without a navigational system now, and she didn't have a clue as to what she was doing, she honestly didn't. She just knew she had to make him understand how much he meant to her. She rocked up into him, giving him her best try-to-resist-me gaze as she slid her arms up around his neck. "I'm done talking now."

"If only I could believe that."

She smiled and smacked him in the chest. He caught her hand in his. "If we do this," he said, "it's going to last all night."

She came undone. "Yes, please." Up on tiptoes, she kissed first one corner of his mouth and then the other. And then full on. If it was possible to take Adam unaware, she did it in that moment. She felt it in every line of his body, and knew she'd done the right thing, making the first move. He'd always been the aggressor. Well, she was done with that. She was her own woman now, and she went after what she wanted.

And what she wanted was to make Adam feel even a fraction of how good she felt when she was with him. He deserved that. She nipped at his lower lip. Not hard, just enough to make him hiss in a breath and have his arms tightening on her as he kissed her.

Deep.

Wet.

Hot.

He kissed her as if nothing else in the world mattered but her, pulling the very breath from her lungs, sending shock waves to her very center, so strong that she had to hold on to him for dear life. He kissed his way up her jawline and licked the shell of her ear, and she lost track of her bones. Her balance shifted, and with a low laugh, she lurched against the door and fell into him. He easily caught her up, taking all her weight.

He wouldn't let her fall. He'd never let her fall. Instead, he turned them and pressed her into the door now. She shifted enough to rub up against the front of his body, which was *heaven*. She couldn't help herself, and she peppered his jaw with kisses, everywhere she could reach.

Growling out her name, his big palm cupped her breast, his thumb brushing over her nipple, which instantly tightened in response, begging for more contact. Bending low, he kissed her through her sports bra before gently using his teeth to worry the turgid tip. With a gasp, she wriggled her hips, desperate for more contact. Feeling how hard he was, she moaned a little. Maybe a lot. She couldn't control herself.

Adam tugged her bra down, freeing her breasts to the cool air and his hot breath, dragging an "oh please" from her, a desperate, hungry plea.

He sucked her into his mouth, pressing her between his wet tongue and the hot roof of his mouth, and gave her a rush a millimeter short of an orgasm. Needing more, her hands slid south past his rock-hard abs and exposed hip bones, all of which were perfectly cut. She dipped into the loose waistband of his jeans but couldn't access enough of his goodies. And damn, he had amazing goodies, so she worked at getting the button free.

He caught her face in his big hands, pressing her into the door so that she couldn't move. "Holly. Jesus." His voice was tight, barely controlled.

"I'm trying to be a bad influence," she said, breathless. "Is it working?"

"Yeah. It's working."

Giddy, she kissed him again, soft and sweet this time, snuggling into him. "I like taking point," she whispered, and his rough laugh caused goose bumps to ripple along her skin. "I'm not doing it wrong, am I?"

He smiled against her. "Hell, if you do it any more right, we're going to finish this right here."

"That's my plan," she said.

Adam's gaze met her. "That's not my plan."

She leaned into him, laced her hands around his neck, and stared up at him. "Well, I don't like your plan. Besides, you're . . . uptight. I have the solution for that."

He didn't say anything to this but his gaze dipped to her breasts, bared now, one of which was still wet from his mouth.

"It's a *really* good solution," she said enticingly, and gave him her best smile. "Admit it, I'm irresistible. And kinda cute."

"The fuck you are. Puppies are cute. You're hot as hell. Hot enough to inspire acts of complete stupidity on my part."

She smiled and he groaned, dropping his forehead to her shoulder. "Tell me what you want from me, Holly."

"I would, but I'm more of a show-not-tell sort of girl." She slid her hands over his shoulders, down his sculpted chest, past his delicious abs. The muscles jumped beneath her fingers. He'd lost a few pounds this past week, but he was still ripped as hell. "Stop fighting it, Adam."

The button on his jeans undone, she helped the zipper along and then slid her hands down the back and cupped his perfect butt in her hands, pulling him flush to her.

They both sucked in air at the sensation of skin to skin. Raining openmouthed kisses over his chest, she stopped to lick each of his nipples, registering his low growl just as he fisted a hand in her hair. "When you touch me," she murmured against him, "I feel it all the way to my soul." She tipped back her head. "Tell me you don't feel it, too."

His eyes darkened and she knew she'd hit a nerve. She pressed her lips to his heart and it kicked hard. She felt her own heart flip-flop in response as she looked up at him through her lashes. "Or maybe you'd rather keep ignoring it."

Ignoring exactly nothing, his mouth covered hers as he pushed her back up against the door. She rubbed up against him, knowing she'd lied. She was here for more than this, and she'd have to live with that. *Later.* "I want you," she whispered. "So much."

"And I want you. That's never been the problem."

She went still, then stared up at him. "So what is?"

He met her gaze, his own unreadable. At his silence, she pushed away from him. He caught her before she could open the door, pulling her back against his chest. She closed her eyes, trying to fight back tears, the frustration of giving to a man who didn't give back.

He tightened his grip on her, and she felt more than heard the words as he breathed them against the shell of her ear. "Damn you."

"You need to let me go."

"You make me crazy," he said.

"Clearly." She shook her head. "I threw myself at you and you turned me down. That sounds crazy to me, too."

Still behind her, he had one hand low on her belly, the other across the front of her thighs. She could feel him, still hard against her.

"I'm not one to fall in love," he said so softly she almost missed it. Again she fought to free herself but he held her still. "I've been in *lust* plenty of times," he admitted against her ear. "But I haven't done love. Not once. Not since you."

Oh, God if that didn't just about kill her, and she fought him again, but for an entirely different reason now. He'd never admitted he'd loved her back then. She'd guessed, but she'd never known for sure. She wanted to turn and face him, wanted to get closer, but it was useless. He had her in his grip. "Adam—"

"You scare the hell out of me, you know that?" he asked. "I could fall for you again, you know. Right into your sweet baby blues and never come back up for air."

She went still.

"Yeah," he murmured, running his jaw along hers. "But it wouldn't be good for either of us. Last chance, Holly. Stop this. Stop me."

Instead, she wriggled free, turned around, and nuzzled his neck until he bent his head, seeking her lips. He hoisted her up, and she wrapped her legs around him as he turned to his bed.

Milo hopped off just as Adam turned and fell backward to the mattress, bringing Holly down with him. He didn't ask again if she was sure, or if she wanted to change her mind. That was one of the things she loved about him. He assumed she could walk and chew gum at the same time. He never second-guessed her, and he didn't try to change her.

He accepted.

Feeling choked up again at the thought, she snuggled up against his broad chest. He took one of her hands and slid it down his stomach and into his jeans.

Decision made.

She never got tired of touching him, but it was Adam who was impatient now. He was one of those men who looked as good out of his clothes as in them, proven when he sat up to kick off his jeans, his abs crunching, folding in on themselves without an ounce of fat, the lucky bastard.

Except she knew it wasn't luck. It was hard work.

With his every movement, the testosterone practically leaked out his pores, making her tingle in her hot spots, and he'd barely touched her. They rolled on the bed, jockeying for position, teasing, stroking . . . Adam's lusciously colored skin always felt so good against her. She loved rubbing herself over him and gasped when he moved on top, sliding a hard thigh between her legs. Mmm, the feel of his unshaven face against her soft skin, the way he quivered when she ran her hands over his taut muscles. Yeah, touching was nice, but tasting . . . even better. It didn't matter what he'd done that day, he always tasted like warm sun and everything male.

He ran a finger over her boy-cut panties. "Off."

She reached for them, but he beat her to it, divesting her of them in one quick, economical move, his eyes taking his own sensory inventory of her body before slipping a hand between her legs. "You should wear a warning label," he said.

"Like you'd heed a warning label."

This garnered her a smile as he lowered himself over her, making her moan with sheer pleasure as the contour of his hard chest met the soft, sensitive skin of her breasts. Pushing her hair over her shoulder, he gently put his lips to the sweet spot beneath her ear. His hands roamed, taking a slow perusal of her body, paying special homage to all her favorite spots, of which he seemed to know every single one.

She tipped her head up, catching his mouth with hers. He let out another of those sexy growls, this one pure hunger, as he slid down her body. Her heart began to pound in her chest as he kissed every inch. Sliding his hands beneath her, he pulled her forward.

To his mouth.

At the first touch of his tongue, she shot straight up as the pleasure reverberated through her.

He pushed her back down, maneuvering her right where he wanted her. Then he lowered his head and went back to driving her out of her ever-loving mind, not stopping for a very long time . . .

Not until she begged him to.

Only then did he surge up, grabbing for the condoms. Together they got him covered, and then he came over her again, kissing her as he slid in deep. With a gasp, she tore her mouth free because it was impossible to kiss through the first delicious slide of their joining.

"Holly." That was all he said, just her name in a low, rough, reverent voice that had her forcing her eyes open to look at him. His head fell back, his face a mask of desire.

Watching him find such pleasure took her to the edge, and she hovered there, moving with him, meeting him thrust for thrust, little whimpers of need escaping her, whimpers she couldn't have held back to save her own life. Finally, she burst with his name on her lips, and with a rough groan, he followed her over, shuddering in her arms.

Gasping for air, damp and utterly limp, she purred when Adam's arms pulled her in close. He held her tight, his lips gliding along the line of her shoulder while his own breathing slowed.

"Wow," she finally managed. "I like your moves while under the influence."

"That wasn't the Jack."

She recognized the tone of his voice—pure male ego—and hid her smile. "No?"

"Hell no."

"Hmm."

He lifted his head, eyes narrowed. "You doubt it?"

"Of course not."

He crooked a finger at her. "Come here." Before she could move, he rolled, tucking her beneath him again, his face intent, his hands even more so. "I'll show you."

She was still smiling in triumph when his mouth claimed hers again.

*Much* later, she was warm, still pleasantly fuzzy with the whiskey, and just about as happy as she could ever remember feeling. Of course, she wasn't sure she could walk again.

And she wasn't sure she cared . . .

# Twenty-two

A dam woke up alone. Well, not entirely alone. Milo was sprawled across most of the entire bed, his head heavy on Adam's pillow.

Snoring.

Adam looked around but nope, there was no soft, warm, sexy female anywhere, and then he remembered. Holly had left at the crack of dawn. Bending low over him, she'd slid a hand down his back as she'd kissed him, whispering that she had an early meeting. Then she'd nipped his ear, slapped his ass, and vanished.

Fair enough. It had been a seduction, after all, and she'd gotten what she'd come for. In spades.

So had he.

But now, in the light of day, he had to wonder what the hell he'd thought he'd been doing. He didn't want a relationship. Never had. He liked being accountable to no one, not having to worry about anyone else's schedule or, worse, feelings. His life was busy and he didn't have time or inclination to fit anyone into it.

And yet . . .

Holly had managed to fit into it just fine.

He rolled over, shoving Milo to make room. His bones felt liquefied, and damned if he wasn't wearing a stupid just-got-laid smile.

Milo licked his ear.

"You big oaf." He glanced at the clock. Eight. He just slept more solidly than he had since getting home. Guess sex till you drop did a body good. Rolling off the bed, he fed Milo and hit the shower, then made his way downstairs. The day had started without him. Jade was at her desk, dictating his and Dell's world with calm efficiency. "Hey, hot stuff," she said.

"Hey, hot stuff," Peanut the parrot repeated from his perch on the printer.

Gertie scrambled to greet Adam and Milo, and there was the usual sniffing and tail wagging as Adam grabbed his messages from Jade. "What?" he said when she gave him a brow waggle.

"You know what. You're smiling," she said.

"No, that's you."

"Because *you* are," she said. "You win the lotto?"

"No."

"Is it your birthday?"

"No."

"Huh," Jade said. "Must have something to do with Holly sneaking down your stairs at the ass crack of dawn this morning."

Jesus. "What were you doing here at the ass crack of dawn?" he asked. "Does Dell need to put more men on the job at home?"

She smacked him. "I was doing month-end accounting."

Adam shook his head and strode out the back. He saddled up Reno and, with Milo and Gertie tagging along, rode out to the lake. There Adam hid various items, including a boot and a sweatshirt, training the dogs under the guise of hide-and-seek.

Actually, Milo trained. Gertie napped.

Two hours later, they were back and Adam closed himself up in his office to get some work done. He had an article to write on rescue dog policy and procedure, a bunch of correspondence to go through, and some S&R training to plan out for several agencies he was visiting next week.

Milo settled on his dog bed in the corner, turning in three precise circles before plopping his graceless ass down so hard the place shook like an earthquake. Two minutes later he was up and setting his large head on Adam's thigh, staring up at him adoringly.

"No," Adam said. "It's not time to eat."

Milo sighed, drooled on Adam's leg, and went back to his bed.

Adam was halfway through the article when Dell poked his head in, holding a tiny puppy in each hand.

"They're here to be checked out," Dell said. "Mama's having trouble feeding them all. Grab a bottle and pitch in?"

Adam followed him to the back and sat on the floor with Dell next to the box of puppies. It took them forty-five minutes to fill the bellies of the mewling, starving crew. The puppies got a little rambunctious after that, playfully chewing on one another's limbs and tails and on Adam's and Dell's fingers. With puppies all over them, Adam asked, "So what's this bullshit about you telling Holly she's my cave?"

"You're afraid of caves," Dell said, as if that were an explanation.

"I'm not afraid. I—"

"And you're afraid of Holly, too, so . . ."

"Jesus." Adam pulled the runt off the biggest sibling, where he'd been trying to start something he absolutely couldn't finish. "You don't know what the hell you're talking about."

"You sure about that?" Dell asked.

No. But he was sure about the urge to pound his brother much like the runt. He was trying to decide how best to do that without hurting the puppies when Lilah picked that very moment to poke her head in. "Dell, I've brought you a rescue—*Awww*." Dropping to her knees between them, she hugged the puppies into her.

"Saved by the princess," Dell murmured to Adam with amusement.

Lilah divided a look between them. "What did I miss?"

*"Nothing,"* Adam said.

"Adam disagrees that Holly is his cave," Dell said.

Lilah rolled her eyes. "She's totally your cave."

Dell sent Adam an I-told-you-so look, which Adam had to ignore because he couldn't very well kill his brother with Lilah sitting right there as a material witness.

"So cute," Lilah said as Adam hugged a puppy.

"They're getting big," he agreed.

Lilah took the puppy from him, set it in its puppy box, and then wrapped her arms around Adam, snuggling her face into his neck as she snorted with laughter. "I meant you, silly. You're both so adorable, sitting on the floor playing with puppies."

Adam tried to untangle himself from her but she held on, laughing at him. "We are not adorable," he said.

"Speak for yourself," Dell said. "I'm adorable as hell." He slid Adam a long look. "And Holly must think you are, too, because somehow you convinced her to spend the night with you."

Lilah nodded her agreement.

There was no use wondering how everyone knew. Not a single one of them could mind their own business to save their lives. But they were smiling at him, all happy and proud of him, and he had to shake his head. "Maybe *she* made the first move," he said. "Maybe it was *her* idea to come over and spend the night seducing me. You ever think of that?"

Dell and Lilah looked at each other and burst out laughing.

"It really was her idea," Adam muttered, and they only laughed harder.

"Let me get this straight," Dell said when he got control of himself. "You telling me you can't get away from her?"

Yes. Exactly. She was taking his classes, showing up at his place . . . He couldn't get away from her. And the scariest part? He wasn't even sure when he'd stopped wanting to.

That night Adam was upstairs on his laptop working when his computer beeped an incoming IM from Grif: *Open Skype so I can call you.*

Adam clicked on the program and waited for the call. When it came, Grif was wearing desert fatigues and a frown. "Hey," Adam said. "You look like shit."

Grif shoved his sunglasses to the top of his head. "Man, what are you doing?"

"Want to be more specific?" Adam asked.

"Sure. My sister. You're doing my sister?"

Adam stared at Grif for a full five seconds. There'd been a time in his life where nothing could have taken him by surprise. Not a sucker punch, not an IED, nothing.

But then Holly Reid had come along and rocked his world.

The Reids were batting a thousand.

Grif leaned a little closer to his screen, distorting his frown. "Hello?"

Adam was trying to figure out how the hell to tell Grif that, yeah, he was doing his sister, when someone knocked at the door.

Grif narrowed his eyes. "That'd better not be her."

"Just . . . wait there." Adam moved to the front door, passing a dozing Milo. "Nice heads-up."

Milo lifted his head. "Woof."

"You're so fired." Adam opened the front door and stared in disbelief at Holly.

"Bad time?" she asked.

"Yes." He moved to block her path, and hopefully also Grif's view of the front door.

Holly went up on tiptoes to see in past him. He rose to his full height to barricade her, but she merely ducked beneath his arm and let herself in.

Adam had held his own through so many back-alley fights he couldn't remember them all, through military training that was as close to torture as a man could get. He sparred with Dell at least once a week, and his skills were excellent. And yet all that went out the open door as he was bested by 120 pounds of nosy, sexy, annoying-as-hell woman.

"Don't worry," she said, laughing at him over her shoulder. "I'm not packing whiskey and condoms tonight."

*Shit.* "Holly—"

"This isn't where you try to fight me off again and then beg me to stay, is it?"

Jesus.

"Holly," Grif said from the desk.

Adam now had two problems, big ones, but Holly was a pro at alpha males. With a wide smile at the sound of her brother's voice, she rushed to the computer. "Hey, you! Looking good."

Grif sent Adam a long look over Holly's shoulder. "So are you."

"Thanks," Holly said. "So what were you guys talking about?" She glanced back at Adam, and her smile dimmed. When she looked at her brother again, the rest of her good humor had faded away. "Okay, what's going on?"

"Nothing," Adam said.

"Oh, it's something," Holly said, dividing a gaze between the two of them. "Someone spit it out."

"Actually," Grif said, "Adam was just going to tell me what's going on."

Adam really didn't want to do this now. He knew what it was like to be right there, right where Grif was, far from home, exhausted beyond reason, tense enough to shatter.

A bad frame of mind . . .

Anything that came out of Adam's mouth right now would only make things worse. And making it worse was fucking dangerous. So Adam exercised his constitutional right to keep it zipped.

Holly gave him a look of disbelief, accompanied by a little push. "Would you stop being all big and macho and stupid and stoic for once? It's infuriating."

Grif smiled at that—until Holly put a finger in his face. "Oh no, don't you do that, look all smug and superior. You're just as big and macho and stupid as he is."

"What, I don't get the stoic label?" Grif asked.

"Stoic would be you being quiet," she said. "And I'm not hearing a lot of quiet out of you. Now what the hell were you two talking about?"

Grif gave Adam a look. "I'd just asked Adam what the fuck he thought he was doing with you."

"Well, Grif," Holly said in a far-too-polite tone that was the equivalent of a tornado siren warning. "As you might have noticed, I showed up here uninvited. So, really, you should be asking *me* what I'm doing with *Adam*."

"So you two are—"

"None of your business," she said, standing in front of Adam as if to protect him.

"It *is* his business," Adam said. "*You're* his business."

Grif pinched the bridge of his nose and drew a deep breath. Then he dropped his hand and gave Holly a long look. "Get out of his way. Let the fucker speak for himself."

Adam gently pushed Holly out of his way and stepped

up to the screen. "I know the shithole you're standing in," he told Grif, "so I'm going to give you a pass."

"I don't want a pass."

No, he wanted a fight. Adam could see that. But now wasn't the time to give him one. "When you come home, I'll give you a free shot at me."

"Oh my God," Holly said, trying to get in front of Adam again, but he kept her behind him.

"So it's already done, then," Grif said. "You've already slept with her. You slept with my sister."

Pain erupted in Adam's shoulder and he clamped a hand to it, twisting to stare at Holly. "Did you just . . . bite me?"

She sent him a smug glance before speaking to her brother. "Sorry, Grif, but you're way off base here. *I'm* the one who seduced Adam. In fact, I *made* him sleep with me. So if you want to take a swing at me when you come home for taking advantage of your friend, go for it. But I promise you, I'll swing back." She started to shut the computer, then ducked down a little and added, "love you" before letting it close.

Then she turned to Adam. He was still holding his shoulder, which was burning like fire. "Christ," he said. "You bite hard. And you hung up on your brother. He was just looking out for you."

"I don't need looking out for!" She gave him a little push, and when he didn't budge, she tossed up her hands. "You keep doing this!"

"I didn't do anything."

"Exactly!"

He stared at her. "Are you speaking English?"

She stormed away, toward the front door. There she stopped, muttering something to herself that might have been a slander on the entire male race before whirling back to him. "You know what I think, Adam? I think you're *trying* to scare me off."

"Hell yes, I'm trying to scare you off!"

She shook her head. "I let you do it once, but there's no way I'm letting it happen again."

She punctuated these words with the removal of her clothing. She kicked first one boot off and then the other. And then her jacket. And her leggings. Her sweater went next, sailing across the room, leaving her in just a black silky bra and a matching pair of barely there string-bikini panties. She was hands on hips, fully pissed off, eyes flashing, chest heaving.

Gorgeous.

"Well?" she asked. "You going to say anything?"

He shook his head, unable to tear his eyes off of her.

She blew out a breath. "I'm *really* going to need you to speak."

"Can't. You took your clothes off and my brain shut down." He strode to her, bent enough to scoop her up, and tossed her over his shoulder in a fireman's hold. Hand on her ass, he turned to his bed.

"I'm trying to talk to you!" she said, squirming.

He gave her a light smack on her very sweet ass and she squeaked in surprise. *"Hey!"*

He tossed her down to the bed, and before she'd even bounced once, he was on her, pinning her to the mattress.

Not that she was struggling anymore. Well, she *was* struggling, he realized, struggling to get closer, to rip *his* clothes off.

"If you can't think," she panted, working open his jeans, shoving them down, "does that mean we're going to . . ."

"Only if you ask real nice," he said.

Which she did. She asked, begged, pleaded, demanded . . . and in the end, she took. She took everything he had, right along with his heart.

## Twenty-three

Holly had been rising early in the mornings, taking the dogs out for her father. She'd been doing this ever since she and Adam had brought her dad home. So it was a surprise when a week later, she walked into the large ranch kitchen after a two-mile sunrise walk and found him waiting for her.

He was standing at the kitchen counter drinking coffee and staring at a big bouquet of fresh roses on the table.

"Wow, Dad. You got flowers?"

"No," he said. "You did. No card. I snooped."

Holly stared at the exquisite bouquet. She'd nearly forgotten about her other nameless delivery. "Huh."

"Adam?" her dad asked.

She'd thought so the first time she'd gotten flowers. Not only had she been wrong, she'd embarrassed herself asking him about it. But she'd seen the regret in Adam's eyes when he'd had to tell her that he hadn't sent them.

So had he sent these? It was possible, especially after the last few nights, which she'd spent in his bed, in his arms.

Panting his name . . .

"I don't know," she admitted.

Her father shook his head. "So all of the Reids suck in the romance department." He looked stronger today but still had shadows of unhappiness beneath his eyes. He'd had lots of company, but he still was missing Deanna.

"And you keep stealing my dogs," he said.

"I've been walking them for you."

"And taking them to obedience training."

"Which, by the way," she said, "they're failing."

"Only owners fail."

She did her best not to roll her eyes. "Dad, I'm just trying to help you out here."

"By treating me like an invalid? I can handle my own affairs."

"You pay me to handle your affairs for you."

"*Business* affairs, yes," he said. "Personal, no. So knock it off."

She let out a low, disbelieving laugh. "You firing me as your daughter, Dad?"

"No. Just as my nanny." He took in the look on her face and sighed. "Listen, I love having you here."

"Good. Because I love being here."

"But . . ."

She arched a brow. "But . . . ?"

Her dad poured her a cup of coffee, handed it over, and then in a rare show of affection, slung an arm around her neck. "But you need to be spending less time taking care of me and more time living your own life."

She looked at the flowers and couldn't help but feel a small ray of hope that they were from Adam. "I'm working on it."

"Work faster."

She looked at him. "Work faster? What's that supposed to mean?"

He grimaced and scrubbed a hand over his jaw.

*"Dad."*

"More coffee?"

"No. Tell me," she said.

"Derek called me."

Her heart dropped. "What? Why?"

"He said he'd been trying to communicate with you, but you haven't responded."

"He's called once or twice." She shrugged. "Texted."

Her dad nodded. "That's what he said."

"We're divorced. There's no reason for me to talk to him. Or for *you* to, either."

"Agreed," her dad said. "But he said he'd been trying to communicate with you and you hadn't responded. He played the concerned ex-husband card pretty good."

"Oh, for God's sake."

He smiled. "I think he wanted me to talk you into going back to him in New York."

Holly stared at him. "He wanted *you* to talk me into going back to him? Is he crazy?"

"That's what I asked him. I said I was *glad* you were rid of his sorry, crib-stealing, gold-digging ass—"

*"Dad."*

"And that you'd already moved on. With a better man."

"Oh my God. Dad, you didn't."

"What? Adam *is* the better man. In every way."

"I'm not with Adam."

Her father gave her a long look. "Heard you come in at three this morning. What were you doing, hanging out at the library?"

Well, hell. And actually, it had been three thirty. And the night before that, four thirty.

She had no idea what she and Adam were doing, but it had involved lots of orgasms, and her body was A-OK with that.

But actually, she knew exactly what she was doing. She knew how Adam looked at her. She knew how his touch felt, and what it meant. He was falling for her. She was just waiting for him to realize it, was all. "If Derek calls you again, please don't talk to him."

"I told him if he calls here again, I'll get a restraining order."

"I don't think you can really—"

Her dad pointed at her. "I told you from the very beginning that he was a bad idea. Didn't I tell you that?"

"So this is an 'I told you so'?"

"Hell no," he said. "It's a fix your damn problems, or I'll fix them for you."

Good Lord. What was it with the alpha men in her life? "Stay out of it, Dad."

"Hmph."

"I mean it."

He eyed her steadily with his ruthless business eyes over his hot coffee. "I will if you will."

Crap.

He nodded to his dogs. "*I'll* take them to class tonight."

"But I . . ." She trailed off when he just looked at her. "What's important here is continuity," she said. "You go only sometimes and then send Red the other times. With me going all the time, they get consistency."

"Consistency," he repeated.

"That's right. You have too much on your plate. I'm just doing what I can. You can thank me later."

"Can I," he said dryly.

"Yes." She took her coffee and escaped to the office, where she kept herself busy until lunch.

She met Kate at the bakery in town, where they sat at a tiny table and inhaled ham-and-cheese croissants, then shared a huge, fresh, warm brownie. Because everyone knew that sharing a brownie meant that the calories didn't count.

Kate looked out the window at the sleet free-falling from the sky. "If I hadn't just used the last of my meager savings to pay my sister's tuition, I'd be going to Costa Rica over winter break," she said. "I'm tired of being all work and no play. I need an adventure. A *warm* adventure."

"They have big bugs in Costa Rica," Holly said. Kate was adamantly opposed to bugs. She'd once called Holly in the middle of the night to come get the spider in her bathroom.

"Well, if there are big bugs . . ." Kate sighed. "But God, I really need to get out of Sunshine. Not all of us get to find our adventure right here, with the hottest guy this side of the Continental Divide, you know."

"You are not talking about me."

"Uh, yeah, I am." Kate used the opportunity to grab the last of the brownie. "You and Adam are doing the nasty. Bumping uglies. Getting jiggy with it—"

"Stop." Holly would have laughed, but she was horrified. "And please, for the love of God, stop watching cable TV."

"You two would make gorgeous babies, you know that? With his skin and eyes and your . . ."

Holly choked on her tea. "My *what*?"

"Sunny, sweet nature." Kate flashed a smile.

"Funny. But we're *not* having kids. The man is relationship phobic, remember? We're just . . ."

Kate's smile faded. "You're just what?"

"Taking it slow."

"Honey." Kate squeezed her hand. "Tell me that you know that you deserve everything your heart desires, whether that turns out to be a Costa Rica zip-line adventure or a diamond ring."

Holly let out a breath and her deepest, darkest fear right along with it. "But what if the very thing that my heart desires can't be had?" she whispered.

"Then, maybe," Kate said softly, gently, "it's time to take a big step back and reevaluate. Go in another direction."

Ninety percent of Holly didn't want to go in another direction. She liked *this* direction. But that last niggling ten percent could admit to wanting to shake an understandably emotionally gun-shy Adam and ask him—wasn't she worth the risk?

Adam had his hands full that night at his dog obedience class. A warm front storm had moved in, bringing rain by the buckets instead of the usual snow. It made things dangerous and had the entire county on flood watch.

He held the class in the reception area of the vet center. It was a big reception room, but things were still tight. Actually, not things. Not even the dogs, all of whom were well behaved.

It was the people.

Gayle was still having trouble being in charge. Liza spent much of the hour making a play for his attention. And then there was Holly. On the surface, she was taking the obedience training very seriously. But there was an undercurrent between them that had the air crackling around them.

When the class was over, everyone but Holly had filed out. She dallied, caught up in Thing One's and Thing Two's leashes.

Jade was still behind her desk, her fingers clicking over her keyboard with authority as she spoke quietly into her ear set on the phone, but she still managed to give Adam a jerk of her chin indicating he should go help Holly.

He did just that, moving up behind her, reaching around to grab the leashes from her.

"She wants in your pants," she said.

"Thing One?"

"Liza!"

He went brows up, then leaned in close, brushing his jaw against hers. "And here I thought it was *you* who wanted in my pants."

Bessie came in through the back, pushing her ever-present broom. She grimaced. "Gonna pretend I didn't hear that."

Holly blushed and glared at Adam as Bessie swept around their feet. The minute she moved away, Holly hissed, "And I've already been in your pants. Remember?"

He wasn't likely to ever forget. "And?"

She crossed her arms. "Are you fishing for compliments? Does the self-made, self-assured, cocky-as-hell Adam Connelly need stroking?"

"Well, I do like stroking."

She gave him a shove and he laughed.

"I'm serious," she said.

"About the stroking?" He ran a hand down her back, gratified to feel a shiver wrack her body. "God, I hope so."

"I'm serious about this class," she said, and elbowed him when his hand drifted south to her ass.

"Uh-huh."

"I am! And it's especially annoying because there are *certain* others who aren't."

"I charge an arm and a leg for the training," he said. "I'm pretty sure *everyone's* taking it seriously."

"Everyone?"

Both their gazes slid to the window. Outside in the pouring rain, Liza was loading her dog into her truck. She was in a clear rain poncho over her very interesting sweater, which had lots of cutouts. The sweater went with her high-heeled thigh-high black rubber boots. Sort of. Either she enjoyed BDSM or she was going to a costume party later as a dominatrix. She climbed into her truck, managing to flash the world what she had on under her miniskirt—a thong.

"Who wears a miniskirt to a dog training class?" Holly murmured.

"She says all the exercise during class makes her warm, so she dresses accordingly."

"Well, you gotta give her props for creativity." She paused. "I got more flowers."

He frowned. Who the hell was sending her flowers?

She took in his reaction. "And they're still not from you."

He opened his mouth, but she beat him to the punch. "No, it's okay," she said. "I don't even like flowers. I mean sure, they smell good and they're pretty and lighten up a room, but I'd rather have candy, anyway . . ."

He didn't know what to do with the embarrassment and unhappiness in her gaze—or the fact that he felt like the biggest asshole on the planet. He wished he'd thought to do the whole flowers thing, but he hadn't. "I—"

Liza popped back into the front door, surprising them both. Eyes on Adam, she smiled. "Hey there, I forgot to tell you, I've made a meat-and-five-cheese lasagna. Why don't you and Milo come over for a playdate tonight? Bring your swimsuit for the hot tub. Or . . . not."

Holly's eyes narrowed to slits, and Adam put a hand on her arm. "Sorry," he said to Liza. "I've got plans tonight."

Liza stepped closer to him, brushing her breasts against his arm. "I'm sure you remember my lasagna. It's . . . mind-*blowing*." She smiled. "You know where to find me if you change your mind."

Adam watched her walk off, and at the snort from Holly, he looked at her. "You have something to say, say it."

"You've been to her place. She cooks for you." Holly studied him, no longer pissed but very serious. "We didn't exactly discuss this, but I have to admit, I assumed that you weren't sleeping with anyone else at the moment. But we all know what assuming makes you, so . . ." She turned to go.

Adam caught her wrist. "It was over a year ago," he told her quietly. "Not too long after I first got back. She had me over for dinner, just a friend thing."

Her gaze met his. "You mean a friend with benefits."

Benefits only, no friendship, but he didn't think clarifying this was going to help his cause. "She wanted more," he said carefully. "I didn't have it to give."

Her gaze locked on his. "And now?"

"You know I still don't."

"And you don't see that changing anytime soon," she said on a slow exhalation. "I know."

Something came into her eyes then that nearly brought him to his knees. Hurt. Regret. And a bone-deep strength of character. She was going to dump him. He'd known it would come to this.

"And if you did?" she asked.

He cupped her jaw, slid his fingers into her silky hair. "You know where I'd be if I did."

"Humor me," she said. "Say it."

He let his knee nudge hers. "I'd be in your bed every night."

She stared at him for a long beat. Then her eyes softened and she turned her face so that her lips brushed his palm. "I never pegged you for being too chicken to go after what you want, Adam. But the thing is . . ."

Oh shit. Here it comes.

"*I'm* not too chicken," she said. "I know exactly what I want. I honestly thought I could do this with you, the whole friends-with-benefits thing." She slowly shook her head, her eyes suspiciously shiny. "But as it turns out, I can't. Not with you, Adam. With you, I want it all."

He felt cold inside at the thought of her walking out that door and having them go back to the way it had been, with little to no contact between them. Somehow when he hadn't been looking, she'd become one of the most important things in his life. And how the hell that had happened, he hadn't a clue. He had more people to care about in his life than he could manage already, and yet there she was. Just as vital to him as his family. "It's not that simple for me," he heard himself say.

"Of course it is. Life is as simple as you make it, Adam.

You're born. You live. You die. I don't plan on dying without doing the living part, though." She moved to the door and then glanced back at him, using Liza's words. "You know where to find me if you change your mind."

He stood there watching her walk away. He stood there until he realized he was the only one in the room, with the exception of Milo, Gertie, Peanut . . .

And Jade.

She was still on the phone, her back to him, thankfully. Otherwise she'd have been on him like white on rice. He reached for the logical portion of his brain. It wasn't as if Holly was the only woman who'd ever mattered to him.

But he could admit that she was the one who'd mattered the most. And she'd gone right to the heart of the matter. His heart.

He looked at Gertie and Milo, both sitting obediently, waiting for a command.

Well, Milo was waiting obediently for a command. Gertie flopped to the ground, rolled to her back, and exposed her belly for a rub. Adam crouched down and obliged her, his mind not on the task.

*I never pegged you for being too chicken to go after what you want . . .*

Holly's words haunted him. He wasn't afraid of much. Life had taught him early to shove his fear deep, and he'd done just that. He no longer allowed himself fear. Except, apparently, when it came to her.

And what the hell was it exactly that he was afraid of, anyway?

Tired of thinking, tired of himself, wanting only to be alone, Adam walked into his office—trailed by Milo, of course—and let out a frustrated breath.

Dell was feet up at the desk, leaning back, helping himself to Adam's laptop.

Adam shook his head. "What are you doing in here?"

"Looking at porn. I didn't want to crash my own laptop."

Adam kicked the legs of the chair. *His* chair. "Get up."

"Please. Get up, *please*."

"Get the fuck out of my chair." It mattered only minimally if Dell actually got up. Adam could feel himself spoiling for a fight. He'd be happy to escort Dell out of the chair.

Dell grinned. "Aw, look at you, pretending to be all tough and grumpy and edgy. And yet you were grinning earlier, I saw it. Now because I'm a good brother, I'm not even going to ask who put that rare expression of satisfaction on your face, but a betting man would guess that—" Dell tore his gaze off the screen and gave Adam a long once-over. "What's up?"

Saving him from replying, Milo plopped to his bed and farted audibly.

"Jesus, dog," Adam said, and had to open the window so they wouldn't suffocate.

"He's handy," Dell said. "You train him to do that on cue?" Leaning back, he studied Adam. "You fucked it up, didn't you?"

"I don't want to talk about it."

Dell sighed. "You had a grand old time watching me fall flat on my face for Jade, remember?"

"Yeah, because you were an idiot about it."

"Well, then, don't look in the mirror."

"I said we're not talking about this."

"Okay," Dell said agreeably. "But we are. Look, things have never come easy for Connellys. Hell, half the time, we made it harder on ourselves on purpose, I think."

Adam shrugged.

Dell put his feet down and leaned over the desk. "Look, we both know that everything that happened to us growing up was fucked-up. And then things didn't exactly get better for you, did they? But you're good now, you've gone through hell to find yourself again and you're good."

Adam scowled. *Why is he talking about this?* "So?"

"So . . . it seems to me that it's all smooth sailing for you, from here on out," Dell said. "All you have to do is let yourself enjoy it."

"It?"

"Life."

"I'm enjoying it plenty." He picked up the chair and dumped Dell out of it.

Dell stood up and dusted himself off. "Nice. You've been bench-pressing again."

Dell had a full gym in his basement, and they often spent time beating the shit out of each other for fun, under the guise of keeping in shape.

"You're in deep with Holly," Dell said. "Everyone can see that plain as day—except you."

Adam shoved his fingers in his hair. "This no longer applies."

"I already admitted I was a complete dumbass when it came to Jade. And I nearly messed it up, too. Remember?"

"Your point?" Adam asked.

"You were always the smarter one of the two of us, so why don't you learn from our combined mistakes and prove just how smart you are?"

# Twenty-four

An hour later, Holly stood in the big ranch kitchen at home, with only the pouring rain for company. She was making her own lasagna and thinking not-so-nice thoughts about Liza's meat-and-five-cheese lasagna. Probably Liza was a good cook and her meat-and-five-cheese lasagna was perfect, but Holly's was . . . not. First of all, she only had two cheeses.

And second of all, she didn't enjoy cooking. Eating, she enjoyed just fine. Preparing what she ate, not so much.

And third of all . . . She sighed. Third of all, she was an idiot. She should have picked something up in town or called a friend. But Kate had a date tonight from her online dating service.

Holly wondered if that would be her soon—resorting to a dating service.

Hope was a strange thing. It was easily kept in check when the very thing she hoped for was pretty much a fantasy, nothing more. But then she'd gone and allowed it to take root in her mind, telling herself it could become real.

She and Adam . . .

And hope had blossomed, taken hold . . . only to be crushed by Adam himself. It wasn't his fault. He'd been brutally forthright and honest with her. As always. The fault—the crushed hope—was all hers. Just as the hurt was.

In tune to the driving rain beating at the windows, she layered noodles, sauce, cheese, then repeated, popping a noodle into her mouth. Overcooked. Damn, she was as bad at this as she was at wearing miniskirts to stupid dog obedience training classes. She looked down at her jeans and the thigh-length oversized sweater she'd stolen from Adam the other night. She'd pilfered it because it was soft and comfy, and . . . because it smelled like him. In fact, it smelled so good she nearly had an orgasm every time she tucked her nose into it and inhaled. She shoved the pan into the oven, hoping the oven would magically fix it into something edible.

The doorbell rang, and her heart leapt with the last of her silly little hope. Adam? She rushed toward the door, but her dad beat her. "Got it," he said, and opened the door. Wind and rain blew in, along with . . .

Not Adam.

*"Deanna,"* her dad said, surprise and pleasure warring on his face at the sight of the beautiful brunette standing there wringing out her long, drenched waves. She wore skin-tight jeans, cowboy boots, and a siren red leather jacket that matched the dinner-plate-size earrings swinging from her ears. She stepped into the foyer like she owned the place and gave Donald a not-so-little shove. "How could you not tell me?"

Donald looked flummoxed, both at her bigger than life appearance and the sheer volume of water coming off her. "Tell you what?"

Deanna went hands on hips, and if she'd not been turning blue from the cold, steam would have been rising from her roots. "You haven't been feeling well."

Donald blinked at the raw, genuine emotion that broke her voice up. "You haven't been around."

She sniffed, patting down her pockets, pulling out an already soggy tissue. "I was out of town on business. Not on the moon."

"You were out of town with your boss," Donald said with that look on his face that men got when faced with a pissed-off, teary woman—*wariness*. "Thomas Pines."

"Yes. On *business*," she repeated, and sniffed again. "I told you that. I told you it was work."

"I thought it was a euphemism," Donald said.

Deanna blinked. "What's a euphemism?"

Donald shook his head and reached into the coat closet where they kept a stack of towels for the dogs. He handed one to the dripping wet Deanna. "Why are you here? You dumped me, remember?"

"Yes, well, it was just a silly fight. I'm un-dumping you," she said, gathering herself together, attempting to dry off.

It was going to take more than one towel. Donald grabbed another and began to help her. "Why would you un-dump me?"

"Why?"

"Yes, Deanna. Why?"

"That's a stupid question, Donald."

His eyes met hers, an unusual amount of emotion in his. "You're half my age. You could get a younger man, a stronger one. A better man—"

Deanna put a fuchsia-tipped finger over his mouth, then went up on tiptoe and kissed him softly. "Baby, I don't want a younger man. I want a seasoned one, who knows exactly what he's doing, one who appreciates life, who's not looking over my shoulder for the next best sweet young thing to come along, one who wants me. Just me."

"I want you," Donald said seriously. "Only you. I thought—"

"I know. I'm sorry." Earrings jangling, water still dripping from her all over the floor, she cupped his face and peered into his eyes. "Are you okay, really? Because they said—"

"They're wrong." He pulled her in against him. "We changed up the meds, and I'm going to be fine."

"But—"

"*Fine,*" he repeated with a gentleness that Holly rarely saw from him. "In fact, now that you're here, I'm going to be fantastic."

"Come home with me," Deanna whispered, leaning into him. "Let me take care of you."

"I can't. I told Holly I'd eat her . . . lasagna?" he said, looking to Holly, who nodded.

"Holly makes crappy lasagna," Deanna said, and then met Holly's gaze. "Sorry."

"It's okay," Holly said. "It's true. I make crappy lasagna. Go, Dad. I'll be fine here."

"Are you sure, honey? The storm's getting crazy and—" He broke off when Holly gave him a shoo-get-out-of-here gesture. She knew he wanted to go, and Holly got it. She really did. She'd be fine. It took more than a storm to scare her. Hell, only a week ago, she'd gone straight into one to go after his sorry ass, and they both knew it. "I'll be fine," she promised. "I'm tired and going to bed early, anyway."

Five minutes later, she'd gotten rid of the lovebirds and gone back to the kitchen to check her lasagna. Five minutes after that, the power flickered and then went out. Damn. She grabbed a flashlight from the junk drawer and was just trying to decide her next move when someone knocked on the door. This time she refused to allow her heart to take another hard leap. It wasn't Adam. It wouldn't be Adam, not after the things she'd said to him.

She was right. She peeked through the front door's peephole and went still from shock. When he knocked again, she nearly leapt right out of her skin. She hauled the door open and stared at Derek. Again, wind and rain slashed at her face, this time cooling off the heat of temper that the sight of her ex-husband brought. "What the hell are you doing here?" she asked.

"Aw. I've missed you, too." He started to come in but Holly blocked him.

"Hell no," she said. He was tall, built, and dressed to impress. He was as drenched as Deanna had been but still somehow managed to look like a million bucks in his New York–sophisticated raincoat, long and slick, collar up.

Two million when he smiled, which he did now. "Aren't you going to let me in?"

"No."

He let out a long breath. "Holly." His voice was low, and he tried the sad eyes—an oft-used trick in his How to Screw Women Over repertoire. "Please," he said.

Once upon a time, he'd been her everything, and she'd been unable to refuse him a single thing, especially when he'd used the soft, coaxing, I'm-so-sexy "please." But she was done letting a man be her everything. Maybe earlier tonight she'd have said otherwise, that she had room in her heart to try again, but Adam had crushed that.

"I only need a minute," Derek promised, shoving the wet hair off his forehead, a gesture of frustration that at one time would have melted her and made her want to stroke that hair from his eyes herself. There was a very good reason the man had been able to charm the panties off her— and every other coed he'd gone after: he was smooth as whiskey.

"No," she said.

"Holly—"

"*No.*" Tired of getting wet, she shut the door in his face, brushing off her hands as if to rid them of unwanted dirt.

That had felt good. Really good. Pivoting, she headed back through the dark house to the kitchen. There she lit a bunch of candles and hoped the lasagna was done. Stuffing her face would be infinitely better than giving too much thought to her life and how she kept screwing it up.

She'd always gone with the flow of the tide, never fighting the current. She'd taken the path of least resistance but no more. Seeing Derek reminded her that she'd come back here to Sunshine to get over herself. To live in the moment. She was determined to follow her own path, to be herself. At first she honestly hadn't known who she might be, but she was getting a handle on that now. She was strong, tough, and—shocking even herself—very able and willing to love in spite of being burned. She had plenty to offer a man, and she wouldn't change for anyone.

And yet . . . and yet she'd wanted Adam to change for her. She wanted him to let her in, to want what *she* wanted— a real relationship.

Which made her a hypocrite. At the realization, her stomach clenched. She was no better than . . . "Derek," she said in surprise as he walked right into the kitchen like he owned the place. "How did you—"

"You've been out of New York too long—you didn't lock the front door."

"That doesn't mean you can walk right on in!"

He looked around with a curiosity he'd never shown when they'd been married. He'd never once come home with her, hadn't shown the slightest interest. "We need to talk," he said.

"Oh, for God's sake." Leaning against the kitchen counter, she picked up a fork and started eating the lasagna right from the pan. At her first bite she grimaced, because Deanna was right, her lasagna was crappy. She pushed the pan aside and sighed. "Fine. Talk."

Derek opened his mouth but paused when a gale of wind battered at the windows. He glanced at them uneasily. "I've never seen wind like this."

"Yes, well, welcome to winter in the Bitterroots."

He eyed the open-beamed ceiling above them as if

worried the entire thing was about to come down on them. "Are we safe here?"

"If I say no, will you leave?"

He made a sound of regret. "I'm sorry, Holly. So damn sorry." Born and raised in Texas before he'd remade himself into New York suave, he let the drawl drip into his voice now. "I was such an ass. Please say you'll come back to me. Say you'll be mine again."

"I haven't been yours in years." She shook her head. "And this doesn't make any sense to me, your sudden play at the doting husband. What's really going on here?"

"We were good together." He moved toward her, turning on the bedroom eyes. "Don't you remember?"

"I do remember," she agreed. "I remember being very happy with you, all the way up until the day your cute little fall-semester TA came to the door, sobbing that you'd broken her heart the night before when you'd left her for your brand-new cute little spring-semester TA."

He sighed. "Well, if you're going to hold a grudge."

Another gust of wind rattled the windows, and Holly shook her head. "You're on the sixty-second countdown, Derek. Get to your point."

"Okay," he said, dropping the good-old-boy act as he came toe-to-toe with her, holding his hands out as if entreating her to really hear him. "I screwed up. I did. But I can make it right."

"No, you can't," she said, backing up into the counter. He was too close, making her feel claustrophobic in the dark kitchen, with only the flickering candles for light.

"Don't," he said softly, not giving her the space she needed. "Don't push me away. We can work all this out, babe. I know I let you down, but I can be the right man. I can be whatever you need. Did you like the flowers I've sent?"

She went still. "They were from you?"

"Well, of course. Who did you think?"

Holly let out a low laugh, shaking her head at her own stupidity as she rubbed her temples.

He pulled her hands from her face. "We can do this, Holly. We can make this work. Just come back with me."

Yanking her hands free, she pushed him. "What's with this sudden need to have me back in New York? What aren't you telling me?"

Something shifted in his eyes. Something that looked suspiciously like guilt.

"Dammit, Derek. Just tell me. Tell me why after years of not giving a shit, you're suddenly sending flowers, spending money to appeal the divorce, flying across the country to see me."

He looked at her for a long moment, then let out a long breath. "Okay, fine. Apparently some word of my . . . indiscretions has leaked out."

She crossed her arms. "And?"

"And it's distinctly frowned on for a professor to sleep with his TA."

"Imagine that."

"Hey," he said stiffly. "It's not like I'm sleeping with my actual students. They're TAs. And they come on to me."

"Uh-huh. And now your reputation's on the line."

He opened his mouth but was interrupted by a knock at the door. She made a move to go get it, but Derek stepped into her, blocking her between him and the counter. "Let it go," he said. "We're not done."

"Oh, we're done." Holly tried to shove past him, but he held her trapped.

"I need you, Holly."

"No, you need someone to put the illusion back together so you can fix your precious reputation. That's not going to be me, Derek. Surely you know that."

"It has to be you." He tightened his grip on her. "I told the review board that we were reconciling."

This momentarily shocked her into immobility. "Oh my God. You have a *case*? You're in *that* much trouble?"

"You have to fix this for me," he said, the façade dropped, replaced with sheer desperation.

The knock came again. Again, she moved to go but Derek pushed her against the countertop, which bit into her back. "Holly—"

"Get your hands off me," she said tightly. "Now."

Instead, he dipped his head, nuzzling at her neck. "We can make this work if we want it enough."

This was true—anything could work if it was wanted enough. Look at her dad and Deanna. Or Kate, going after her own happiness. Even Adam knew how to make things work for him, and she'd been wrong to push for more just because that was what *she* wanted. "You're right Derek, but I don't want it, not with you."

"Holly—"

"No, Derek. I don't love you. You can't make someone love you the way you want to be loved, no matter how badly you want it to be so. Trust me, I know."

He stared at her. "There's someone else. You love someone else."

"Yes, I love someone else. And to be honest, I always have." Again, she shoved at him, but he couldn't be budged. His fingers were digging into her arms hard enough to leave bruises and the counter was hurting her, and for the first time, she began to get scared. "Let me go, Derek."

"No. You're mine."

Wrong. So wrong. Furious at him, at the situation, she simply reacted—with her knee to his crotch, dropping him to the ground like a sack of wet concrete. Holly whirled to run out of the kitchen and gasped.

Adam stood in the doorway, soaked to the skin, eyes hard and cold, body tense. Milo was at his side, alert, his fur standing straight up at his neck, eyes on Derek.

But it was what was in Adam's hands that caught Holly's attention—a bouquet of wildflowers. They were dripping water like he was, a wonderfully brilliant rainbow of colors that were so beautiful it only further infuriated her because it mocked romance. It mocked her divorce. It mocked everything she was feeling in that moment, which explained her juvenile reaction. She snatched the bouquet from Adam's hands and whirled on Derek. "Are you kidding me? More stupid flowers? What is this, a bad romantic comedy?" She threw the bouquet at Derek's feet and stomped on them.

"I . . . didn't send those," Derek said through clenched teeth, still cupping his family jewels.

Oh God. Holly turned back to Adam.

"You okay?" he asked, voice low and calm enough to get past the adrenaline rushing her system.

Was she okay? Her answer depended entirely on how long he'd been standing there and what he'd heard. Her mind raced backward, trying to remember exactly what she'd said. *You can't make someone love you the way you want to be loved . . . Trust me, I know . . . I love someone else. And to be honest, I always have . . .*

Oh God. She had to figure by the light of barely banked anger in Adam's eyes that he'd heard it all, every bit of her dirty little secret. Embarrassed, horrified, she kept moving, grabbing her purse, leaving both men in the kitchen as she made for the door.

She ran out into the night, into the rain. It didn't seem so bad now. Or maybe that was just compared to the storm brewing inside the kitchen. She thought she heard Adam call her name, but she kept going. She jumped into her Jeep, slamming and locking the door as she pulled out of the driveway. She was on the street before it occurred to her that leaving Derek and Adam alone might not be such a smart idea.

She didn't care. She turned her concentration to the road because the night was pitch-black. No city lights, no streetlights, nothing but the slick roads.

And the wind beating at her Jeep.

The rain seemed to amp up now, viciously slashing at the windshield, and she began to doubt her sanity for leaving the relative safety of her house. She debated turning around, but at this point Kate's place was just as close. If she was home . . . Since the last thing Holly wanted to do was be the stupid chick who drove off the road trying to get to her phone, she pulled over to fumble through her purse. When her fingers closed around it, she made a sound of relief that was short-lived.

Low battery.

Damn stupid smartphone, with only enough battery to get her three-quarters through a normal day. What the hell was wrong with technology? "Please work," she said, and hit Kate's number, sagging with relief when she answered. "Hey, you're home."

"Yeah, got a sick brother acting like a baby."

"How does an ice-cream pity party sound?"

"Perfect," Kate said. "On a night like this, we need something hot to go with it. I'll heat the fudge. Be care—"

The phone died. Holly tossed it aside and carefully pulled back onto the road. The *isolated* road, with no other cars in sight.

Driving straight into a storm.

Seemed she was the stupid chick, after all.

The road was slick, the water flowing across it in sheets now, past the rails on her right, down the embankment to the river rushing below. She slowed down, way down, not wanting to be a statistic. It happened out here all the time. The people of Sunshine were a hardy bunch, but they also thought they were invincible.

She did *not* think she was invincible. She had a healthy sense of preservation and a will to live for that ice-cream pity party with Kate, so she slowed down even more. She crossed the bridge—the one that washed out every few years at flood time—and gulped in relief when she got over it. Another gust of wind hit and she fought the steering wheel as she headed into the next hairpin turn. In spite of her low speed, the Jeep slid, and both right tires rolled off the edge of the asphalt. She jerked on the wheel but her tires didn't respond. Adam's words flashed in her head.

*Steer into the slide . . .*

She could hear him plain as day in that low, authoritative voice. But before she could do that, there was a loud POP— her tire, she thought—and her Jeep hit the railing. The railing broke. She screamed as she went airborne off the ice-slicked surface and over the embankment.

# Twenty-five

Adam heard the front door slam signifying Holly's departure, and it galvanized him into action. He strode across the kitchen floor and squatted before the man curled in a ball on the tile floor, still clutching his gonads. "Derek?"

The guy wheezed and nodded.

"You all right?" Adam asked.

Derek let out a shuddery breath. "I think so."

"That's too bad."

Derek's eyes flew to Adam's face. "Who the fuck are you?"

Adam was tempted to say "your worst fucking nightmare," but he didn't want to sound like a bad movie line. "You touch her?"

"She's my wife."

Adam grabbed Derek by the front of his shirt and pulled him up, possibly banging the back of his head on the cabinet just a little bit.

"Hey, man, watch it."

Adam did it again, harder.

"Ow, Jesus! What's your problem?"

"You," Adam said. "You're my problem. You're still worked up over the divorce?"

"Yes."

"Wrong answer."

"You threatening me?" Derek asked.

Adam got a little closer, and this time when Derek's head banged into the cabinet, it was his own doing as he tried to move back.

"You're the guy," Derek said slowly. "The one she loves."

Against all odds and disbelief, yeah. He was. He'd never been worthy of that love, but he was going to work on that.

"Did you know she was coming off a long-term relationship when you took up with her?" Derek asked.

Adam purposely took his hands off Derek so he wouldn't be tempted to strangle him. "You want to talk? Let's talk about what a college professor was doing hooking up with a vulnerable nineteen-year-old."

Derek swallowed but didn't look away.

"Drop the appeal," Adam said. He rose and headed for the door.

The storm had intensified, but he was already drenched, anyway. He started toward his truck.

Holly was long gone already. Not surprising. He'd seen her expression when she'd turned to him. Embarrassment, and hurt, which killed him. He pulled out his cell and called her, but he went right to voice mail.

He had no idea where to look for her. He called Dell. "Where would a really pissed-off woman go?"

"You're asking me?"

"You're with Jade, and I figure you piss her off daily, so yeah, I'm asking you."

Dell let out a breath. "Jade wouldn't go anywhere—she'd stay and kick my ass."

"Not helping."

"Holly, right?"

"No, the Tooth Fairy."

Dell laughed softly. "Okay, so you pissed her off and she stormed out. Give her some space. Then grovel. She's a hell of a good woman, and she's worth a little time on your knees."

Adam hung up. Fuck space. He'd given her enough space over the years. He was done with space.

But most of all, he was done holding back how he felt about her. He'd long ago learned to shelve his emotions, long before he met her, in fact. No amount of training could have prepared him for her, and no one could have told him that he would be brought to his knees by a woman.

But that's what she'd done, brought him straight to his knees.

He'd always told himself that there was a better man for her, and that man wasn't him. Even though deep down inside he'd wanted to believe that he was the only man for her.

She'd believed it all along, and he finally believed it, too.

All he had to do was find her and tell her he'd caught up. He told himself this, knowing it wasn't going to be that simple, nothing with her ever was. He drove out into the storm, figuring he'd take the only road into town and wing it once he got there.

One hundred yards later he was thinking he was insane to be out in this. And so was Holly. The road was an exercise in concentration, and a disaster waiting to happen. Deeply concerned for Holly, he crossed the bridge, then hydroplaned on the next curve, swearing viciously when he saw the broken rail.

It hadn't been broken on his way here, which meant that it had just happened.

A car had gone over.

He called 911 and then pulled to the side of the road. Grabbing his Maglite, he hit the ground running, the storm beating at him. At the broken rail, he flicked the light below, trying to take in what he was seeing. The riverbanks had flooded, and Jesus Christ, there was a car at the bottom of the embankment, nose in, the water rising toward the doors. An old memory nearly knocked him to his knees. That long-ago night, drag racing, watching the cop car skid out and go over the embankment . . .

Fuck.

He didn't see anyone moving around, but he needed to get down there for what would hopefully be a rescue and not a recovery. It would take emergency responders at least twenty minutes to get here. But whoever was in that car didn't have twenty minutes.

He ran back to his truck for rope, tying one end around a sturdy tree at the top of the embankment, the other around his waist. Two cars had driven by him and not even slowed. He was on his own. No Kel, no Milo, no anyone but his own wits, which were weak at best.

He rappelled down the bank. Normally the river would be at his knees, but tonight it was raging and about to take the vehicle into its greedy grasp. Closer now, he shined the light on it and his heart stopped.

Holly.

Holly opened her eyes and panicked. She couldn't breathe. She couldn't move, couldn't see. Disoriented, confused, she couldn't even tell which way was up or down. She was reaching out, trying to feel around when she saw a shadow move outside her Jeep. She flinched with instinctive fear, but that was quickly replaced with knee-melting relief because it was a man, and he had a flashlight. He flicked the light inside her vehicle and she realized her Jeep was nose down, her seat belt holding her suspended between the seat and steering wheel. Water was swirling around her, filling up the interior of the Jeep.

"You okay?" the man yelled through the wind and slashing rain.

Holly jerked in stunned disbelief because either she was hallucinating or it was the one man she didn't want to see right now. "Adam?"

He knocked on the window. "Unlock your door."

She blinked and took better stock. She was still having trouble breathing, no doubt because she was hanging from her seat belt, the nylon cutting into her chest. Water was filling the Jeep at an alarming rate as she fumbled for the door lock control—but it was underwater and she couldn't find it. Straining forward, she ran her hands beneath the surface of the water over the slippery controls on the door and accidentally dunked herself. "I can't—" She choked on fear. "It won't unlock!"

"All right, it's okay." His voice was calm, suggesting that this was no problem at all. "I'll come to you."

But then he was gone from her view.

Her head was pounding and her eyes drifted shut. She shivered and tried to be patient but panic gripped her. "Adam!"

"I'm not going anywhere without you, Holly, I promise." His voice came disembodied in the dark. "Cover your head with your arms."

When she'd done so, he smashed in the back window with his flashlight. He jabbed at the glass with the butt of his flashlight until it was clear and reached in for her. "Take my hand."

"I can't reach you. I . . ." She fought her seat belt but still couldn't get free. And the water was rising. She choked on another mouthful and coughed. The next thing she knew, Adam, water running down his face in rivulets, was inside the Jeep with her. "Why are you here?" she murmured, heart tight.

Or maybe that was the seat belt, still cutting off her circulation.

His eyes locked on hers. "For you."

In all his big, bad, pissed-off glory. His jaw was tight, his eyes glittering with some emotion she couldn't even begin to decipher. But he was steady as a rock as he reached for her.

"I'm stuck."

He came up with a knife. The blade glinted in the air as it sliced through the seat belt and then she was in his arms. He hauled her out through the back window just as the river swallowed up the Jeep.

On solid ground, he ran his hands over her, assessing for damage.

"I'm not hurt," she gasped.

That wasn't true, and they both knew it. She had a gash above one eye that was bleeding, and her ribs were killing her—proven when Adam pulled her into him, his arms closing tight and hard around her, holding her close. She felt a fine tremor go through him, and her heart squeezed at the realization that he'd jumped into yet another rescue— for her. "You should have waited for your team."

He shook his head. "It's not that. It's you— Christ, Holly, I was almost too late."

She pulled back and looked into his face. His usual calm was shattered, and in that one brief second, she could see every emotional wall he'd constructed come tumbling down. His gaze was eating up the sight of her, the lines around his eyes and mouth drawn tight. She put a hand to her aching head and tried to take it all in but she was having trouble putting thoughts together. "I want you to know, my driving like a so-called granny was a good thing tonight. How did you even find me?"

"The broken rail. I saw it and knew someone had gone over."

Someone. He hadn't even known it was her and he'd stopped. Fate, pretty much hand-delivering him to her. Made sense. Fate had always had a sense of humor when it came to their relationship.

He pulled off his jacket, then his T-shirt, which he balled

up. Pulling her hand from her head, he pressed the cotton to her forehead over her right eye, making her wince. "Hold still," he said. "You should have waited for me—"

Oh, that's right. She was pissed off at the entire male race. She'd almost forgotten. "I didn't want to be with you," she said, pulling back. "I wanted to be alone."

"In this storm? Jesus, Holly, if I hadn't come along—" He broke off and tried pulling her into him again, but she fought him and then slipped on the wet embankment and went down in the mud and sleet.

"Godammit." Squatting before her, he put his hands on her arms and held her still. "You're bleeding. You need to calm down—"

*"Calm down?"* She pulled free. "You heard things I didn't want you to hear! And then when I went over the edge, I thought I was going to die before I got to tell you how mad I was at you for eavesdropping!"

"I wasn't eavesdropping. You didn't answer the door and I was worried."

"No one stopped," she repeated, suddenly exhausted. Dizzy. Shaking. She closed her eyes and dropped her forehead to his chest. "Except the one person I *didn't* want to stop . . ."

Then she horrified the both of them by bursting into tears.

"Ah, Holly. It's okay." He hauled her up into his arms. "It's going to be okay."

"No, it's not. You saw me at my worst," she said soggily into his shirt. "And you brought me flowers, which I accidentally stepped on!"

"Accidentally?"

She began to cry harder, unable to stop. It hurt her head, as did her chattering teeth.

"Holly. Holly, listen to me." His hands were on her arms and he ducked down a little to make sure they were eye to bloody eye. "I'll buy you more flowers. I'll buy you all the damn flowers you want, in the entire town, in all the land. Just please, God, stop crying." His voice dropped, his hands softened. "And besides, you've seen me at my utter worst, too, remember? You saw me in that cave. You saw me completely lose it. That didn't seem to change how you felt about me, so how can you possibly think I'd judge you?"

She stared up at him while he stroked her matted hair from her face. He looked at her injury, grimaced, and pressed his T-shirt back against it.

She winced and tried to back away, but he tightened his grip. "Oh, hell no," he said. "I'm not letting you go, not ever again."

"Ever?" She sniffed. "You don't do ever, remember?"

"We'll talk about this after I get you to the hospital."

"You don't do talk, either."

He dropped his head to his chest, and then looked at her. "That was me being that chicken you accused me of being," he said. "I'm sorry, Holly. So fucking sorry. I'll straighten my ass up, but I'm going to need help. I'm going to need to learn how to share more of myself with you."

She ignored the apocalyptic moment of an Adam apology for a moment to concentrate on the prize in that statement. "*All* of you," she said. "You have to share all of you—the good *and* the bad."

"Yes, but only if you do it, too."

She pressed her face into the crook of his neck and nodded, smearing blood, tears, and rainwater on him.

"Did you just snot me?"

She let out a watery laugh and nodded.

"Just checking," he said, and because she was shivering, quite violently now, he pulled her in close. "Time to get you up the embankment, Holly, and then warm and dry."

Her limbs were boneless, she could barely control them. Shock, she figured, and it was damn annoying. "How are we going to get up there? I'm tired . . ."

"No problem. I've got you."

He might be the most stubborn man she knew, but he was also the best man she knew. If he said he had her, he had her. She managed a weak smile. "I owe you."

"I like the sound of that." He wrapped her up in one strong arm and used his rope to begin to pull them up the embankment, just as, from above, flashing lights approached.

The cavalry had come.

# Twenty-six

When Holly woke the next morning, it was still dark. She could see Adam asleep in the chair by her bed, head resting on his hand, long legs sprawled out. When she struggled to sit up, he came instantly awake. Standing up, he moved to her bed. "Hey."

"Hey." After getting her up the embankment, Adam had called her dad and Kate, who'd met them at the hospital. Holly had been cleaned up, poked, prodded, and x-rayed. Her ribs were bruised, she'd received four stitches above her eye—which was also black and blue by now—and she had a mild concussion.

But she'd slept in her own bed.

"How do you feel?" Adam asked.

She had little men jackhammering in her head and her ribs felt like she'd gone ten rounds in the ring, but she was breathing. Breathing was good. "Like I drove over an embankment."

"Your head hurt?"

"No."

His eyes smiled, but not his mouth. "Liar."

She scooted over and he sat on the bed facing her, a hand on either side of her hips, his gaze running over her as if reassuring himself she was in one piece.

"I'm okay." She touched her bandage. "Just a little bump."

He drew a deep breath, his eyes never leaving hers. "Then you're right, you *are* okay, since you've got the hardest head of anyone I know."

He was the same solid, warm presence he'd been last night. The same solid presence he'd always been, with several days of stubble on his face, making him appear even darker, more dangerous.

At least to her heart.

Looking into his eyes, she could see how tired he was, but she saw something else, too. Lifting her hand, she cupped his jaw. "Did you sleep?"

"Not yet. Your dad went into town to get some food. He'll be back in an hour, and then I'll get some sleep." He turned his face and pressed his mouth to her palm. "We need to talk, Holly."

Her stomach dropped. "Are you sure?"

"Yes."

She closed her eyes. Because that made it so much better. "About?"

"Relationship etiquette."

Her eyes flew open. "Relationship etiquette?"

"Yeah. See, when you're in a relationship, you charge your cell phone so that the person that you're in the relationship with doesn't have heart failure when he knows something has gone FUBAR and can't get ahold of you."

She must have hit her head harder than she thought. "What?"

"FUBAR. Fucked-up beyond all recognition."

"I know what FUBAR means," she said. "I'm stunned

over the word *relationship* coming from your mouth. We have a relationship?"

"We have a relationship." He didn't exactly sound thrilled about it, either. He pushed her hair from her face and eyed the bandage on her head, mouth grim. "Not that we seem to have any control over it."

And, oh, how he hated that. Anything that wrestled precious control away from him was a cause for concern. Her warrior didn't like to be vulnerable. "I scared you," she said softly.

"Took at least ten years off," he admitted.

She pulled him down to her, cupped his face, and kissed him. His lips were soft, a sharp contrast to the hardness of his body. He let her have her way with him for a minute, but when she tried to tug him over the top of her, he resisted. "No," he said. "You're hurt."

"Either come down here or I'm going to get up and climb you like a tree."

"Holly." He lay alongside her on the bed, his hands gentle. But she didn't want gentle. She bit his lower lip.

He responded without hesitation, deepening the connection, devouring her mouth with his.

Wanting even more, she again tried to pull him over her, but he shook his head.

"I won't hurt you," he said, voice thick.

She slid her hands into the back of his jeans and rocked him into her. "You won't."

He groaned once and then again when she sucked on his neck while attempting to work his shirt up and off. He lent his hands to the cause, tugging it over his head.

"Now mine," she demanded.

"Holly."

Oh, hell no. "You can't say we're a bad idea anymore. Because you're here, Adam."

"I am." He came over the top of her, supporting his

weight on his forearms. His fingers slid into her hair and he lowered his head to brush his lips over the bandage covering her stitches. "I'm here."

"Why?"

He shook his head. "You know why."

"Humor me."

Quiet now, he ran his thumb over her jaw, then he swallowed hard. "When I saw your Jeep trapped in the river, with the water filling up the interior . . . I thought I'd lost you. I thought I'd lost my chance to tell you how I feel and that I'd have to live with the regret for the rest of my life."

She felt his words all the way to her heart. "You didn't lose me. You saved me."

"Luck." He shook his head again. "I can get through almost anything, and have. But losing you isn't something I'd be able to get through. I'm crazy about you, Holly. You've worked your way under my skin." He closed his eyes. "Into my heart."

She pulled him down and softly caressed his mouth with hers. "You love me," she whispered, not quite successfully keeping the triumph out of her voice.

He choked out a laugh. "I do. I love you. I think I always have."

"Show me."

His gaze darkened. "Your injuries—"

"You won't hurt me."

He stripped her out of her pj bottoms with little effort. "Don't even think about moving," he commanded. "Not your ribs. Not a muscle." He stared at her until she nodded with a secret thrill that his simple male strength could both arouse and protect her.

In the blink of an eye he had his jeans off and then spent long moments kissing every inch of her, and some inches twice. When she'd shuddered and cried out his name, he made himself at home between her wet thighs.

The sure and solid weight of his body was as comforting as it was arousing.

Holding her gaze, he entered her. She cried out again, unable to help herself. Still panting for breath, she watched as he dropped his head, taking in the sight of them joined, then lifted his head and met her gaze again. She tried to see herself as he must. Hair wild. No makeup. A black eye . . .

"You are so fucking beautiful," he whispered hoarsely, one hand sliding up her back to cup her head, his touch gentle and sure, tempered by his care of her injuries. "And you're mine now."

"Always have been." She struggled not to rock up into him like she wanted to do. "And you're mine now?"

"Always have been." Holding her gaze, he began to move. It was heaven. He'd had her every way she could have imagined, and every time felt like the first.

The thought took her over the edge, and she took him with her. After, still breathing hard, he lifted his head, his gaze searching hers. She put her fingers over his lips to still any questions of her comfort, because in truth she'd never felt better. Sated male satisfaction lit his eyes and they lay together, waiting for their heart rates to return to some semblance of normal. "I waited a long time for you," she finally said.

"I know." He wrapped his arms around her and buried his face between her breasts. "Turns out I'm a little slow on the uptake." He breathed her in deeply—taking comfort from her, she realized, her heart swelling. He'd never allowed himself to take comfort from her before, but he did now.

"Sometimes I think about my life before I let you in," he said. "I was afraid that loving anyone this much would make me weak."

"So I take it since you've dropped the *l*-bomb, you're longer worried about that?" she teased.

His arms tightened. He wasn't playing. "I'm going to drop more than the *l*-bomb, Holly. I want you. The forever kind of want. No more messing around."

*Forever*. The air left her lungs, and something new replaced it. Hope. Affection. And a love that warmed her from the inside out. He had a way of erasing all her doubts, of reinstating her confidence. He could make everything right in her world with one word, a touch. She hadn't been sure a man could do that for her, but he did, and she thought maybe he was offering to do it for the rest of her life, but she had to be sure. She'd been wrong before and couldn't bear to be wrong now. "Maybe you should define forever."

"Is there more than one meaning for the word?" he asked.

"So . . . you mean forever like a diamond ring and white picket fence, that kind of forever?"

"Yes. But not white picket," he said with a head shake. "Rail-horse fencing."

She just stared at him. "Let me get this straight," she said. "You went from worrying about being weak to wanting a fence with me?"

"I don't give a flying fuck about being weak. You're the only thing I care about. You make me whole. You make me feel. You make me . . ." He searched for the word. "Everything." He pulled her tighter to him. "It's always been you, Holly. And it always will be. Say yes."

"Yes," she said instantly. "To everything."

*Dear Readers,*

*Hi there! I hope you all enjoyed* Rescue My Heart. *I wanted to thank each and every one of you who wrote me begging/ pleading/demanding for Adam's story over the past year. I had so much fun torturing—er, writing—his and Holly's long, passionate, windy road to their happily-ever-after.*

*So what's next? Well, I was thinking Griffin and Kate should get a story. I'm going to start their book at Adam and Holly's wedding. I plan to bring Griffin home on leave for the festivities and torture him a little bit with the one girl he's always secretly dreamed of but never dared to have. Their story will be coming your way in August 2013.*

*In the meantime, if you haven't already read* Animal Magnetism *and* Animal Attraction, Brady's *and* Dell's *stories of finding happily-ever-after with a special woman, why not? To entice you, here's an excerpt from* Animal Magnetism, *the first book in the series.*

*Happy Reading!*
*Jill Shalvis*
*www.jillshalvis.com*
*facebook.com/jillshalvis*

One

~~~

Brady Miller's ideal Saturday was pretty simple—sleep in, be woken by a hot, naked woman for sex, followed by a breakfast that he didn't have to cook.

On this particularly early June Saturday, he consoled himself with one out of the three, stopping at 7-Eleven for coffee, two egg and sausage breakfast wraps, and a Snickers bar.

Breakfast of champions.

Heading to the counter to check out, he nodded to the convenience store clerk.

She had her Bluetooth in her ear, presumably connected to the cell phone glowing in her pocket as she rang him up. "He can't help it, Kim," she was saying. "He's a *guy*." At this, she sent Brady a half-apologetic, half-commiserating smile. She was twentysomething, wearing spray-painted-on skinny jeans, a white wife-beater tank top revealing black lacy bra straps, and so much mascara that Brady had no idea how she kept her eyes open.

"You know what they say," she went on as she scanned

his items. "A guy thinks about sex once every eight seconds. No, it's true, I read it in *Cosmo*. Uh-huh, hang on." She glanced at Brady, pursing her glossy lips. "Hey, cutie, you're a guy."

"Last I checked."

She popped her gum and grinned at him. "Would you say you think about sex every eight seconds?"

"Nah." Every ten, tops. He fished through his pocket for cash.

"My customer says no," she said into her phone, sounding disappointed. "But *Cosmo* said a man might deny it out of self-preservation. And in any case, how can you trust a guy who has sex on the brain 24/7?"

Brady nodded to the truth of that statement and accepted his change. Gathering his breakfast, he stepped outside where he was hit by the morning fresh air of the rugged, majestic Idaho Bitterroot mountain range. Quite a change from the stifling airlessness of the Middle East or the bitter desolation and frigid temps of Afghanistan. But being back on friendly soil was new enough that his eyes still automatically swept his immediate surroundings.

*Always a soldier,* his last girlfriend had complained.

And that was probably true. It was who he was, the discipline and carefulness deeply engrained, and he didn't see that changing anytime soon. Noting nothing that required his immediate attention, he went back to mainlining his caffeine. Sighing in sheer pleasure, he took a big bite of the first breakfast wrap, then hissed out a sharp breath because damn. *Hot.* This didn't slow him down much. He was so hungry his legs felt hollow. In spite of the threat of scalding his tongue to the roof of his mouth, he sucked down nearly the entire thing before he began to relax.

Traffic was nonexistent, but Sunshine, Idaho, wasn't exactly hopping. It'd been a damn long time since he'd been here, *years* in fact. And longer still since he'd wanted to be here. He took another drag of fresh air. Hard to believe, but he'd actually missed the good old US of A. He'd missed the sports. He'd missed the women. He'd missed the price of gas. He'd missed free will.

But mostly he'd missed the food. He tossed the wrapper from the first breakfast wrap into a trash bin and started in on his second, feeling almost . . . content. Yeah, damn it was good to be back, even if he was only here temporarily, as a favor. Hell, anything without third-world starvation, terrorists, or snipers and bombs would be a five-star vacation.

"Look out, incoming!"

At the warning, Brady deftly stepped out of the path of the bike barreling down at him.

"Sorry!" the kid yelled back.

Up until yesterday, a shout like that would have meant dropping to the ground, covering his head, and hoping for the best. Since there were no enemy insurgents, Brady merely raised the hand still gripping his coffee in a friendly salute. "No problem."

But the kid was already long gone, and Brady shook his head. The quiet was amazing, and he took in the oak tree–lined sidewalks, the clean and neat little shops, galleries and cafés—all designed to bring in some tourist money to subsidize the mining and ranching community. For someone who'd spent so much time in places where grime and suffering trumped hope and joy, it felt a little bit like landing in the Twilight Zone.

"Easy now, Duchess."

At the soft, feminine voice, Brady turned and looked into the eyes of a woman walking a . . . hell, he had no idea. The thing pranced around like it had a stick up its ass.

Okay, a dog. He was pretty sure.

The woman smiled at Brady. "Hello, how are you?"

"Fine, thanks," he responded automatically, but she hadn't slowed her pace.

*Just being polite,* he thought, and tried to remember the concept. Culture shock, he decided. He was suffering from a hell of a culture shock. Probably he should have given himself some time to adjust before doing this, before coming here of all places, but it was too late now.

Besides, he'd put it off long enough. He'd been asked to come, multiple times over the years. He'd employed every tactic at his disposal: avoiding, evading, ignoring, but nothing worked with the two people on the planet more stubborn than him.

His brothers.

Not blood brothers, but that didn't appear to matter to Dell or Adam. The three of them had been in the same foster home for two years about a million years ago. Twenty-four months. A blink of an eye really. But to Dell and Adam, it'd been enough to bond the three of them for life.

Brady stuffed in another bite of his second breakfast wrap, added coffee, and squinted in the bright June sunshine. Jerking his chin down, the sunglasses on top of his head obligingly slipped to his nose.

Better.

He headed to his truck parked at the corner but stopped short just in time to watch a woman in an old Jeep rear-end it.

"Crap. *Crap.*" Lilah Young stared at the truck she'd just rear-ended and gave herself exactly two seconds to have a pity party. This is what her life had come to. She had to work in increments of seconds.

A wet, warm tongue laved her hand and she looked over at the three wriggling little bodies in the box on the passenger's seat of her Jeep.

Two puppies and a potbellied pig.

As the co-owner of the sole kennel in town, she was babysitting Mrs. Swanson's "babies" again today, which included pickup and drop-off services. This was in part because Mrs. Swanson was married to the doctor who'd delivered Lilah twenty-eight years ago, but also because Mrs. Swanson was the mother of Lilah's favorite ex-boyfriend.

Not that Lilah had a lot of exes. Only two.

Okay, three. But one of them didn't count, the one who after four years she *still* hoped all of his good parts shriveled up and fell off. And he'd had good parts, too, damn him. She'd read somewhere that every woman got a freebie stupid mistake when it came to men. She liked that. She only wished it applied to everything in life.

Because driving with Mrs. Swanson's babies and—

"Quack-quack!" said the mallard duck loose in the backseat.

—A mallard duck loose in the backseat had been a doozy of a mistake.

Resisting the urge to thunk her head against the steering wheel, Lilah hopped out of the Jeep to check the damage she'd caused to the truck, eyes squinted because everyone knew that helped.

The truck's bumper sported a sizable dent and crack, but thanks to the tow hitch, there was no real obvious frame damage. The realization brought a rush of relief so great her knees wobbled.

That is until she caught sight of the front of her Jeep. It was so ancient that it was hard to tell if it had ever really been red once upon a time or if it was just one big friggin' rust bucket, but that no longer seemed important given that her front end was mashed up.

"Quack-quack." In the backseat, Abigail was flapping her wings, getting enough lift to stick her head out the window.

Lilah put her hand on the duck's face and gently pressed her back inside. "Stay."

"Quack—"

*"Stay."* Wanting to make sure the Jeep would start before she began the task of either looking for the truck's owner or leaving a note, Lilah hopped behind the wheel.

She never should have turned off the engine because her starter had been trying to die for several weeks now. She'd be lucky to get it running again. Beside her, the puppies and piglet were wriggling like crazy, whimpering and panting as they scrambled to stand on each other, trying to escape their box. She took a minute to pat them all, soothing them, and then with her sole thought being *Please start*, she turned the ignition key.

And got only an ominous click.

"Come on, baby," she coaxed, trying again. "There's no New Transportation budget, so *please* come on . . ."

Nothing.

"Pretty sure you killed it."

With a gasp, she turned her head. A man stood there. Tall, broad-shouldered, with dark brown hair that was cut short and slightly spiky, like maybe he hadn't bothered to do much with it after his last shower except run his fingers through it. His clothes were simple: cargoes and a plain shirt, both emphasizing a leanly muscled body so completely devoid of body fat that it would have made any woman sigh—if she hadn't just rear-ended a truck.

Probably *his truck*.

Having clearly just come out of the convenience store, he held a large coffee and what smelled deliriously, deliciously like an egg and sausage and cheese breakfast wrap.

*Be still, her hungry heart . . .*

"Quack-quack."

"Hush, Abigail," Lilah murmured, flicking the duck a glance in the rearview mirror before turning back to the man.

His eyes were hidden behind reflective sunglasses, but she had no doubt they were on her. She could feel them, sharp and assessing. Everything about his carriage said military or cop. She wasn't sure if that was good or bad. He was a stranger to her, and there weren't that many of them in Sunshine. Or anywhere in Idaho for that matter. "Your truck?" she asked, fingers crossed that he'd say no.

"Yep." He popped the last of the breakfast wrap in his mouth and calmly tossed the wrapper into the trash can a good ten feet away. Chewing thoughtfully, he swallowed and then sucked down some coffee.

Just the scent of it had her sighing in jealousy. Probably, she shouldn't have skipped breakfast. And just as probably, she'd give a body part up for that coffee. Hell, she'd give up *two* for the candy bar sticking out of his shirt pocket. Just thinking about it had her stomach rumbling loud as thunder. She looked upward to see if she could blame the sound on an impending storm, but for the first time in two weeks there wasn't a cloud in the sky. "I'm sorry," she said. "About this."

He pushed the sunglasses to the top of his head, further disheveling his hair—not that he appeared to care.

"Luckily the damage seems to be mostly to my Jeep," she went on.

Sharp blue eyes held hers. "Karma?"

"Actually, I don't believe in karma." Nope, she believed in making one's own fate—which she'd done by once again studying too late into the night, not getting enough sleep, and . . . crashing into his truck.

"Hmm." He sipped some more coffee, and she told herself that leaping out of the Jeep to snatch it from his hands would be bad form.

"How about felony hit-and-run?" he asked conversationally. "You believe in that?"

"I wasn't running off."

"Because you can't," he ever so helpfully pointed out. "The Jeep's dead."

"Yes, but . . ." She broke off, realizing how it must look to him. He'd found her behind her own wheel, cursing her vehicle for not starting. He couldn't know that she'd never just leave the scene of an accident. Most likely he'd taken one look at the panic surely all over her face and assumed the worst about her.

The panic doubled. And also, her pity party was back, and for a beat, she let the despair rise from her gut and block her throat, where it threatened to choke her. With a bone-deep weary sigh, she dropped her head to the steering wheel.

"Hey. *Hey*." Suddenly he was at her side. "Did you hit your head?"

"No, I—"

But before she could finish that sentence, he opened the Jeep door and crouched at her side, looking her over.

"I'm fine. Really," she promised when he cupped and lifted her face to his, staring into her eyes, making her squirm like the babies in the box next to her.

"How many fingers am I holding up?" A quiet demand. His hand was big, the two fingers he held up long. His eyes were calmly intense, his mouth grim. He hadn't shaved that morning she noted inanely, maybe not the day before either, but the scruff only made him seem all the more . . . male.

"Two," she whispered.

Nodding, he dropped his gaze to run over her body. She had dressed for work this morning, which included cleaning out the kennels, so she wore a denim jacket over a T-shirt, baggy Carhartts, boots, and a knit cap to cover her hair.

To say she wasn't looking ready for her close-up was the understatement of the year. "Do you think you can close the door before—"

Too late.

Sensing a means of escape, Abigail started flapping her wings, attempting to fly out past Lilah's face.

She nearly made it, too, but the man, still hunkered at Lilah's side, caught the duck.

By the neck.

"Gak," said a strangled Abigail.

"Don't hurt her!" Lilah cried.

With what might have been a very small smile playing at the corners of his mouth, the man leaned past Lilah and settled the duck on the passenger floorboard.

"Stay," he said in a low-pitched, authoritative voice that brooked no argument.

Lilah opened her mouth to tell him that ducks didn't follow directions, but Abigail totally did. She not only stayed, she shut up. Probably afraid she'd be roasted duck if she didn't. Staring at the brown-headed, orange-footed duck in shock, she said, "I really am sorry about your truck. I'll give you my number so I can pay for damages."

"You could just give me your insurance info."

Her insurance. *Damn.* The rates would go up this time, for sure. Hell, they'd gone up last quarter when she'd had that little run-in with her own mailbox.

But that one hadn't been her fault. The snake she'd been transporting had gotten loose and startled her, and she'd accidentally aligned her front bumper with the mailbox.

But today, this one—definitely her fault.

"Let me guess," he said dryly when she sat there nibbling on her lip. "You don't have insurance."

"No, I do." To prove it, she reached for her wallet, which she kept between the two front seats. Except, of course, it wasn't there. "Hang on, I know I have it . . ." Twisting, she searched the floor, beneath the box of puppies and piglet, in the backseat . . .

And then she remembered.

In her hurry to pick up Mrs. Swanson's animals on time, she'd left it in her office at the kennels. "Okay, this looks bad but I left my wallet at home."

His expression was dialed into Resignation.

"I swear," she said. "I really do have insurance. I just got the new certificate and I put it in my wallet to stick in my glove box, but I hadn't gotten to that yet. I'll give you my number and you can call me for the information."

He gazed at her steadily. "You have a name?"

"Lilah." She scrounged around for a piece of paper. Nothing, of course. But she did find five bucks and the earring she'd thought that Abigail had eaten, and a pen.

Still crouched at her side, the man held out his cell phone. Impossibly aware of how big he was, how very good-looking, not to mention how he surrounded her still crouched at her side balanced easily on the balls of his feet, she entered her number into his phone. When it came to keying in her name, she nearly titled herself Dumbass of the Day.

"You fake numbering me, Lilah?" he asked softly, still close, so very close.

"No." This came out as a squeak so she cleared her throat. And, when he just looked at her, she added truthfully, "I only fake-number the jerk tourists inside Crystal's, the ones who won't take no for an answer."

"Crystal's?"

"The bar down the street. Listen, you might want to wait awhile before you call me. It's going to take me at least an hour to get home." *Carrying the mewling, wriggling babies* and *walking a duck.*

He paused, utterly motionless in a way that she admired, since she'd never managed to sit still for longer than two minutes. Okay, thirty seconds, but who was counting. "What?" she asked.

"I'm just trying to figure out if you're for real or if you're a master bullshit specialist."

That surprised a laugh out of her. "Well, I *can* be a master bullshit specialist," she admitted. "But I'm not bullshitting you right now."

He studied her face for another long moment, then nodded. "Fine, I'll wait to call you. You going to ask my name?"

Her gaze ran over his very masculine features, then

dropped traitorously to linger over his very fine body for a single beat. "I was really sort of hoping that I wasn't going to need it."

He laughed, the sound washing over her and making something low in her belly quiver again.

"Okay, yes," she said. "I want to know your name."

"Brady Miller."

A flicker of something went through her, like the name should mean something to her, but discombobulated as she was, she couldn't concentrate. "Well, Brady Miller, thanks for being patient with me." She reached for Abigail's leash, attaching it to the collar around the duck's neck.

"Quack."

"Shh." Then she grabbed the box of babies. It was damn heavy, but she had her dignity to consider so she soldiered on, turning to get out of the Jeep, bumping right into Brady's broad chest. "Excuse me."

He straightened to his full height and backed up enough to let her out, helping her support the box with an ease that had her envying his muscles now instead of drooling over them.

Actually, that was a lie. She managed both the envying and the drooling. She was an excellent multitasker.

"You're really going to walk?" he asked, rubbing his chin as he considered the box.

"Well, when I skip or run, Abigail's leash gets tangled in my legs."

"Smart-ass." Brady peered at the two puppies and pot-bellied piglet. To his credit, he didn't so much as blink. "They potty trained?"

"No."

He grimaced. "How about the duck?"

"She'd say yes, but she'd be lying."

He exhaled. "That's what I was afraid of." He took the box from her, the underside of his arms brushing the outside of hers.

He was warm. And smelled delicious. Like sexy man and something even better—breakfast wraps and coffee.

"What are you doing?"

"Giving you a ride." He narrowed his eyes at the duck on the leash. "You," he said, "behave."

"Quack."

Without another word, Brady strode to his truck and put the box inside.

Lilah looked down at Abigail. "You heard him," she whispered, having no choice but to follow. "Behave."